THE TERROR OF THE SIMULACRA

VOLUME TWO: BULBOUS CHUNKS

THE TERROR OF THE SIMULACRA

VOLUME TWO: BULBOUS CHUNKS

ROSS CHANNING REED

OzarkMountainWritersGuild

Library of Congress Control Number: 2013952411

ISBN – 13: 978-1-940514-07-9

ISBN – 10: 1-940514-07-X

Ozark Mountain Writers Guild

Salem, Missouri 65560

ozarkmountainwritersguild@gmail.com

Dedicated to Dr. John Ellsworth Winter and Dr. Richard J. Westley, freedom fighters.

CONTENTS

FOREWORD

In these United States, through diligence, perseverance, and hard work, we like to believe we have the opportunity to create our lives as we choose, in harmony with the interests of others. And if you happen to have the good fortune of a wealthy family, a first-tier college education (even if it's only as a legacy), and connections with powerful corporate interests, then the great brass ring called the American Dream is yours for the taking.

For the rest of us, the American Dream is an American Nightmare, thick with American Despair. If we are lucky, we get to work at two or three part-time jobs, without health benefits, with co-workers we want to choke and Powerball lotteries we can never seem to win. We work ourselves into early graves just to make ends meet, build relationships that make us long for the comfort of an asylum, eat bad and cheap fast food, clog our arteries, have strokes, have heart attacks, eat more fast crap, obsess over Hollywood celebrities, and do anything to be like those skinny supermodels who "have it all."

This book, the second volume in the *Terror of the Simulacra* trilogy (*Vituperous Cleavage, Bulbous Chunks, Evisceration*), is not meant for the faint of heart. It makes no appeal to a mass audience. Its audience is serious, but not solemn. Ostensibly a curious story about high school cross country runners, its protagonists convey energetic ideas and steadfast ideals readers will affectionately recognize as part of their own lives and, if you are who I think you are, continue to affirm today. At bottom, this book is for thoughtful readers, readers engaged in the art of living – a book for free spirits.

I met Ross Reed in Chicago in the fall of 1986. We were fellow graduate students in Loyola's doctoral philosophy program. We share an uncommon passion for existentialism – regarded by some "professional" philosophers as having already worn itself out as a philosophical movement. Of course, Ross and I both know this is patently false. The only philosophy worth its salt is lived philosophy, philosophy with its boots on the ground, dealing head on with those questions that continue to animate the human imagination. If you don't understand this, even if you have a Ph. D. in philosophy, you might *think* you're a philosopher, but trust me – you aren't.

Philosopher Reed's perception of the issues he presents in this book punches "conventional wisdom" in its collective face. He is uniquely qualified to make his case: he has supplemented his formal philosophical training with fifteen years plus as a philosophical counselor. He knows both the laudable and the loathing of what it means to be human, from both a theoretical and more importantly an experiential point of view. Contrary to popular belief, wealth and fame are not what life is about. Life is about family, life is about friends, life is about love. Be as cynical as you want – no one is more cynical than I am – but these are fundamental truths that none who are honest with themselves can deny. Against the backdrop of these truths we learn about Tommie, Monica, and the people that matter to them. With unflinching eyes we see in these characters' lives their pain, their goodness, their suffering, their beauty. This is the stuff meaning is made of, a few of the qualities that make life worth living. Like us, these kids and their families live in difficult economic times, where the American Dream is at best indefinitely delayed, more often altogether denied.   Their stories present a reality far different from the media's derisive condescending portrayal of the Occupy Wall Street movement, dismissing the protests of "the ninety-nine percent" as the well-intentioned naïveté of ordinary people who just don't seem to be able to understand the intricate complexities of world finance.

I have the good fortune of being both a formally trained philosopher as well as a financial analyst with over fifteen years of experience with a global financial institution. I wanted to write this forward because this book squarely lands in the overlap that is, for better or worse, my life. I cannot emphasize enough the importance of the story you are about to read. If you suspect a handful of *über*-venture capitalists believe they are "too big to fail" and are gladly playing us for a bunch of fools, trust that intuition – it's remarkably close to the truth.

The Terror of the Simulacra is an all-too-human narrative of young hearts and minds facing the evil wrought by pathological greed. If you've ever wondered what "we are the 99 percent" really means, read this book. Its truth shines a sorely needed light on an inhumanity we need to grab by the throat and choke to death – before it kills us.

Chris "Breakneck" Broniak, Ph. D.
Chicago, Illinois

18

NOTHING LIKE A GOOD PISS

"You guys totally suck! Slow it down. Slow it down." Ferris was yelling at Harlan and Tommie, as per usual. Or, more specifically, at the backs of their heads, as they slowly faded into the distance down Owl Bridge Road. The weather was perfect for a long run to nowhere. Harlan slowed to a jog, then turned around and jogged backwards, smiling at a distant Ferris. Ferris was maybe 120 meters back. At this point, he was losing about a tenth of a meter for every meter traveled. It was time to get him back on track.

"Yeah, we know, Ferris. You suck too, you big wuss. Why don't you get up here and kick my ass?" Harlan shouted, jogging a couple of slow 360s.

"You mean your no-ass?" Ferris bellowed. He was starting to get pissed, and when Ferris gets pissed, look out Usain Bolt. Ferris was maybe 110 meters back. Harlan turned around and sprinted back up with Tommie.

"Shut up, Harlan. Let him alone. He'll get up here if he wants to," Tommie said, without looking over at Harlan. Tommie's role in this situation was to make peace when it was absolutely unnecessary.

"You mean if he has the nuts. I'm just coaching him, you know. It's no big deal," Harlan said, trying to catch his breath.

"It's no big deal—as long as he doesn't

actually kick your ass. He's got probably triple your muscle mass—just a conservative estimate, Harlan. No offense."

"None taken. I'll have to kick your ass after I kick Ferris', if you've still got the Nuggets." Ferris was bringing up the rear, pounding the pavement in his fifty-pound Brooks running shoes, really slamming it down. Now he was maybe ninety meters back. Harlan started doing the 360 degree turn thing again, tiptoeing backwards and yelling at Ferris, lifting his arms in the air and jumping around like he was doing some kind of Lakota rain dance.

"Who's looking stupid now?" Tommie called over his shoulder.

"Shut up, Tommie. I'll bust ya later, so shut up," Harlan yelled. This time, Tommie stopped, turned around and jogged back toward Harlan. Sometimes, making peace meant trying to get somebody to shut up.

"Wow, I'm so scared, wimp. Don't scare me like that. How 'bout if you shut up and run, Harlan?"

"What's the matter, gonna piss your pants, Tommie?" Tommie was close enough now to kick Harlan in the ass, but instead he just jogged in place, watching Harlan do his Lakota rain dance.

Harlan and Tommie were running side by

side, still a good seventy-five meters in front of Ferris. "I'm gonna piss *your* pants, Harlan. Lay off Ferris, dude. If we get separated, he knows how to get back from here. He doesn't need your input, so just lay off. We could run back to Ferris and go his pace, you know. We don't have to stay right out of his reach." Needless to say, Harlan wasn't taking any advice. He turned and yelled again at the not-quite-so-distant Ferris.

"Hey Ferris, you girl. Kelsey Stoltzfus and Kevin Klinefelter are about to pass you, dude. They're right off your left shoulder. C'mon, wuss pussy," Harlan yelled louder than ever. The cattle on the field to the south started a stampede of sorts away from the noise, and who could blame them? The ground started to rumble as a good thirty head bounded down a fairly steep slope, at a pace far exceeding that of Tommie and company. Clearly, they sensed danger, or maybe they recognized a stench other than their own. The cloud formation overhead suggested a subtle, ubiquitous mockery.

"You'd make a great cheerleader, Harlan." It then occurred to Tommie that Harlan's legs would have disqualified him for said position posthaste, unless you were going for the ugly squad. Harlan's freakin' knees stuck out all around, thought Tommie, protruding mightily beyond his meager thighs and calves. He was a bony SOB. He might even get turned down for the ugly squad. Tommie laughed to himself, giving up some of the precious little oxygen he had left.

"You'd make a great buffalo chip, Tommie. Oh, wait! Excuse me, you *are* a great buffalo chip," said Harlan. Tommie and Harlan could hear the pounding. Ferris was maybe fifty meters back.

"Shuh up, Harlannn! Youh suhck," Ferris bellowed in a gasp. His words echoed in the approaching valley. Ferris was obviously out of breath, given his hoarse five-word pidgin rebuttal. They were way out of town now, and Owl Bridge Road was a hilly sucker. It would be a good thirty minutes or more just to get back. Tommie and Harlan started down a long grade, maybe six hundred meters or so. The pounding was getting really loud. Instantaneously, Ferris was there, sprinting like a maniac, down the hill and up on his tormenters. His breathing was on the order of a small scale steam engine. For thirty seconds, he had exceeded four minute mile pace. He was on the crown of the deserted country road, right between Tommie and Harlan, shoulder to shoulder, before they knew what had happened. Tommie and Harlan each turned to look at the red-faced Ferris. It was almost as if they had seen an apparition. Ferris was smiling a sadistic smile of victory, pain and dementia, a smile every cross-country runner has seen, or better yet, worn. He was about to make somebody pay for all the time he had spent in the hall of shame, just beyond the pale of running respectability. If running was going to suck this much, the least he could get was a little respect, even if he had to pound somebody for it, and even if that somebody he had to pound was a 115 pound bony kneed twirp with a chicken breast. Sheer determination could only make you run so fast, and he was running that fast. It didn't seem fair that some people got all the glory and didn't feel all the pain, while all he ever seemed to get was all the pain and all the shame. But maybe shameful recognition was better than no recognition at all? Undoubtedly the allure of cross-country.

"Okay...losers. Who...wants to get...pounded first?" His stuttery, breathless voice was mighty close for comfort. Tommie knew that if any pounding was going to take place, Harlan was gonna be the hapless recipient, but who would pound a guy who couldn't even make the ugly squad?

"Save your energy, Ferris. We've got four and a half miles to go," said Harlan in the calmest voice he could muster, a voice that had an edge of carefully concealed alarm. He should have been a United Nations peace negotiator, the way he spinned it. Maybe in spite of it all, he did deserve a pounding. Ferris knew how far they had to go. It was just a bluff of sympathy and concern. The tip off, for Ferris, *was* the sympathy and concern.

"He doesn't need a tour guide, Harlan. He knows where we are, dude," said Tommie, imitating Harlan's U.N. peace negotiator voice.

"Yeah, anyway. I was trying to save my energy, Harlan, you dork. You're the one racing," said Ferris, momentarily overcoming his shame. Ferris was still breathing like a steam locomotive, but more like a steam locomotive at idle. They *were* still on the downhill.

"Yeah, maybe you should hit me. Go ahead. I deserve it. Hit my chicken breast," said Harlan. The description was nearly spot on: it was the breast of a Cornish hen. Ferris looked over at the running chicken breast, Cornish hen, bobwhite quail or other nondescript game fowl. Even Harlan's protestations of guilt were so pathetic that Ferris found it hard to consider giving him a slug.

"Naw, I think I need to conserve my energy. Maybe later," said Ferris, trying to keep his feet from slapping on the asphalt. The downhill sections were particularly bad and, in some cases, each slap sounded like the discharge of a rifle echoing through the ridges and valleys. Once in a while, Ferris even startled himself, thinking the sounds were coming from somewhere else and not his ostensibly perambulating feet. When he was alone he would often practice smoother footfalls, but the net effect was usually to make the sounds of contact even louder. In the end, he quit trying to manipulate what came naturally and just went back to the slapper he figured he was meant to be.

"You mean if you live through this workout?" said Harlan, not one to shy away from the precipice.

"No, if *you* live through this workout. You're the wuss, wuss," said Ferris, looking over at Harlan as if he was pushing his luck, which he was. "In fact, the more I think about it, the more you don't look like a chicken. You look more like a great blue heron. Especially the legs. Wuss."

"God, that hurt. Man, dude. You're cruel. Okay, now we're even," said Harlan. Harlan attempted to negotiate once again, once again very badly. Some people never learn. The real problem was that Ferris couldn't keep up with Tommie and Harlan unless they slowed down for him, and they had a way of rubbing it in. If they'd just shut up, the situation would be manageable. But that scenario was unlikely.

"Yeah, right. We're even if *you're* buying the pizza. And I'm getting fries and a Greek salad and an extra large coke with my extra large extra cheese anchovy Canadian bacon hamburger green pepper jalapeno pepperoni spinach thick crust Sicilian pizza. And you're buying, right Harlan?" said Ferris, getting his wind back.

"What about the onions, dude? We *gotta* have onions. And he's buying for you and me, right Ferris?"

"Yeah, Tommie, and if he doesn't we'll both kick his no-ass-at-all."

"Deal. Give me five."

"Five." Tommie and Ferris did the Owl Bridge Road victory dance. That would be like the victory dance they did on all the other deserted crowned roads in Lancaster County: a couple of 360 degree turns, slowly, so as not to fall (they were, undoubtedly, coordinationally challenged), waving their arms in the air, and going "Oh, yeah, Oh, yeah. Woooo! Woooo!" They didn't do it with reckless abandon; it was a controlled victory dance, not a Dionysian frenzy but an Apollonian pseudo-frenzy. And this for two reasons: first, too much frenzy could lead inadvertently to an accident, spoiling said victory dance, kind of like the time on Sickman's Mill Road the previous summer where Ferris was on about his fourth or fifth 360 and tripped over a rock or an imaginary rock and catapulted himself right onto the crown of the tarry road, face down. There was a copious amount of blood, especially from the nose, but no real injuries. This reason would be sufficient, but it is followed by a second: Tommie and Ferris would never make Harlan pay anyway; that would just plain spoil the fun. Besides, no one liked anchovies with Canadian bacon and hamburger, so that combo was definitely out.

"You guys sound like a bunch of psychotic owls in heat. Woooo! Woooo! My ass," said Harlan. He had it right, but that still didn't mean he had an ass.

"This is *Owl* Bridge Road, dirt bag, and dinner's on you. Let's get an order of onion rings too, Ferris, what do you think?"

"Two orders. One for you and one for me. Harlan doesn't need any because he'll be out running an extra five."

"Oh yeah, deal." They proceeded to do another victory dance, as if adding two orders of onion rings to their already voluminous order was somehow a separate victory in itself, and as if Harlan had the dough to pay for either order, and as if they were going to actually make Harlan pay for the whole order even if he could, which they weren't, even if he could, which he couldn't and wouldn't even if he could.

This dance exhibited an eerie similarity to the victory dance Tommie was doing last October on Silvermine Road. That was the best laugh Harlan and Ferris had had in a long time, but with these guys, you didn't have to wait long. Tommie was on a particularly hilly and rough part of Silvermine Road, trying to do multiple 360s as per usual, it being a victory dance, when the tip of his Asics caught the edge of a pothole, launching him forward at a speed heretofore never even imagined by the likes of Tommie. He flew into a dirt embankment before he even had the chance to get his hands up, and as it had recently rained a good two inches, he was essentially plastered into the six foot mud wall. It was a moment to remember. And all because he just *had* to do a victory dance to signify his satisfaction at his recent humiliation of Harlan. As they say, it ain't over 'till it's over. So true in long distance running. So true in life. The real problem was cleaning the mud off of his glasses. What the heck was he going to use to do that? A sweaty nylon singlet? Let's just say he groped his way back. Now that was really livin'. As far as making Harlan pay—before and after this run—Ferris and Tommie had not yet finished rubbing it in.

"If you don't have enough money for yourself, you can just watch us eat, Harlan," said Ferris, leveling a blow without taking a punch. "That is, if you're not out running the extra five." For a moment, he is king of Owl Bridge Road. "Oh, and another thing, keep the pace down for the rest of the workout, or I'll sprint after you and snap your femurs like oak twigs in a winter forest.

Got it, Harlan dude?"

"Shut up, Ferris. You suck. I got it." Harlan is probably crying behind his shades, but who wants to know? He'll give his ego a rest and go along with the program. They've backed off to a comfortable eight-minute pace on the hilly route. Thoughts of pizza dough danced in their heads. They floated and slapped and pounded a few minutes in silence, cresting one of the bigger hills on the course. If you slog it right, no hill is insurmountable, provided you've got endless patience, nerves of steel, a massive ganglionic pain threshold—and all afternoon with nothing better to do.

They were all slogging just fine, whether or not life has a meaning. If life has no meaning, then slogging meaninglessly up a meaningless hill in the middle of nowhere can hardly be construed as a waste of time, and if life does have a meaning, slogging to the crest must in some sense be a meaningful subset of some larger set, even if the set itself remains hidden from view. To summarize, apparently pointless activity cannot be effectively condemned whether life does or does not having a meaning. A lesson for bowlers, rowers, and long distance runners.

Anyway, they had backed off and all were well within their comfort zones, if life can in any sense and at any time be said to be comfortable.

This allowed them to do one of the things they always liked to do out there: have an actual conversation without having to look at each other. Actually, it was usually a combination of factors: not having to look at each other, being out in the country, low blood sugar and general exhaustion, not having their mobile devices, and no chicks within view.

Ferris first crossed the line between abuse among friends and actual conversation. He could do it because, according to them, Harlan was already paying for lunch.

"Hey Harlan, not to change the subject, but is something bothering your dad? He doesn't seem like himself. Is he sick? Last week when we came over to run, he just looked up but didn't say much. Same with this week. He didn't start boring us by talking about Prefontaine or Frank Shorter or Emil Zatopek or Henry Rono and asking us a bunch of questions like he usually does. Is he okay or what? Did we do something to piss him off?" All was forgotten with Ferris. Part of running was the ego fencing, and they were all taking a break.

"No, no, you guys didn't do anything to piss him off, and, if you did, he probably wouldn't even notice it. And as far as I know, he's not sick. He's just got a lot on his mind. I'm not sure what's really bothering him. But I think it's some

kind of financial thing. Some kind of debt service
or something. I saw some notice on his desk in his
office not too long ago. I think that could be it. I
was trying not to think about it. If that's not it, I
guess it could be a bunch of stuff. Who knows?"

"Notice? Debt service? Harlan, do you
mean debt consolidation service? I always see
those ads on TV where they say they're gonna
help bail you out," queried Tommie.

"Yeah, that's it, dude. Yeah. Debt
consolidation service. Yeah, exactly."

"Debt consolidation service: It provides no
service, but it puts the con back in con-solidation,
said Ferris. My parents got screwed by one of
them." For a moment, Ferris was king, only this
time it was king of Sheep Lane. He was getting a
little bit more oxygen back in his cerebellum, but
little to his corpus callosum, so his left foot didn't
know what his right foot was doing. And it
showed. But right now nobody was thinking
about running.

"How do you know this stuff, Ferris? I
wish my dad knew that before he got involved
with that shit."

"I wish mine did too—but he didn't either.
Like everyone else who gets suckered into those
scams, if they knew then what they know now,
they wouldn't have done it. So the people who
sign up, they don't know it's a scam.

But it is. Anybody that works for a living's got to be suspicious of all that crap—cash advances, title loans, payday lenders, debt consolidation services, credit cards. All of it is predatory. They're all vultures pretending to provide you with a needed service, when the only people they service are themselves as they help themselves to your money—whatever money you've got left," Ferris said, clearly agitated.

"Don't vultures prey on the dead?"

"That's true, Tommie, but if you've ever watched those big giant turkey vultures, they circle before the thing is dead. They smell out the vulnerable." Ferris's feet weren't even slapping anymore. He'd lost sight of trying to correct his form—and it was working. The impediment of the mind had dropped off; he was thinking about the disintegration of his family. The smell of cow manure was pungent.

"Now there's one of my favorite smells," offers Tommie.

"Oh yeah, asphyxiation by cow manure."

"At least we're not racing—or, we're no longer racing," said Ferris. "So your dad is upset because he got involved with a debt consolidation service?"

"They asked for a shitload upfront, but they let you pay in installments. Sooo merciful. They can't take it if you ain't got it. So, they take it *as* you get it. It's just an elaborate legalized front to take your money while pretending to help you get out of debt. Five thousand bucks, in installments. That's what my dad is supposed to pay. I'm not supposed to know that, but like I said—I saw the statement. I guess I barely knew what I was looking at. They're just taking it out of his account every month, and then letting him know, like a burglar sending you a list of stuff he ripped off so that you can file an insurance claim. I was like 'what the hell is this?' At first, I thought it was some college savings plan for me or something, something really cool I didn't know about. That's why I was curious. But it wasn't.

"It was some billing statement for consolidation services. Now that's a goddamn euphemism for a box of shit. When I saw that stupid statement on his desk, I felt like I had less oxygen than I do now, in the middle of a nine mile run on some nasty hills. I almost felt dizzy. I thought our finances were cool. It almost felt like the earth was moving underneath me as I actually looked at the statement and processed what the damn thing was. My first reaction was to think it was a mistake, but I can tell now by my dad's behavior that it's real. Yeah, it's real. That's gotta be why he's been acting so out of it lately. Real sick. He doesn't want me to know, I'm sure. I guess my mom has to know, but does she really know what it is? Does my dad really know? They're not going to find out the truth by listening to the company that stands to benefit a whole lot by them not knowing the truth, that's for damn sure. Now how are people with a bunch of debt supposed to pay money to clean up their debt?"

Harlan continued to speak and by speaking work out what the hell he thought was really going on. As he did so, his hopes were slowly diminishing, replaced by anger and despair, just as his glycogen levels were slowly diminishing and were being replaced by lactic acid and pyruvic acid. The illumination of his consciousness was as a darkening of his dream.

"It's stupid. They are supposed to be paying all your bills for you—that's the consolidation part—and they're supposed to be negotiating with your creditors to cut you a deal on what you owe. But they take control of your money too, like you're giving them the right to pilfer your accounts, like they were doing with my parent's account. All that we really got was the $500 a month service fee or whatever, in installments for ten months, and behind in our credit cards, with no reduction in principle. I know, because I've seen the statements, and we're now behind on the two I've seen, and the principle hasn't gone down. It hasn't gone down. Is that absurd or what? And now my dad isn't able to get out of the contract. Plus he'd lose at least $3000 bucks if he could get out right now. I'd be depressed too. No wonder he's not saying much to you guys. He's not saying much to anybody right now. He goes to work, comes home, grade papers, prepares classes, and once in a while stares at the TV. He and I don't even have to do any yard work, since we're in the crappy rental unit. The financial hole we're in has just gotten deeper since he went to those scumbags."

The one thing Harlan realized was how much it was all bothering him. He not only realized how much it was bothering him, but he also realized that it hadn't ever even occurred to him to actually talk to anybody about it.

"Man, Harlan, dude, that's terrible. That stuff shouldn't be legal, but as long as it is, the sharks will be right there pretending to provide a so-called service. Your dad's really smart, so he'll find a way to get out of it. I guess you don't think it would be a good idea for you to say anything to him, right? I mean, if he thinks you don't know and all."

"There's no way, Ferris. I can't say anything to him, but I see what you mean. The shit shouldn't be legal. It's like somebody offering you a contract to help provide self-mutilation services."

"I think it sounds more like a legal contract

to get your uninformed consent to allow them to mutilate you, only the way they write the contract, it looks like you have given your informed consent," said Tommie, jumping in.

"That's it, Tommie, that's it. You've got it right. I hope we get out of it soon. We've got to. This totally sucks, " said Harlan. "And forget about my college fund. Oh yeah, that fund that doesn't exist."

"What doesn't exist? You don't have any college fund, dude. None of us do."

"You've got it, Tommie. Exactly. And my family's got the *con*-solidation service. That's what we've got."

"I hear you, Harlan. It's a deal with the devil. Get out before it's too late, and learn your lesson," said Ferris, emphatically. He had gotten his second wind, without a doubt. It was like it almost wasn't even Ferris. Ferris knew what he was talking about. He knew because his dad had done the same thing years back when Ferris was little, but he still remembered what it did to his dad. Things were never really the same after that, but Ferris wasn't aware of that yet. He still hadn't put it all together. He didn't and wouldn't know that the debt consolidation effort was part of the reason his parents split up, and why he had had to live with his dad since he was ten, and why his dad smoked a god awful lot of big ass cigars and looked broken. He hadn't always been defeated, but he got kicked one too many times when he was down. He was down and sought help and the so-called service kicked his ass, and then kicked it a few more times until, out of exhaustion and fear and the inability to afford a lawyer he just gave up and gave them what they wanted, and after the parasites had had their way with him, he was never the same.

He worked double shifts to get out of the 10,000-foot-deep hole, but there's only so many feet a man can climb in a day, continuing to slip back with every step, and the life of mortals is only so long. He didn't want to talk about it, or much of anything else after that, and finally his wife left him. After that, Ferris only saw his mother about once a week or less, but he was used to it by now. And no matter how much he hated the debt consolidation service, he never connected their self-serving perniciousness-masquerading-as-philanthropy to the breakup of his family. He never traced the unraveling back to this man-made disaster, the Katrina of their lives.

At least not consciously. But he did have that pervasive feeling of dread since the unraveling of everything he'd ever known. Some may say that the order of events is otherwise, that the divorce precipitated the desperate measure of the consolidation service, but that analysis would be wrong. They've got it backwards. Ferris's mom had that operation in about 1999 and that set them back, and after his sister was diagnosed with juvenile diabetes, they were set back again.

They had like a million co-pays and add on fees, even with insurance, and it all piled up to so much that by the time Ferris was eight, his parents were in such bad shape that his dad called the number that he saw on his screen during the late night movie commercial break. It was about 12:45 a.m. and he was too tired to go to bed. Ironically, he was watching a rerun of *The Razor's Edge,* with Bill Murray. He was depressed about money, as usual, and couldn't work any more hours at his two jobs, or he would just keel over. He was already at about sixty hours a week, and sometimes it was closer to seventy. He was trying to figure out how to boost the family's income, but it just seemed hopeless. He was thinking about the financial hole they were in when the commercial came on.

He stared at the TV. He thought, "What do I have to lose?" He had just enough time to dial and request information, since he wasn't too hip on looking it up online. It seemed like an answer to prayer. But apparently, a serpent can sometimes appear as an answer to prayer. No, the last straw was the consolidation service that reamed the Ferris family and shredded their pedestrian hopes like a balsa wood airplane in a cyclone. Why talk about it now, running down Sheep Lane, when there's nothing left to say? Ferris knew what Harlan was talking about, that's for damn sure, and he felt a sense of despair and desperation slowly overcome him, like a cold wind sending shivers down his spine. He also felt the anger rising in his blood. He felt the hope drain out of his body, limb by limb, but then the anger flooded his body, limb by limb.

"Harlan, your parents *have* to get out of it. Your dad has to tell your mom. That's what these vultures do: divide and conquer. They count on shame to keep people quiet while they do the looting. That way, shame makes you complicit in your own downfall. Your dad has to tell your mom. Tell your dad you saw the statement. Get it out in the open. There may be time for your mom and dad to work together before things get really bad. They want everybody to keep quiet out of shame." Ferris seemed so serious that it was kind of scary to both Harlan and Tommie. They could barely remember him ever being this serious, even at Surekill.

"My mom might know. I'm not sure. But how do we get out of it, Ferris?" asked Harlan. He was realizing the gravity of the situation. It was weird because he thought he had done that before, but he didn't really understand and didn't know that he didn't really understand.

"Look bro, I'm no expert. Our family was victimized by these predators. I don't know if I learned anything about how to handle them. But keeping quiet because you're ashamed of having gotten involved with them is playing right into their hands. They create traumatic stress in their victims and then count on the effects of this abuse to allow them to continue to abuse them. It's a form of psychological torture, a war tactic, pure evil. You can get your parents together—*today*—to talk about it. If they're not at work."

"Ferris, I may need your help. Is there anything specific you would do if it happened to you?" asked Harlan. They took a right on Letort Road and began the trek back toward town. They still had plenty of time to hash it out. They were still slogging out the easy eight minute miles over the rolling hills. The weather was still perfect; nevertheless, Ferris felt the chill in his spine. The chill demanded that he continue to speak.

"Well, here's what I might do, but you need to work it out with your parents. It might not work. I don't know. But I do know that I've been thinking about this for a long, long time. I don't think my parents did any of this stuff. They were caught blindsided, I'd say. If it were me, I'd close all of my bank accounts, and open an account at the local credit union and put whatever money I had left in there—but keep some out in cash in case somehow they got to the new account. If necessary, you could give the money to somebody you trust to put in their account, just so it's out of reach of the long arm of El Diablo. If you have direct deposits going into any of the accounts that you are going to close, make sure you deal with them first. Maybe you can go back to a paper check and have it mailed to you, or see if you can have it deposited into your new account.

"I'd contact the States Attorneys Office and file a claim against the company, however you would do it. I don't know, but you could figure it out. If I could, I'd freeze all my credit cards and stuff like that, so no charges could be made against them. I'd call the con-solidation disservice every day at least twice and ask for all of my money back, and I'd try to get specific names so that I can call those specific phone extentions every time, and I'd tell them I'm taking notes every time I call and that I'm documenting every conversation. I'd have a representative with all my account information call to get to those same people, and I'd have them ask for my money back. I may do the same thing by email, day after day, although phone may be more effective."

"Representative?" asked Harlan.

"The representative could be anybody who sounds authoritative and who you trust. You need to talk with the same people every time, and so often that after they leave work, they're still thinking about *you*. If possible, I might pay them a visit in person, with or without my representative, and ask for all of my money back. Of course, if they're in India or something, that won't work. But try to find out where they actually are, because they sure as hell know where you are. Your representative could be an uncle or two uncles, or a couple of friends. Just leave us out of it, bro. Just kidding. The point is, it doesn't have to be someone you pay. The con-solidation disservice doesn't need to know who these people are. It's none of their damn business. You've got to do whatever seems best to let them know you mean business and to let them know that they screwed with the wrong people."

"I hear you, bro. I think I'm getting it," said Harlan.

"Don't ever expect them to tell you the truth, and don't give them any information—ever. You're not having a conversation. You're having a power struggle. It's war by other means. It is a struggle for your hope, your dignity, your self-respect, your future. If necessary, change your phone numbers—home and cell, and then don't call them from your new numbers. Find an alternative way to call them. Use a throw away phone, one you can put minutes on without a contract. You could even get a special throw away just for them if you have to. Do what you have to do before you and your family are screwed up for life.

"Go after them every single day, multiple times a day, and like I said, have different people call. Be professional and clearly state the same thing over and over. Do not negotiate or give the impression that you will ever negotiate. Avoid expressing emotion, no matter how rude or unprofessional or duplicitous they may be. This will take practice and resolve. This is what I imagine I would do in my mind, and I've had six or seven years to think about it. Maybe I wouldn't do any of that if I were actually in that situation. Maybe I'd capitulate in shame, remain silent, and help them sell me down the river. But I'd like to believe otherwise. And I know you guys would help me if I needed it. At least, you'd better help me, or I'd have to pound the crap out of both of you losers." Ferris got that sadistic cross-country runner's smile. His feet were so silent he sounded almost Kenyan. The less he thinks about it, the better off he is.

"We *would* help you, Ferris. And we're gonna help Harlan too, if he needs it. He can't pound the crap out of us. No way. But we'll still help him."

"Thanks, dudes. I appreciate it. And I

won't pulverize you with my powers. I'm gonna talk to my dad the next time I see him. Hopefully tonight. You really take this stuff seriously, eh Ferris?" Harlan was looking over at him with a new curiosity. "Is it really as bad as you're making it out to be? Can it really be that bad? I really appreciate you being upfront with me and all and telling me how you feel, but maybe you're overstating the case a little?" Harlan felt bad about the hole his father had dug for himself and his family, but he didn't completely get it. The egregious unfairness and the corresponding helplessness were still not fully realized. The fact was that Harlan still retained a shred of dignity, and his sense of humor.

"Harlan, I don't want you to have to live through it to know. I'm taking a risk and talking about it now so that you can get out before it gets that bad. It's important that you do something now, before it does get bad. I'm telling you from experience—it can get so bad that it's a nightmare, and you feel like you're never going to wake up. Acting now may save you a lot of pain and suffering. If you don't do anything now, it could affect you for the rest of your life. It could affect your children for the rest of their lives too, if you've got the sperm count to have any."

Harlan elbowed Ferris in the ribs. Ferris didn't even flinch. "Hey, the flies are getting bad out here," he said, without missing a beat. "Back to my point, dudes. I think it can be that serious. It can wreck you economically so that you never recover, and it can break your spirit so that you're never the same. Hey, it happened in my family, I can tell you. It's poison."

For once, they were all three running shoulder to shoulder and almost stride for stride. The hill had flattened out. They hadn't seen a car for over a mile.

"Yeah, okay, Ferris, I believe you. I admit, I felt sick looking at that statement. It was like a blow to the abdomen, and the feeling hasn't really gone away since I found out. I guess I was kind of blocking it out, but it was always there, I just didn't want to admit it. But like you were saying, I didn't even think about talking about it. I think it's the shame thing. It's weird. Like I made sure not to even consider that option. And I wasn't even aware of how it might be affecting me until now, when I started talking about it. I can't even imagine how my dad feels. No wonder he hasn't said much in months. Man, it's got to suck. I wouldn't want to tell Mom."

"He'd feel a lot better if he could tell your mom the truth," said Ferris. "It may not seem like it now, but it's true. He *will* feel better if he tells her the truth. He won't be alone with the secret, and they can work on it together. When you're alone surmountable things can seem insurmountable. Help break the silence by speaking out first, dude. You've got the balls, even though I keep telling you you don't. Don't listen to me if I tell you you don't, dude. You've got the nuggets. If I'm not telling you that, don't listen to me. Okay, man?"

Harlan was feeling uncomfortable but glad he brought it up. His bony knees ached a little from the downhill sections on the nine-miler. "Hey man, we're not even listening to you now. What was all that shit you were talking for the last mile and a half?" said Harlan. "Tommie, did you hear a word he said?"

"What? Was Ferris speaking? Damn. I hope it wasn't important. I guessed I missed it. I thought it was just the sound of cattle farting."

Ferris was less than amused. "Harlan, that's it, dumb-ass. Why do I bother? I was talking to *you*, dude. Do you think I'm just in love with the sound of my own voice? You are going to pay for two big ass dinners at the House of Pizza. Hey, Tommie, and you suck too. Thanks a lot, dipstick." Ferris was starting to slap again. They were a good seven miles into the run, with plenty of road left to travel.

"Did you say you dudes have big asses? piped Harlan. No argument here. And my no-ass-at-all always kicks your big asses, just like it did at

Schuylkill Haven. You guys were smoked."

"You're smoked, Harlan. Smoked chicken breast," said Tommie.

And then it all happened so fast. Ferris ran up behind Harlan and grabbed both sides of his nylon shorts, pulling them straight down, below his knees. Harlan's forward motion was arrested in mid-stride. He careened forward, to the right side of the road, arms outstretched like Frankenstein, and fell forward straight into the ditch, about half a meter deep, rutted with mud and crabgrass, his bare white ass pointing skyward, to be blessed by the endless blue. There was first a thud and then the sound of the wind. Then the sound of Tommie and Ferris, laughing so loud that the cattle again began to stampede, only this time toward the sound. Maybe it was the scintillating reflection off of that bare porcelain white ass.

Harlan was moving. He lifted himself just enough to pull up his shorts. His face, torso, arms and legs were sliming around in the grass-accented mud as he tried to push himself up to a standing position. He was nearly up when his back legs slipped and again he fell forward into the slimy sediment. He was still silent, as were his companions, save for the wheezing sounds of laughter bordering on asphyxiation. Tommie farted. It was loud. Then he farted again. This time even louder. Ferris and Tommie were bent double with laughter. It couldn't be a better day. Finally, some verbiage from the ditch. Everyone knows it's hard to shut Harlan up.

"Damn, you guys suck. Oww. Oww." Ferris and Tommie were still unable to speak. They could barely breathe on account of the overwhelming laughter. They hadn't laughed that hard since the last trick they played on Harlan. They stood in the road, choked with laughter, eyes fixed on the ditch in which Harlan still remained, face down. Harlan made a second valiant slow and unsteady attempt to stand, and this time he was successful.

"You're lookin' awesome, dude. Isn't he, Ferris?" Tommie managed to say between gasps.

"Without a doubt. Best you ever looked, Harlan," Ferris choked out.

Harlan looked like he had taken a mud bath de-luxe.

"Oww. You guys suck," Harlan said, weakly. His pants were back up past his no-ass-at-all, hiked a good six inches too high, crooked and twisted to the degree that a self-induced wedgie was clearly inevitable.

"Yeah, we know, but you're still paying for dinner," said Tommie, who was starting to get some oxygen back into his blood. "Now that we're stopped, I'm taking a leak."

"Good idea. Me too." Ferris and Tommie walked over to whizz in the ditch at the edge of a small bluff. Harlan steadied himself for the same purpose. All was silent save the sound of the wind, a few bellowing cows, and three runners urinating. All in all, it was turning out to be a fine day.

19

ORANGE SHAG CARPET

I'm in bed with someone who bears a faint resemblance to Avril Cheyenne. We are not in a log cabin. There is no fire in the fireplace. Looking out the window, I do not see distant mountains. I see a faded blue Hyundai Accent in a bumpy dirt driveway, '03 or '04. I look over at the sleeping woman again, wondering if there is any way she could be Avril. Naw, she looks too old and beat up to be Avril. From what I can see, she's naked. I know I am. I wipe my eyes again. They're pasty and my mouth tastes nasty. I keep thinking that she looks like Avril, but I must be dreaming. Holy crap, she sure looks like Avril, but then again, not Avril. Don't I see traces of… black lipstick? I feel like I've been here before. Damn, it's gotta be Avril. Or not.

I roll over toward her and she reeks. God does she reek. Even worse than I do. She doesn't wake up, but she rolls over on her left side so that I can't see her face. She starts to snore. Then the snoring starts getting louder. I stumble out of bed and my bare feet hit the cold uneven floor. The bed is really a ratty mattress on top of a squeaky box spring up against the short wall. A beat up wall with what look like punch or kick holes. A magenta nightstand with cigarette burns and ashtrays sits on either side of the mattress/box spring combo. The magenta looks like the tenth coat of paint. We're in a room that must be eight by nine, or less. My stomach starts to cramp up. I stand up slowly, feeling unsteady.

I notice that I have a large blue and green tattoo on my right forearm. I don't remember seeing it before. It is written in this weird-ass decorative script: "Avril Forever. 2011." What the...? Underneath, it looks like Chinese characters or something. Am I supposed to know what the hell this says? I start to feel really shaky. That's Avril? What the...? No. How...? No. I break out in a cold sweat. I glance at my other arm, then my legs, then everything else I can see. Nothing.

I look like shit. My skin looks like a rhinoceros. I walk up to the window and look outside. I notice a couple of bumper stickers on the back of the Hyundai. "Life Sucks Even More Than You Do." What the hell does that mean? It must be Avril's car, or the Avril imposter, whoever she is, since there's no way I...then I notice another bumper sticker. I can barely make it out. I almost want to go outside, but then I remember that I'm naked. I stumble over to the next window. "Monster Truck Drivers Make Better Lovers."

I look back at the bed. Is it really Avril, and is this her car? It is cold as hell in here. I'm feeling the cold sweat dry. I walk to the bedroom door. I open it. I realize that we are in an old single-wide trailer in the middle of nowhere. I look out the window in the narrow hallway. I press my hands against the wall as I shuffle toward the bathroom. I make it to the bathroom and find the light switch. The switch plate says "Come to Mama". I slap myself, just to make sure. As I shuffle past the dirty mirror on the vanity, I take a glance. This brings me to a dead stop. The face looks so not me that I feel like I am being watched. I don't want to look at it again. I avert my gaze.

I find myself standing over the toilet bowl, leaning forward with my right hand on the wall and my left hand holding what's left of my manhood. The uneven stream is dark, but not as dark as the rusty cigarette butt-filled toilet bowl. There are three crumpled beer cans, a beer bottle, a hair dryer, and an opened, half-empty box of tampons on top of the flush box. There is no toilet paper in sight. I suddenly get the urge to pull back the mold-infested shower curtain, which I do, but I nearly fall forward onto the toilet. No dead bodies. I feel myself sigh with relief, as if I had imagined the worst. I start thinking about my problem. I don't know if that's Avril. I have reasons to believe it is, which is a problem in itself.

I find myself at a loss when trying to think through the implications of this possibility. I find myself at a loss when trying to think through the implications of any other presently conceivable possibility. But really, maybe there's a bigger problem: who the hell am I, and what am I doing here? I start shaking my penis to get the last drops in the toilet, and not on the orange shag carpet. I wonder why I care. Then I wonder if I only think I care, but don't, and that the whole thing's just habit.

I fumble for my fly. Then I remember that I am naked. I look down and wince. I feel a lot fatter than I remember, but what the hell do I remember? Is it actually *me* doing the remembering? This is my life? I stumble back out to the hallway and accidentally kick a beer bottle that was buried in the shag. I yell out something, but it is lost to me. My left big toe starts hurting. I look out the next sliding window. I see the Hyundai from another fine angle. The passenger side door has sustained major damage. I also notice the license plate for the first time. AAC – TRC. I freeze and break out into another cold sweat. Is that me and Avril? Is it? What? Did I miss something? Or did I miss everything? Then I notice something more. It says NORTHWEST TERRITORIES. The first thing through my mind is "At least we're not in California" and then I think that maybe I could check out any time I'd like, but I wonder if I could ever leave. Weird. I wanna leave even before I've figured out where I am. I hear stirring in the bedroom and a loud grunt.

"Hey, are you gonna make the coffee or what? Can you hear me? Hey!" It is a cross between sleep speaking and a loud moan, but it's edgy just the same. I walk back down the eight foot long hall and back through the doorway, this time scanning my path. Right now, I really don't need any more surprises.

"Uh...are you Avril Cheyenne?" I sound like a freakin' unmitigated moron. I'm an idiot. Just shut the hell up.

"No dude, I'm Lady Gaga, and you're Elton John. Are you gonna make the coffee or what, rock star? I'm not gettin' out of this freakin' bed. It's gotta be forty degrees in here." I realize that it is freezing and that I'm freezing my ass off. I see a thermostat on the wood paneled wall only feet away. It must be broken 'cause it's already set at eighty-five. I feel a wave of unhope.

"Damn. Hey, where are my cigarettes? Can you get me my cigarettes? I don't know where they are," says whoever it is in the bed.

"Uh...maybe." I walk out into the other two so-called rooms in this fancy-ass place. There is another small bedroom and a combo living room/kitchen, separated by a half-wall with spindles. At the far end of the trailer, there's a three-piece angled picture window over the kitchen sink. The half-wall separating the living room from the kitchen is about three feet high, with a gap where you can pass between the two rooms, such as they are. There are spindly, decorative wooden posts from the top of the half-wall to the ceiling, the wood looking like three snakes wound around each other. Two posts are missing completely, and one is broken just above the wall and dangles precariously, at about a twenty-degree angle from the ceiling. Only five of eight spindles actually make it from half-wall to ceiling. 62.5 percent, I think. That's passing. And this trailer sure beats camping outside, 62.5 percent to zero. If those were the only two available choices, I mean. I think about the not-so-good Avril impersonator in bed at the end of the trailer. I won't ask her any more questions. I look around for cigarettes. I find five packs, two in the kitchen, two in the living room, one in the bathroom, all empty. I walk back to what is clearly the master bedroom.

"Avril, I can't find any cigarettes." No response. She's rolled back over to face the wall.

"Avril?" I walk over and stand over her. She appears to be asleep. Her hair looks like it got hit by a cyclone. I'm guessing it has a dozen knots. I am silent for a moment. Breathing. Then soft snoring. Then louder snoring. It stinks in here. Man, does it stink. I give up and stumble back down the hall. My right calf cramps up just in time to fall onto the stained red sofa. It also has cigarette burns. Damn. The sofa is uneven on the floor. As I massage the cramp in my calf, I lean forward and discover that the left front two-inch sofa leg is missing. There's green shag carpet in this room. About twenty-five percent of its synthetic fibers are missing. Both of my bare feet are sticking to something on the carpet. I wonder why I notice what I notice when the big picture seems to have escaped me entirely.

Beer bottles and cans are strewn liberally throughout the living room. Obviously, someone has done some living, after a manner of speaking. There is one lounge chair, beige, across the room from the red sofa. It looks like one of its arms is about to separate from the chair's torso. There's a lamp stand with no lampshade beside the red sofa, with a nice round wood veneer table encircling the gold lamp post. On it sit five or six lottery tickets, presumably drained of all hope. A faint flicker of hope lights my consciousness, but vanishes before I know what it was. Other than the wind and the hum of the refrigerator, it sure is quiet out here. Eerie. I notice strands of multicolored Christmas lights festooned at the top of each wall in the double room, taped down to the paneling.

I wonder what day it is. I hear noise from the bedroom.

"Hey…hey Bubba…would you get my pills?" A loud voice from the master bedroom. I want to know if I am Bubba, but I don't think this is the time. "Is my name Bubba" just sounds stupid, like if you don't know, your name must be Bubba. "Bubba. Do you hear me? Bubba…Bubba? What're you doin' in there?"

"I'm comin' Avril. Hold on a second." I don't think yelling about my calf cramp will elicit much sympathy, so I abstain. I finally get up and hobble back to the scene.

"Whatcha need, Avril?"

"Come on, lay off. I don't wanna fight about it again. Just get 'em. I'm sore."

"Okay, okay. Are they in the medicine cabinet?" I am really trying to go along with the program. Avril rolls over and stares me down. She doesn't say anything, and she doesn't need to. Obviously, the pills are either certainly in the medicine cabinet, or certainly not in the medicine cabinet. I hop down to the bathroom to check it out. I creak open the rusty cabinet door. Not much in here. Some eye liner. Black lipstick. Old Spice from about 1997. An empty box of Band Aids. Some nasty looking loose Q-tips. Saline nasal spray. Generic aspirin that expired six years ago. Something gooey that has melted on the top shelf and dripped down to the other two shelves. I'd say I'm about striking out here. It sounds like Avril is out of bed. When I go out to the hall, she grinds past me without making eye contact. I notice bruises on her back, rear end, and on the back of her left arm.

"Thanks for nothin'. You suck," she says loudly as she clomps by. Then I notice something on her ankle. An electronic ankle bracelet? WTF? She goes into the kitchen and gets a chair from the five-piece dinette set, red vinyl and metal. She places it near the tripartite picture window, and proceeds to stand up on the chair. It is then that I realize we are both naked. Well, it's true, I realized this before, but in a less overt sense. Now, with Avril three feet off the ground, bruised back turned toward me, electronic ankle bracelet and all, I realize that we are naked and not ashamed. Or if we are ashamed, it must be for some other reason. Yeah, it's for some other reason. "Shut up, Bubba, you asshole. Makin' me stand up here and get my shit. How hard would it have been...? You suck."

"I would have gotten them for you, but—" Then I realize that nothing I was going to say was gonna make a lick of sense, so I just trail off.

"Yeah, you would have gotten them, but–. That sounds just like ALL of your other empty promises... That's all you ever do, give me a bunch of empty promises. You're just a big dick, you big dick. You're just trying to control me. It's always gotta be your way, dick. God. What an asshole."

Her voice was quivery. She sounded pretty pissed off at me. She was opening a small cupboard over the left side of the sink, and then removing a small wooden panel on the inside of the cupboard, behind which she retrieved an amber colored plastic prescription bottle. "Hey, make yourself useful. Don't just stand there. Bubba! Take the bottle so I can get back down." Now here's something I can understand. I hobble over and take the bottle. Oxycodone. *Roderick Terrance Mayfield.* Then she put the panel back, closed the cupboard, and stepped down off the chair.

"Who the hell...?" I stopped myself again, again not in time.

"Why don't you just shut up and give me my pills?" She has pretty much already grabbed them out of my hand. She gets the top off and swallows a pill, without water. Then she moves the chair back to the dinette set and sits down. I follow her and sit across the table. The vinyl is cold on my ass, but I haven't bothered to see if I have any clothes anywhere in the joint. At this point, it doesn't seem to make a damn bit of difference.

"Avril?"

"Bubba? Do you just like sayin' my name, or hearin' yourself talk, or what?"

"Where'd you get those bruises, Avril?" It is already cold in here, but if you can imagine an arctic blast, full in the face, that's how it feels now. She gives me the AK-47 look. I grit my teeth and my face contorts, all before I know what's happening. She looks so pissed, I feel like running right out into the cold. Hell, it might be warmer out there.

"Quit playin' games. I'm sick to death of it. Quit askin' questions you already know the answers to." Her face looks so dark, so dark. Those black rings under her eyes aren't old makeup, I'm pretty sure. She looks so dark, and livid, and tired. I feel like I want to burst out into tears, but I don't exactly know why. She looks so small on the other side of the table. I feel the tears well up in the back of my eyes.

"You're the one that oughta be wearin' this goddamn ankle bracelet, not me. You piece of shit. You're the one that oughta have it. Where the hell're my cigarettes? I'd be outta here, but *I'm* not allowed to leave. Why don't *you* get the hell out? You're like a goddamn stalker. You won't leave. You act like you want me to leave, but you won't let me get away. So here we are, in the middle of fuckin' nowhere. We're nowhere, alright. Happy now?"

"Where would I go?" It is a pathetic line, I know it as I hear it coming out of my mouth, but it seems like a safe bet, although I am feeling less and less sympathy for myself.

"How would I know, dumb shit? Go wherever you go when you're cheatin' on me. That should give you plenty of options, unless you take 'em all to the same place. Call one of your girlfriends. Maybe they'll come over and pick you up. Quit trying to play dumb and innocent. You're just a jerk and you know it." Her voice has an edge of pain, desperation, disgust, and hatred.

Now she looks like she wants to cry. I wish I could at least find her cigarettes, but it seems like we are way beyond that. I have absolutely no idea what to say. Anything that smacks of attempted self-defense doesn't seem like a good idea. So I just sit there and look at Avril. Suddenly, I feel really sick to my stomach. Before I know what I'm doing, I'm running and hopping to the bathroom. I make it almost in time. The vomit hits the floor right in front of the toilet, with the second wretch making it in. By that time, my knees are slipping on the orange shag carpet, which is slimy from the first wretch. I wonder if I am in hell. Then I notice what appears to be a tampon and a condom, both used, both behind the toilet bowl, secluded for what may have been an eternity. Unless someone knelt before the bowl. I wonder if they are ours.

"Asshole. I told you not to drink that shit when you're takin' those pills. If you're dead, what'm I gonna do? You don't care about me at all."

It's Avril standing over me kneeling over the toilet bowl. God I feel like shit. I feel like I have the flu, only ten times worse. My head is pounding like a mother. A firing squad right now might be a good idea. Avril is still standing over me. She probably thinks the same thing.

"I didn't mean to—"

"Like hell you didn't. I was right up in your face yelling at you not to do it, but you just laughed like a chauvinist asshole and push me out of the way. There's some love for ya. But it ain't love for me—or you."

I feel my muscles doing some more involuntary contractions and I wretch up whatever is left of my guts and my pride. Invisibility would be an improvement. Who the hell wants to be seen, anyway? I feel what seems like self-hatred rise up within me, and I want to vomit again. But that, apparently, is not so easy to expel.

"Avril...why do you hate me?" It is so pathetic. There I am, naked, on my knees in my own vomit on the orange shag carpet, drool and vomit running down my chin. Avril is still standing over me.

"Shut up, Bubba. Stop talking. You're sick. I...don't hate you, Bubba...it's just that..."

"You do hate me?"

"No...that's not it."

God, I need general anesthesia.

"Thanks for clarifying."

"Quit being such an asshole. Asshole." I feel hands under my arms. Avril is helping me get on my feet. I feel tears well up in my eyes. With all the vomit and such, they should be undetectable. By the time I get on my feet, her head is below my chin. She is so small.

"Thanks for the lift," I manage to say, weakly.

"Anytime. But if you didn't do that to yourself last night, you wouldn't be in here. It's a goddamn death wish, I tell you."

"Yeah, I was thinking that too." I have no idea what the hell I'm saying.

"What, Mr. Perfect made a mistake? Are you sure? Maybe you've made a mistake about making a mistake? Or are you just trying to kill yourself? Whatever it is you're doing, I can't take it anymore." Her voice is dripping with sarcasm and pain. I need to sit down. I am feeling mighty weak.

"I've got to sit down. I'm feeling dizzy."

I stumble out to the living room.

"Get in your chair."

Avril is looking at the ratty beige recliner with the ready-to-bust-off arm, so I shuffle over there and fall into the chair, which feels like it is going to give out at any second. I forgot to rinse my mouth out. Well, it's not much worse than before I vomited. I decide to remain in the chair. Besides, I'm too weak to make it back to the bathroom. I need more information. I feel vulnerable sitting here naked in the classic beige recliner. What do I have to lose?

"Avril, do you have any tour dates coming up?"

Avril shoots me a look of disgust and irritation. "Listen, Bubba. We've already been through all this. We've gone over it and over it. What don't you understand? You're going to have to stop it. No more fantasy life. It's time to face reality." She was still pissed off, but the knife edge was off her voice.

"So you don't have any upcoming tour dates?" I sound like what I am: clueless.

"Cut it out, you asshole. You KNOW I haven't played a concert in over ten years." She is practically yelling. Her bloodshot eyes flash with pissedness. "*Why* do you want to keep rehashing ancient history? *Why*? *Why*, Bubba? Why do you want to torture me?"

"Avril, I don't want to torture you, it's just

that—" She cuts me off.

"It's just that you do want to torture me, even if you don't want to torture me. You just can't stop yourself. You don't even know what the hell you want, Bubba. And you know who suffers the most? Me, that's who, and you know it."

"Avril, I'm sorry for making you suffer. I never wanted to make you suffer—"

"Really, your intentions don't mean shit."

"I'm still sorry." There is a good thirty seconds of silence. It feels like we are on some kind of sadistic movie set. Fuck, this just can't be real. Avril breaks the silence.

"Okay, I admit it. I went down in flames, and now we're here in this antique single-wide piece of shit in the middle of nowhere. Happy now, dipshit? God, you can be mean. God. Sometimes I just don't know what the fuck's wrong with you."

I think about the fact that we are both still naked. I don't feel cold, but it almost seems like I can see my breath.

"Are you cold, Avril?"

"Yes and no. Let's go with the no. Like you care."

"I…me neither." Avril looks at me from the stained red sofa.

"Look, Bubba. What don't you

understand? There's no hidden money, so quit insinuating that there is. You're lookin' for nothin'. Quit lookin'. Give it up." Her voice had softened, so I went with the flow.

"What happened to the money, Avril? Was it my fault?" This is the only thing I can think of that might elicit more information, but then again, maybe not.

"Bubba, dude, you might have a freakin' big ego, but you're not that powerful. We got screwed. That's all there is to it. Face it. It was a colossal clusterfuck. Now we're here. Nowhere, that is. We got screwed by the shitty record label, my agent, my PR people, those two fucking lawyers, those big tour assholes, the crooked accounting firm, and finally, the goddamn government. Those bastards taxed money we didn't even make, but we were set up by the other motherfuckers so that it *looked* like we made it. Shit, you know we still owe at least 1.4 million to those sons of bitches. Goddamn government. How're we ever gonna dig out of that hole? How can we prove we don't owe it? Shouldn't they investigate? Anyway, they didn't. Shit. Why the hell am I talking about this? Why did you trick me into talking about this? Why do you want me to go over it again? Accept reality, or die, that's it. Bubba, just shut the hell up. I mean it. Unless you want to be out on your ass." The softness had receded.

I feel like the trailer has started to spin, and I'm right in the vortex. I think I might vomit, but there is nothing left. I feel pressure behind my eyes, but there is no crying in the desert. The wind howls its emptiness. I have absolutely nothing left to say. Maybe that is a good thing. We sit there staring at each other, with only the warped low coffee table between us. There are about six or seven low fat candles on the coffee table, with hardened wax spilled over onto the table. There are also matches, a lighter, a half dozen beer bottles, a few beer cans, a can of diet coke, an empty canister of Pringle's potato chips, or what pass for potato chips, and a half-empty can of dried up bean dip.

I make eye contact with Avril. God, is it painful. I feel it in my gut, in my heart. The blackness around her eyes engulfs her; she seems to be vanishing slowly, and the harder I look, the more she seems to go. It seems as if her spirit is leaving her body. I want to hold on, but it seems impossible. Avril Cheyenne, international star? Avril Cheyenne, international recording artist? That is all I remember of Avril Cheyenne. I almost jump when her voice pierces the silence.

"Why don't you quit being an asshole and make some coffee?"

"Okay. Sure. Yeah, I'll make some

coffee." I figure I can probably stand by now, so I start to get up. Damn. I fall back into the chair. It feels like a stale Dorito or something is poking me in the ass. I hold onto the soon-to-break-off arms, and carefully stand. Man, am I feeling shaky. I notice the white plastic coffee maker out in the kitchen and head that way. It isn't a Dorito, but close. There's a piece of hard pretzel stuck to my ass, which I pull off on my seventeen-foot slog to the kitchen.

"I've gotta take a piss. Make the coffee, will ya?" Avril gets up and starts to unsteadily fumble her way to the bathroom. I watch her move unevenly toward the hallway, knotted hair, bruises and all. Her small frame fades smaller. Something reminds me of a scene from Dante's *Inferno*.

"Well yeah, that's what I'm doing." I am trying to keep it upbeat, positive. I mean, at least we're talking and having a real conversation. The topic—our lives, or their simulacra—just sucks, but other than that, one might construe the turn of events as positive. I wouldn't, but one might. I am hoping I can find everything I need to actually succeed in making the coffee, but there isn't much on the kitchen counter besides the coffee, coffee filters, sugar, and nondairy creamer, so I get it going. Even an asshole can make a decent cup of coffee once in a while. I hobble to the metal and vinyl chair in anticipation. All I hear is the wind, the hum of the refrigerator, and the sound of coffee brewing. The trifecta gives at least the illusion of progress, an illusion, apparently, I've nursed all my life.

I look around a bit more at the wood paneled piece of shit trailer. This would make a great hunting cabin. There is a clock over the Trinitarian picture window, the kind that doesn't actually have any numbers, but has lines marking the passage of time. I am having trouble focusing. I stare at it for a hell of a long time. Finally, I give up in frustration, get up, walk over, and look up from three feet away. Four…twenty or so. Four twenty? No second hand. I watch for a minute, then a few minutes. Four…twenty or so. Okay, the goddamn clock isn't working. I walk back to the metal and vinyl, sit down, and stare at the clock. Alerted to the location of the hands, I can see their absence of movement. The absence feels invasive.

I can't take my eyes off that clock, like it is gonna start keeping time or playing *Sweet Child 'O Mine* or some shit. I start getting pissed off, like I was robbed of time. Robbed of time by a stopped clock? Right, it doesn't make any freakin' sense to me either. Finally, I give up and stare straight ahead at the warped paneled wall. I start thinking about Avril and who the hell I am and what the hell I'm doing here and if I'm ever really going to know and if I'm just going to have to pretend and fake my way through 'till the end, since I can't find any other way out. Does what I do now make any goddamn bit of difference at all? I mean, at all? Maybe it never did, but how would I know?

How long have I been sitting here alone in the kitchen in this red vinyl and metal chair in this single-wide trailer in the middle of nowhere in what appears to be the Northwest Territories, although for all I know it could be another planet entirely? Was I ever really sure at any time that I was living on planet earth? I mean, really? How the hell would I be sure? Because I saw a few NASA photos? Wow, I'm convinced. Nobody could fake those photos, and besides, our government would never do a thing like that, would they? My ass is sticking to the vinyl, but I don't feel any Doritos or pretzel chunks, so there's something to be said for that.

I don't feel the least compunction to get up again and find something to wear. I'm gonna sit here until time stands still. Or until I have to vomit again, in which case I'll probably have to run right out the side door and wretch, since Avril's in the loo. God, my stomach hurts. And my throat feels like a sewer pipe. Damn. Where's Avril? I'd better leave her alone. She's mighty pissed at me. My stomach starts to cramp up. This is so not cool. My vision seems to be getting blurry, but maybe I'm wrong. I feel so tired. Suddenly, I hear a loud crash. I am awakened from my cosmic stupor. I look around. I don't see anything. I remember Avril. I almost run to the bathroom. My calf hurts like a mother. The door is locked. I body slam with all I've got, which isn't much, but the lightweight door pops open on the third hit. Avril is on the floor beside the toilet, on her side in a nearly fetal position. She's sort of wedged between the toilet and the wall, not moving.

"Avril! Avril!...Avril? Can you hear me...Avril?" I touch her face and she feels really cold. I grab her wrist. There's a faint pulse. "Avril?"

"Wha do...youuu...want?" she almost yells. Her speech is slurred. Her body becomes rigid.

"Are you okay?"

"I was...okay 'til youuu got here...Leave me alone...Leave me alone."

"Avril, you're on the floor between the toilet and the wall. Can I help you get up?"

"Whas it to you, Bubba? If it wassn't for you, I wouldn't be here, ashhole." She makes a feeble effort to slap me away, but misses.

"Avril, if it weren't for you, I wouldn't be

here either. Let's call it even. How 'bout if we get you up? Where are your pills?"

"Forget it, man. None of your damn binness. Leave me alone." Her speech is still slurred, but her resolve is intact. She gradually starts to fade.

"Avril, how 'bout if we get you to the bed?" A grunt of resistance.

"God, I feel awful…oh God…oh…oh my God."

"How 'bout if I tuck you into bed? You can be under the covers in a minute. You don't want to sleep on the bathroom floor if you can be under your covers in the bed, right? It'll just take a minute."

"Okay. Okay…God…holy shi—"

"I'm gonna lift you up by your armpits and stand you up, and then we can both walk to the bed, alright?"

"…Yeah." She acquiesces. I manage to get back into that tight spot and lift Avril up, but her legs are bent at the knees and she doesn't make any effort to hold up her own weight. She is completely out of it. I feel that sick feeling in my stomach, the same thing I felt before I rushed into the bathroom last time. I need to get Avril to the bed. There is just no way she is gonna help with getting her there. Once I get her a few feet from the walls, I bend down and put my left arm behind her knees. My right arm is on her bruised back, below her armpits. I lift her up and steady myself. If my calf cramps again, we're both going to be SOL. I carry her, very slowly, to the bed. She makes a few moaning sounds. I get her into the bed and manage to get her under the covers.

"There. That's a lot better." I pull the covers up around her and look at her face, and I can't help but feel sorry—sorry for what I've done, sorry for what I haven't done, sorry for all the things I don't even know about, which is just about everything. It was my life, I guess, but I wasn't even ever really there. I look at her face, her face with her eyes closed, and I can't hold back the burning tears. I see her, but she doesn't see me. She is already asleep.

20

IF YOU'RE A FATTY AND YOU KNOW IT CLAP YOUR HANDS

I fuckin' hate being fat. It sucks big time. But the even shittier part is that I can't remember a time when I wasn't fat, which means I'd like to forget just about everything. That's so pathetic. God, is that pathetic. Fat: it's an indelible part of my identity, or so it seems. Why couldn't something *good* be an indelible part of my identity? Oh yeah, right. Like that's gonna happen. Absolutely not. And fat is so goddamn intransigent. It's like a lame-ass loser friend with nowhere else to go. Fat people are invisible, unless you're fat or you're looking for somebody to mock. Hey, and I know what I'm talking about. Invisibility is the best you can hope for, and even invisibility sucks. Well, okay, there are a few exceptions—very few--but they exist. They don't disprove the rule. Tommie sees me and he's not fat and I don't think he's mocking me, but he's the exception. If he's an exception, he's one gigantic exception. Maybe he only feels sorry for me, which I guess could be construed as its own form of subconscious mockery.

In fact, that hypothesis gets my vote. All I'm ever doing is whining like a baby when he's around, so no wonder he listens, 'cause he feels sorry for me. That makes him a decent human being, but not me. And I'm fat and he isn't. The essence of the ontological condition of fatness is that it sucks. But you sure as hell don't need a lesson in medieval metaphysics to know that. That's its *essence*, so it ain't gonna get any better than this. And this sucks. Oh yeah, ontology is a fancy philosophical term for being. I know that, even though I'm fat. I can do a lot of things even if I'm fat, but I'm still a fatass, and my mom still has cancer and I've still got just about no friends and I'm just smart enough to know all this shit and to figure out that it ain't gonna get any better, 'cause the essence of fatness is to suck. Life already sucks enough without the essence of fatness hanging all over your body and draggin' you down down down to *terra firma*.

You can't ever get away from it. I know that sounds obvious, but unless you've experienced what I'm talking about, it just sounds like some kind of obvious truth, a tautology if you're Dr. Winter, not some form of twenty-four seven torture—which it is. The goddamn antidepressants don't do shit for the depression, unless by "therapeutic" you mean soul deadening numbness without end. The happy pills do help you lose weight for awhile, until the whole thing turns around and bites you in the ass. That's when you put it all back on, and are even more depressed as hell, even though you're still taking the goddamn happy pills. Only now, you're taking 40 milligrams instead of 20 milligrams and the numbness just engulfs you like a black hole from beyond time and space, and from somewhere beyond the land of the living, a beckoning icy hand, a feeling of slipping, slipping, sliding soundlessly, soullessly toward the abyss, your silent scream vanishing as it passes your drug-laden lips. The only time you could possibly feel okay is when you're drunk with delusion, floating on a sea of selective serotonin reuptake inhibitors or dopamine enhancers or epinephrine boosters or oxytocin infusers or drop-dead gorgeous demiurgic designer neurochemical phase shifters.

God, I feel tired. I feel so fucking tired. I'm either asleep, finishing up a yawn, yawning, or getting ready to yawn. Maybe I'm just bored. What the hell's the difference? I even have trouble keeping my head up. I just want to put it down. On a pillow. On a desk. Whatever. Forever. The weight of existence is so goddamn heavy it's excruciating. But what the fuck choice do I have? Other than just plain checking out, that is. Let's take today for example. One hell of an existence. All I did today was get out of bed about 9:30 and eat toast with grape jelly, drink three glasses of weak orange juice, eat a stale bagel and then go back to bed and read Kafka's *The Trial*. Oh, and I had a brown sugar cinnamon frosted pop tart. Now it's afternoon and I'm ready for a fuckin' nap. How 'bout a nap for like 10,000 years, after which time I'll be dead, how about that? Waking up is always such a...letdown.

God, I'm tired. I can barely keep my eyes open. Today, there's no point in even getting dressed, so why bother? It's a weekend. It'll be dark before you know it. So much easier to stay in my pajamas. Who the hell cares, right? Definitely not me. Weekends suck even more than weekdays. Or maybe I should get dressed, just in case the A team girls pay me a visit. A couple of cheerleaders and homecoming queens? Oh, yeah, you're fuckin' dreamin'. B team? Dreamin', bitch. C team? Yeah, now we're down to the band nerds and that shit. Nope, they won't be visiting any time soon. D team? The losers that still give a shit but shouldn't? Still dreamin'. F team? That would be me. The Fuckin' Losers. They don't visit anybody. And nobody visits them unless it's an accident. Like I said, no reason to get out of the pajamas. They're cozy too, by the way. Polar fleece. Nice. This pair's got pink with white trim with a few gold sequins in a design on the top, right over where my heart would be. Put that in your fashion column, you goddamn Fashion Fascists. Go blow yourself. Popularity may have its travails, but it doesn't hold a candle to unpopularity. Shit.

Ever heard Janis Ian's *At Seventeen*? Yeah, that's goin' way back into the archive of pain, but it's a bad-ass song—a bad-ass song for losers. It's kinda the loser's theme song. If we even rise to the level of having a theme song. Now that's an awesome thought in itself: a losers' theme song. It almost makes me feel like less of a loser. Oh yeah, I almost forgot for a minute: I'm not just a loser, I'm a fat loser. I'm a goddamn fat loser. What? Am I being redundant? God, I'm so sleepy. It's like sleepiness rather than oxygen is permeating every freakin' cell. Well, lying here in bed isn't exactly waking me the hell up, but like I said, consciousness sucks. Boy does it ever suck. Dostoevsky was right, consciousness *is* the origin of suffering. Or maybe he meant reflective consciousness: awareness of awareness. That blows on a whole new level.

Awareness of awareness. It's shittiness to the second power, when you're a fat loser. I'm fat. I'm aware that I'm fat. That sucks in itself. But what really sucks is the fact that I'm aware that I'm aware that I'm fat. You're fat, and you know it. And you know that you know it, and you can't forget that you know it. And the whole world is screaming at you, tapping you on the shoulder every second of every freakin' day, reminding you that you are a fat fatass and don't you ever forget it, fatass. And while you're being accosted by the external barrage of unmitigated hatred, there's the internalized assault right there, keeping you company when you'd rather be alone.

It's that big goddamn neon sign in your brain flashing over and over: HEY, I'M FAT, I'M FAT, I'M FAT. Don't forget that you're fat, fatass. Keep remembering who you are, fatass. Fat. Fucking godawful fat. You can forget everything else, but don't forget that you're fat. Or, you don't even have to *know* anything else, as long as you *know* you're fat. That's all you really need to know. Forgetting everything else because you're focusing on the fact that you're fat—that just proves that you're stupid—and fat. And if for one goddamn second you forget, there are always a bunch of people out there to remind you. *If you're a fatty and you know it clap your hands (clap, clap), if you're a fatty and you know it clap your hands (clap, clap), if you're a fatty and you know it then your face will surely show it, if you're a fatty and you know it clap your hands (clap, clap). If you're a fucking fat sonofabitch clap your hands (clap, clap), if you're a fucking fat sonofabitch clap your hands (clap, clap), if you're a fucking fat sonofabitch and you know it, then your face will surely show it (undoubtedly), if you're a fucking fat sonofabitch and you know it clap your hands (clap, clap).*

Oh, God, I feel *so* much better now. So much better. Whenever you put your woes into song, it lifts the burden. Yeah, that's what Negro spirituals were all about. I'll bet they felt sooo much better after singing a few of those spirituals. Kinda like "Yeah, I'm a slave and all, but singin' that there song made me feel so much betta! Singin' 'bout freedom is tha nex bes thing to bein' free! " And the blues too. Hey, throw away your happy pills, just listen to Muddy Waters or B.B. King or Jimmy Reed or Koko Taylor or Dion Payton or Buddy Guy. Woo ho! Oh yeah. It's so easy. I feel the unbearable lightness of being that only comes from sad songs that portend hope for some ethereal future. Is everything we imagine as good too perfect for this world?

Is there a future for fat people? Dumb people? Ugly people? People who can't make change at the grocery store? People who get their electric shut off because they can't pay the freakin' bill? People whose mothers have terminal cancer? People who don't have any friends, or only one half-friend who just feels sorry for them? People who are illiterate? People who are hungry and thirsty and can't find food or clean water anywhere? People who live in a war zone? People who are just plain mean? What about the Big Daddies suckin' at the trough—do they have a future? Those Wall Street motherfuckers? They'd kill a million babies just so that they could make another billion bucks. Oh, I've forgotten myself: they've already done that. That was just the warm up, the propaedeutic.

Thinking about the future is depressing the hell out of me. And it's making me so tired, so tired. Why can't I just get the hell out of here? But where would I go? I guess getting the hell out of my bedroom might be a propitious start, but I can't seem to manage. But I'm not really talking about my bedroom, I'm talking about this whole goddamn town. I think about moving a lot, to someplace cool, but then I think that that place only seems cool because I haven't been there, and if I *actually went* there, it would suck, probably just as much as it sucks here, which is a whole hell of a lot, a colossal amount of suck, all added on top of the fact that I'm fat, which makes the suck exponentially greater because humans have a boundless capacity for shallowness. I know I do. Fuck it. Besides, I haven't really been anywhere, so how would I know? Yeah, how *would* I know? How would I know about *anything*? Winter was spouting off the other day about the one thing Descartes knew, the one Archimedean point upon which he could construct everything else, was that he knew he existed, even if he doubted he existed. That's to die for and all, but I can take it one step further, with twofold epistemological indubitability: I know that I exist, and I know that my existence sucks. Beyond that, one might say, my certitude is exhausted.

Lunch time. I'm gonna have a grilled

cheese sandwich on rye with ham and a quartered dill pickle, some ruffle chips and some nice-ass Southern style sweet tea with extra goddamn sugar. What the hell, we're close to the Mason-Dixon line. So close. And with all that reading, I've really burned up the carbs. I'll have to get back out of bed if I want to eat. That part sucks. But we don't seem to have room service around here. I didn't read much Kafka, I can see that now. I think I fell back asleep. Now that's a surprise. Hell, it's nearly 3:00 o'clock. Fuck. What a shitty wasted day. Alone in my room, alone in the house. Dad took Mom in again for a radiation treatment, and with the drive and everything, it's always a long shitty time. And then they try to do something "fun" afterwards. After a radiation treatment for cancer? Are you kidding me? Is that for real? It sounds like some kind of tragic cosmic joke to me. How many treatments has this been? Dozens, for sure. Something "fun" afterwards? *What could that even mean*? God, do I feel sad now. I should have kept sleeping in. But then it would have been tomorrow. Maybe it should always be tomorrow, 'cause I never seem to like today. But then, tomorrow is the next shitty today.

Who the hell set us up for this bullshit anyway? Some kind of sadistic god looking for cheap thrills? How the hell could this be a part of some divine plan? Oh yeah, not Plan A or Plan B; more like Plan T for Torture, or Plan S for Sucker. I mean, it could be soooo much better, but no, it has to suck, and then when you think you're out of the woods there's a goddamn endless swamp, and it has to suck some more.

They said that the radiation and chemo worked last time. That was bullshit. Then, they'll get it with surgery. Now, it's post-op and we're back on radiation and chemo. Basically, all of their vague-as-hell predictions turned out to be wrong, even with the most charitable of interpretations. I can see what I've got to look forward to: my mom's not even fat, which as we know, is the root of all evil. What the fuck did she do? If it's not a punishment, then why does it feel like a punishment?

Yeah, I know, life's not fair. If we said, yes, life is fair, because in the end, everyone gets screwed royally, that would make more sense. Equal opportunity when it comes to getting screwed. Because there are two kinds of people: those that get screwed royally and show it, and those that get screwed royally and don't show it. Who hasn't gotten screwed royally? Oh, you mean all those lucky rich and famous people who escaped the royal screw like Elvis, Marilyn, James Dean, Jimi Hendrix, Martin Luther King, Jr., Gandhi, John F. Kennedy, Amy Winehouse and all the other rich and famous people who didn't get screwed? Oh, and I left out the poster child of Neverland, Michael Jackson. Yeah, he had a hell of a life. If it was so great, Mister Genius, would you trade places with him—or anybody else on the list? That's what I thought.

Who were all those people who didn't get screwed? Oh, I remember, the empty set. Zero. Nada. Nichts. Come on people, get with the program. This is it, and it sucks. Everybody seems to keep thinking that there's this nonsucky part right around the corner, and in a sense they're right—it *is always* right around the corner. Which means you'll never get there. It's a mirage. The ontological empty set. There's that word again. Can't get away from it 'cause it is the shit, man— all of it. The bogus essence of hope. Zeno's paradox. Boy, does this suck, whatever *this* is. Maybe I'm cheering myself up with all this bleak talk, just like listening to the blues? Fuck that. And it sucks even more if you're fat. Because the essence of fatness is an ontological condition that sucks. God I'm so freakin' tired. Shit. Why do I keep going off on a tangent? Lunch time, goddamn it. Get on it.

I'm having that grilled ham and cheese on rye with quartered dill pickle and ruffle chips and Southern-style sweet tea, and I'm feeing a whole shitload of anxiety. Don't ask me why. Hell, it'd just make me anxious. The more I think about the future, the worse I feel. And I can't stop thinking about the future. When is that whip gonna come down? Would you rather know that you're gonna get hit in the head with a ten pound sledge or not know that you are gonna get hit in the head with a ten pound sledge, if you're gonna get hit in the head with a ten pound sledge, that is? Which would it be? Maybe being in the dark would be better. I'll take the dark. But I'm not quite there. Maybe letting me remain in the dark is the only truly merciful act one could bestow on me in this sphere, and it is an act of omission. That is, a nonact. All action is flawed, which means sooner or later we're gonna have to repent.

I'll go first: I repent that I exist. My autonomic nervous system is keeping me alive, so I repent of that. Autonomic means out of my control, right? True, but I could quit feeding the beast. But no, I'm back at the trough day after fuckin' day, feeding the hell out of the beast until it's ready to burst. So I repent of that too. I repent that I feel the need to repent. Goddamn reflective consciousness again. There's always that freakin' mirror, staring you right in the face. It's cruel. And it's you. You can't get away from the mirror, no matter what you do, because it's part of your goddamn loathsome consciousness. Shit. Oh, I've overstepped the bounds of propriety. Forgive me. Pardon me, I'm thinking with my mouth full.

You, on the other hand, have got a lot on your plate, so to speak. A whole hell of a lot. Well, maybe you're not fat, but that's just the absence of something bad, not the presence of something good. I may be the one eating, but you've got a lot on your plate. Illuminating the darkness seems to be my specialty, if by illumination one means shedding absolutely no light on the situation. Because you can't shed the unsheddable, and it ain't possible to see in absolute darkness masquerading as light. You're in Plato's cave, but as you sit shackled facing the shadows, you only see the images on the wall. You collude with the puppetmaster in branding the imagery as real, the only reality you will ever know, 'cause it's way too scary—out there. I merely point to the existence of said situation, a situation others would prefer not to acknowledge, lest their cover be blown.

There are things I would prefer not to acknowledge as well, obviously, and lots of them. Let's start with my being 5'4" and 172 lbs. Getting stabbed in the back by people I barely know is another, as is being pissed off as hell that said nonpersons stabbed me in the back. While we're at it: my mom's goddamn evil cancer is another, and the fact that the university is working really hard not to be supportive. I was under the mistaken impression that an institution of higher education would take a more humane approach. I was operating under the delusion that a liberal arts university would at least attempt to appear compassionate when we really, really need the help, when it's a matter of life and death. What a bunch of shit. Money, money, money. Humans are just a tool to make the money. Just another tool. Goddamn. Sick. What the hell happened to my childhood?

It's still dawning on my recalcitrant consciousness that a university in America is just a business with a bunch of Latin-scripted slogans on stuff. It's just a business that runs by hiring a bunch of academic sharecroppers to peddle their wares to the consumer, where the consumer really decides what kind of product they want to buy. If the sharecropper breaks a leg? Too fucking bad, Jose. Gets cancer? Time to put you out to pasture, Nellie. Go ring your bell. If you trip over a fuckin' rock out there, we won't pay you no mind, 'cause we won't hear a goddamn thing. Yeah, all that fancy Gothic architecture? Built and maintained with the blood of the totally forgotten pedagogic martyrs. Luckily, the snake masquerading as a university has its endowment, and it'll never forget about that. Just like every other shithole corporation in this great faux free market economy—all controlled by the nobility and run by slaves. Guard that pot of gold with your life. Yeah, but it's my life, and their pot of gold. What the fuck is wrong with this picture? I just want somebody who can actually do something for my mom to actually give a shit. And if there's one thing they have proven over and over again it's that they sure as hell don't give a shit and they're willing to hide behind their empty corporate structures in order to protect their right not to give a shit. Does anybody anywhere who actually has the power to do anything positive give a shit? That's got to be the crux of the contradiction of modern society, exemplifying its moral bankruptcy: if you give a shit, you're not in a position to do anything about it, and if you are in a position to do anything about it, you don't give a shit. Which one am I? I tried not giving a shit, but guess what? It didn't work out so well. I'm so confused that I don't even know. Maybe I don't give a shit but I think I do, just because I want to lie to myself about what a great person I am. Well, if that's it, I really fucked it up big time.

What the—? Yeah, this Southern-style sweet tea is absolutely exquisite. Ten teaspoons of sugar per pint and really kick-ass strong black tea is the charmer, and it goes great with the dill pickle. Shit. I think I'll have another glass.

21

BABE MAGNET

"Hey Tommie, what's up? I thought you'd be out on a date or something." It's 7:06 p.m., Saturday night. Monica's still in her pajamas. She decided to call Tommie rather than have another snack.

"Hey Vera! Oh yeah, I go out six or seven times a weekend. I don't *ever* get any sleep. Make it short. I've got a date in ten minutes." Tommie is looking forward to a night of absolute nothingness. He took another nine-mile run with Ferris and Harlan this morning, after which they hung out at the House of Pizza. No one got injured—at least not physically—so all in all, it was a good day.

"I can believe it. You're just a babe magnet." It was news to him.

"Yeah, I know. A real babe magnet. Ugly is seductive." He didn't mention the smelly runner stench.

"You're not ugly, Tommie! It's just that smell…"

"…That smell?…ah…?"

"I'm just kiddin' with you, Tommie. Lighten up, dude. Geez, I thought *I* was bad."

"I do stink. You're right. That's what Sammie is always saying: 'You stink, Tommie.' I mean, what's the world coming to if you can't trust your big brother to set you straight?" Tommie always knew he could count on Sammie when it came to identifying Tommie's runaway stench. Sometimes, Sammie called Tommie the meister of stench, but usually he wasn't so charitable.

"I'm just kidding, Tommie. You don't stink. You're not *that* dense—are you?"

"Ahhh……………"

"I'm just kidding, dude! C'mon!"

"Yeah, I know. It was funny. I am kinda dense. Almost as dense as you are."

"Hey you……………"

"I'm just kidding, Vera! Now look who's serious. What's up, anyway? Are you callin' just to say 'Hi'?"

"Just to say hi."

"Are you gonna hang up now?"

"Not unless you want me to."

"No, I don't want you to hang up. I wasn't doing much of anything. Looking at a couple of running magazines, contemplating existence, wondering if my dad is ever going to get another job. I hardly get any calls on my cell phone. I'm glad you called."

"Me too. Sorry about your dad. What happened?"

"He got laid off a while back, and he's been looking all over for a job. I mean all over. I'll bet he's sent in at least fifty applications, maybe more. I don't really know how many, but it's a lot. He's really getting depressed. It sucks.

I couldn't imagine being his age and going all over five counties groveling for a job. And I'll bet he's overqualified for most of them. Or at least that's what they tell him, you know. Talk about taking a lot of shit. It really sucks. But, ahh...how's your mom doing?

"Not that great, if you want to know the truth. My mom and dad just got back from the hospital in Harrisburg. My mom had a radiation treatment today, and she got some test results back from some tests she took a few weeks ago or something. She's...she's not getting better, Tommie." Monica paused and swallowed a couple of times to try to get rid of the lump in her throat. "She's had surgery, radiation and chemo, and now she's back for more radiation and chemo, and she's not getting better." The lump was still there. "She's in bed now because she feels so sick and exhausted. I saw her when she got back, and it looked like the life was drained out of her. I felt sick just looking at her, and now I feel bad about it."

"I'm really sorry to hear it, Monica. I'm really sorry. I know you're very upset. I think I'd have a really sad and helpless feeling too if it were my mom."

"That's it, Tommie. Helpless, hopeless, frustrated, angry, confused, lonely and a lot of feelings that I can't identify. Can't trust the doctors, can't trust the hospital, can't trust the insurance company. All the people you need to be able to trust, and there's one thing you know—you can't trust 'em. The bills keep coming in for co-pays and things that are somehow not covered by insurance, and like I told you, my mom is on unpaid medical leave. You know how those insurance companies have their inscrutable codes when they calculate what's covered—and what's not covered. They always side in *their* favor. Imagine that? We've got at least three dozen bills on the desk in the study right now, and there are a bunch more coming in. The financial thing is pretty scary. We won't be able to get the care for her that she needs. What's even worse is: she's leaving us by degrees. And I wonder if one day she'll be past the point that she's knows she's leaving, and it will be too late to say goodbye."

Tommie, feeling uncomfortable, cleared his throat. "Maybe you've got to—Vera, I'm really sorry if I offend you—start saying it now."

There was a lengthy pause. "I…know…but I can't. I just can't. I will break down. I won't be able to function. I'm just trying to hold it together as it is. This is the best I can do." Monica felt like she was barely hanging on, so the only thing that could happen now would be for things to get even worse. Her stomach was cramped up with anxiety. She wanted to jump right out of her skin and fade into oblivion.

"I hear you. It's a nice night. Ah, do you want to take a walk down by the river?" Tommie asked. He wasn't much for a night of entertainment staring all alone at an electronic screen, but that was all he'd come up with before he heard from Monica. Or maybe Dad would come home and they could sit in silence and stare at the blaring screen together.

"Tonight?"

"Yeah, right now. I'll walk over to your place and we can walk down from there. The moon's out. We'll be able to see—a little."

"Sure. Yeah, I'd like to take a walk."

"Cool. I'll be there in ten minutes and we can keep talking. Is that long enough?"

"Sure, Tommie. I'll be out on the driveway." So much for makeup, she thought to herself. I'll be lucky if I'm out of the pajamas by the time he gets here.

"Awesome. Bye."

"Bye."

Tommie watched the moon gradually rise as he headed over the back way toward Monica's.

22

SALUTE YOUR INFINITE POTENTIAL

"*Every action and every choice aims at some good. The good, therefore, has been well defined as that at which all things aim.* This is the opening passage of the *Nicomachean Ethics*, written in the fourth century BCE, long before the time of Christ. It is one of the greatest works of ethics in the history of humanity, and it's going to be your new favorite. What does Aristotle mean here? The good has been well defined as that at which all things aim. That everything we do is good? That would be kind of crazy, right? He's got to mean something a little less obvious, don't you think? Does anyone want to hazard a guess as to what Aristotle might mean here in this passage? Just take a guess."

Dr. Winter was giving another lecture laced with the Socratic method, a combination of pontification and interrogation. Just when you get to thinking that he's on a roll and you can relax a little, he pauses and stares you down. And then he asks you a question that sounds like something you'd read in the U.S. tax code about business property depreciation recapture—something I'd hear about in that oh-so-boring fifth period Business class. Just being present in Winter's class is a form of weight loss, what with all the anxiety and humiliation. It's like learning to run through a dark forest, naked, at midnight, with a big-ass bag of rocks on your back. There is no sleeping in this class. Crying is optional.

The one thing I can say: he's teaching us how to read. No, I don't mean it like that, smart ass. I mean really read. For example, look at Aristotle's sentence again. Ruminate. Now think of all the possible interpretations of this sentence, Aristotelian or no. Get creative. How many could there be? Are some better than others, and some just plain erroneous? It's really hard, isn't it? Then imagine having to interpret the sentence in the light of all the other sentences in the book, all of which you must scour and wring out for possible meanings before putting the analysis all back together into some kind of coherent overall synthesis. Yeah, I admit it, he's got me—us— hooked.

Did my explanation give it away? I mean, it's a pain in the ass and all, and so is Winter, but isn't everything worth doing a pain in the ass, a big pain or at least a moderate pain in the ass? Take cross-country for example. Now, there's a spectacular pain in the ass. On the best day, it hurts like hell. And the start and finish are most likely in the exact same place. Go figure. The only reason you can even get yourself to be dumb enough to go out there and do it again is because the pain from last time has killed off something like one-hundred million brain cells—specifically in the areas of memory and judgment—so you don't remember a whole lot about the last horrifying debacle and what with your newly impaired judgement, you ain't about to launch an investigation.

So there it is: you find your candy ass back out there toeing the starting line. And for what? It's kinda like getting out of bed every day. So maybe I just like making myself suffer? Maybe. But if so, it looks like a trait I share with most of the human race. Making yourself suffer is one thing. It's when you step over that line and inflict pain on others for your own purported benefit that it gets my attention. What would Aristotle say about that? Damn. See, I'm already screwed up for life. Thinking for yourself is a nasty habit, a hard one to quit. It could get you killed, just like smoking. Maybe faster. Better to think you're thinking for yourself without actually risking anything by *actually doing* it.

If people who stand to benefit from manipulating you can train you to think what they want you to think while at the same time training you to believe that you are actually thinking for yourself, what then? You'll know if you're thinking for yourself, so that whole scenario is purely hypothetical, you say? How can you be so sure? How can you be so sure that you're thinking for yourself right now? You can think for yourself without being able to read, and you can write a Ph.D. dissertation and not be able to think for yourself. By the looks of all the dissertation abstracts out there, a lot of highly educated people have trouble realizing that they're not thinking for themselves.

Damn, I wasn't thinking for myself right there. I was just parroting off what I heard Winter say a few days ago. I don't even know exactly what a dissertation abstract is. I guess some kind of a short summary, the plot, if you will, to see if it will keep you awake. Or the lack of plot, to ensure your choice of soporific. Okay, enough rambling about the merits of thinking for yourself. You'll have to think for yourself on that one. Or not. I'm thinking for myself right now. I'm thinking that I do a hell of a lot of parroting off, but maybe I'm just parroting off about parroting off.

We're all in our hard-as-cement chair/desk combos, except Winter, who is sitting (for once) on his desk, facing us with his blue Bette Davis eyes. Today, they look like a cross between the eyes of Rodrigue's *Blue Dog*, Clint Eastwood in *The Good, The Bad, and the Ugly* and Bette Davis. He has on a black vest, black cuffed pants, a gray button down shirt with the sleeves rolled up like he's going to work on a '57 Chevy, and these super retro leather lace-up boots. Looking at the boots, I keep thinking he is in a time warp. His white beard and side burns look recently trimmed, but the gray mane in back is looking wild as ever.

"Hey, here's a try. Nobody else is jumpin' up with the answer, so here goes." It's Monica Leblanc. Who else would go for that bait? Now I know without having to turn my head. I feel like somehow I have special knowledge on this one, even though I don't. She can be bold. Bolder than I can. What the heck were we even talking about, anyway?

"Miss LeBlanc, please proceed."

"Aristotle is saying that any creature that makes choices chooses what seems like the good for them, but what they think is good may not turn out to be so good. Their 'good' could even be bad, in some larger context. But we don't always have the larger context. Maybe we never have the larger context." I can tell you right now that there were a lot of people in there—and this class has pretty much the smartest people in the school—if you don't count Ferris and Harlan—who were really amazed by Vera's intelligence, and the way she expressed herself. There was a general silence, just soaking it in. She'll probably rerun it later in her head when she gets home, and kick herself because it wasn't even more brilliant, but as far as I was concerned, it was absolutely perfect.

"Monica, that is a wonderful reading of

that passage! Thank you. So, Aristotle is not saying that whatever you think is good is *in point of fact* good. He's saying that there *is* a good, and you could miss it. You could be *absolutely mistaken* about what this good is. That, of course, does not mean that this good will somehow vanish simply because of your denial. Aristotle goes on to say that whatever good we choose, the ultimate goal is to achieve the final end or the final good, that toward which all other goods are said to lead. What is this good? Does anyone remember? After your reading and rereading of this text, this shouldn't be a problem." I'm sure everyone has read and reread the text. As I'm sure that I'm gonna win the meet this Thursday with Annville-Cleona, right after a herd of monkeys flies out of my butt. Skip Garnet has obviously done his reading. I have and I'm still afraid to say anything.

"The final end—or goal—is happiness. That's what we're going for." Maybe a herd of monkeys will fly out of my butt. As for the win over A-C, that will probably have to wait. Especially if Garnet is in the meet. Or Harlan, or…okay, I'll go with the monkeys.

"Exactly, Mr. Garnet! Happiness. Now here it can get a little tricky. By 'happiness' Aristotle does *not* mean pleasure. Pleasure seeking alone, for Aristotle, is the lowest form of life. No, by happiness, or *eudaimonia* in the Greek, Aristotle means something like 'living well' or 'faring well'. This is only possible by living a moral life—a life of virtue. What he's saying, ladies and gentlemen, is that *you can't be morally bad and be truly happy.* Only morally good people can be truly happy. Aristotle is not necessarily saying that virtue will ensure happiness, although some assert this. He is saying that virtue is a necessary precondition for the possibility of happiness. Aristotle, living in the ancient Greek city-state of Athens, had a collective notion of happiness. It wasn't a zero sum game, where my gain is necessarily your loss and your gain is necessarily my loss. A real benefit to me is a real benefit to you, since we share a collective destiny.

"This is radically different from our 21st century Wall Street winner-screw-all mentality. In order to live well individually and collectively, Aristotle maintains that we must first have the correct idea of the good. It's not just something that we can pick out of thin air. We get the right idea of the good only through rationality and virtue. You could say that to be rational means to be virtuous, or to be virtuous mean to be rational. This is a different notion of rationality too, one indelibly imbued with humanism, a notion imbued with value, with prescriptive as well as descriptive elements. The good person is the rational person, and the rational person is the good person. They are coextensive. Let's break it down. What is Aristotle saying about the relationship between moral virtue and happiness? Anyone? Mr. Harlan, give us your elucidation."

"My e...lu...cid...a...tion?" Harlan looked up like he had been spacing it big time.

"Yes, your elucidation. Your elucidation should make the issue lucid, it should throw light on the subject, capish?" Winter raised his eyebrows.

"I'll throw something on the subject, but I don't know if it'll be light," said Harlan with his typical mixture of sarcasm and false humility.

"Excellent. Well said. Continue." Winter looked amused.

"Aristotle is saying that you can only hope to be happy—or live well—if you are good, but being good doesn't necessarily mean you will be happy."

"And bad people?"

"Morally bad people have ensured that they will never be happy. But they still think they are aiming at the good, so I guess in some twisted way, they think that they are aiming at happiness. But they are aiming in the wrong direction, only somehow they don't know enough to know this. Hey... I think that sounds like most people I know." There were audible groans but Harlan acted like he didn't hear them. He just got the same crooked smile he gets when he's passing me at about 137 meters out on a 5000 meter course—about twenty-seven seconds into the race.

"Harlan, my man! Beautifully said! You did throw something on the subject!" Winter looks very pleased. He looks so happy that it is somehow unnerving. "Ladies and Gentlemen, I want you to stand up—everybody up!" Yeah, I knew he was up to something.

Winter is now standing in front of his desk. He is starting the perambulatory portion of his lesson. People are looking all around to see who would stand up first. Nobody wants to make the first move. Bahh Bahh. Sheep. I, of course, am craning my neck while remaining firmly planted on my ass in the elementary school hard-as-cement chair/desk combo. John Raush stands up. Jason Lake. Tosha Monette. Kenny Zeferino. Waylon Waites. Christine Geist. Winterfield. Rebecca Stoltzfus. Haley Cooper. Ferris punches me as he stands. Okay, I'm ready to be bold and follow the crowd. The hell with thinking for myself when it actually comes down to doing something. What a wuss. I'll never be happy. And now Aristotle has convinced me of this. No wonder I love philosophy. Schmuck.

I start to stand up. My left knee cracks.

Shit. My left hamstring cramps up on me. I try to muffle my pain, while messaging the hell out of the ham without looking like I am playing with myself from behind. Luckily, Winter is perambulating on the other side of the room just now, and he doesn't have Bette Davis eyes in the back of his head. I manage to stand. The ham is twitching. I steady myself by holding onto my desk. By now, everybody is standing, something like twenty seven people.

"Ladies and gentlemen, I want you to contemplate your potential today, both individually and collectively. You are standing here to salute your infinite potential, a potential limited only by your imagination and by false beliefs. Now, I want you to raise your right hand to your brow, and salute your own singular infinite potential." There is a wave of laughter. Winter stops and looks even more serious than usual. "Don't you dare laugh at your own potential! Don't you dare laugh at yourselves! If you don't take yourself seriously, who will? Don't ever laugh at your own future. That's just cynicism masquerading as realism or as humor or some other form of pseudo-rationality.

"Once your mind is in a box, you're gone. Once your mind is in a box, your future is no longer yours—you now 'choose' whatever external forces induce you to choose. Once your mind is in a box, there is no longer a living, breathing, vibrant self with limitless potential, but a self in despair, a nonself, the antithesis of a self. And for Aristotle, happiness, goodness and wisdom are linked. You destroy your ability to think when you deface your moral nature. Your capacity for rationality is impaired as you fail to develop your capacity for virtue. Virtue, wisdom, and happiness—*eudaimonia*—are inextricably intertwined. When you cut corners in life, you destroy yourself—as you destroy others." I'm saluting on the inside. But I'm still afraid to salute on the outside.

Everybody is still standing, becoming more self-conscious by the second. Especially the cross-country runners, for whom self-consciousness is like heavy breathing.

"Okay, people, right hand to your brow. Now. Salute your infinite potential, and that of your colleagues. Go." Winter looks at us with anticipation, or what passes for anticipation. He has more hope in us than we do in ourselves.

Hands start going up.

"Salute your infinite potential. Make a commitment to it. Protect and preserve it. Don't let anyone rob you of your potential or your belief in its existence." Winter is emphatic, almost pleading.

Hands all around me are going up. Winter

is walking behind me somewhere in the hinterland of the classroom, and it's really starting to make me nervous. At about the last possible second, right before I imagine that the whip comes down, I get my hand to my brow and affect a salute.

"Keep your hands up! Keep 'em up. *Salute your infinite potential*," Winter bellowed, walking within inches of my saluting right arm as he made his way back to the front, whereupon he pivoted and faced us as he raised his arm in salute.

"*I* salute *your* infinite potential," he said. Nobody laughed. We just stood there, saluting our infinite potential, waiting for the bell. Then he dropped his arm and relaxed.

Alright, ladies and gentlemen, have a seat. Thank you for caring about your future and the future of our planet."

We're sitting there, recovering from our infinite potential, and Ferris actually raises his hand. Yeah, even Ferris is getting the fever.

"Mr. Ferris? A question, or are you just stretching your deltoid?"

"A question, Dr. Winter. I'll stretch later. What about meth cookers?"

"What about them? Go on. Formulate a complete question."

Ferris slumped down in his seat, but then sat straight up.

"Well, if all things—every action—aims at

the good, what about someone who sets up a methamphetamine lab in the mountains and cooks meth? Is that guy aiming at the good too? It seems like a stretch, Aristotle promoting meth cooking." Ferris looked around like maybe he was making an ass of himself. I thought it was a good question. Better than anything I'd thought of, that's for sure. Actually, I haven't come up with much of anything, so his question had to be better than that.

"Great question, Ferris. Anybody want to answer, based on everything we've already said? The answer is there, if you distill it from our text and discussion. You simply need to extrapolate from what you already know. Now, that's what I call thinking for yourself!" If Harlan and Ferris and Garnet were jumping into the fire, I thought "Why not"? How bad could it be? I raise my hand. I get the BlueDogGoodBadUglyBetteDavis eyes.

"Go right ahead, Mr. Tommie Boy," said Winter, raising his eyebrows, I'm sure. Or maybe it was just me.

"Okay, I'm gonna think for myself, so if I'm way off, at least I'm thinking for myself." I was already second guessing my desire to express myself. I was breaking out into a monster sweat.

"Your point is duly noted, Tommie. Please proceed." Holy crap, isn't it time for the bell? It's gotta be time. I clear my throat and dive off the Socratic cliff. And I volunteered? Dumbass. I'd rather be at Surekill with three miles to go.

"Well, if *all* actions aim at the good, then the meth cooker *has* to be aiming at the good, right? But it can't be the real good, since meth cooking destroys rationality, virtue, and lives. If we can't agree on that, we can't get anywhere with this. So I mean, ah, the meth cooker must be seeking the good as he sees it, and he is delusional about the real good, okay? He still thinks, in some perverse way, that he is aiming at the final end—happiness. He wants to be happy, and he thinks, somehow, that cooking meth is going to be a part of getting him there."

"Holy shit, Tommie, that was beautiful! Beautiful. Stand up! Get up, right now." I can barely even remember a thing I was just saying. There must've been something at least remotely good in there to warrant the "holy shit." Good thing this isn't a fundamentalist academy or this class would be cancelled. Probably for the same reasons the Athenians sentenced Socrates to death in 399 BCE. See, there I am, thinking for myself again. I'm also thinking about my left hamstring. I know I'm gonna have to stand up. I carefully maneuver myself to my feet while hanging on to the oh-so-prosthetic chair/desk combo. If you're brainless, the chair is there to support your thirteen-year odyssey through the military-industrial socialization process that fronts as education in this corpocracy. With a few exceptions. Like right now, and a major pain in the ass. Literally and not. I mean, who really wants to think, if you can rely on your prosthetic? As I was saying, I knew I had to stand, so stand I did. I saluted without being asked to do so. It was easier than suffering through the insufferable Madame Xero karaoke. Anything but that.

"Well done, Tommie. Have a seat. Beautiful. Beautiful." Winter looked so happy.

23

THE TREE DID NOT FALL IN THE FOREST BECAUSE NO ONE WHO MATTERED WAS THERE TO HEAR IT

Here we are again, back in the Winterzone. A great place to freeze your brain off. Winter's out in the hall, harassing students as usual, giving them the Rodrigue *Blue Dog* Clint Eastwood *Good, Bad, Ugly* Bette Davis stare. In here, in my cement chair/desk combo, a moment's peace, if you could call it that. I mean, if you can ever get a moment's peace in this life. Before the freeze out. All of the runners in here are looking pretty electrolyte depleted, but that's nothing new. They've got that low electrolyte blank stare, a beacon of imbecility. If your car battery had their combined electrolyte level, you'd be walking. By the way, I didn't win at Annville – Cleona. I was fourteenth. Pretty damn good for me. Must be all those argumentative eight and nine milers with Ferris and Harlan. A 5,000 meter mudfest in 17:36. Not too bad for a talentless slogger. I do think, however, that a herd of invisible monkeys did in fact fly out of my butt. Maybe that made all the difference. And it's hard to believe, but we did actually win the meet, 25-30. Oh yeah.

It rained like hell all day and the course was a freakin' mud hole, so I'm sure that helped me. No lightning, so the show had to go on. We were all completely covered with mud by the time we finished. Guys had mud in their eyes, mouths, everywhere you can imagine. A couple of the girls were crying, but they would have done that even without the rain. It's just part of the performance. A bunch of people bit the dust during the race, figuratively speaking, since there wasn't a lick of dust to be seen anywhere. Some of them really bit the dust, but no broken bones. One of the funniest things that happened was Cameron Moyer lost a shoe in this giant mud hole at about the two mile mark. The mud hole was gigantic. You had to run through it for at least a hundred feet because there were small bluffs on both sides and it was in a narrow valley. Anyway, Moyer lost a shoe somewhere in the middle of the mud hole. I didn't see it, but that's a good thing, since he was like a half mile behind me when it happened, but Klinefelter and Kevin Huber were right behind him and they saw the whole thing. You come down this path straight into a mud soaked field in a low spot. It really looked more like a lake, and by the time Moyer got there, I'm sure it looked like a *mud* lake since a bunch of people had already run through it. According to Klinefelter and Huber, Moyer started sinking down into the mud and started to panic, flailing his arms and legs around like he's got a cattle prod up his ass. He was almost running in place with this stupid high knee lift, throwing his arms back and forth across the centerline of his chest like he's gonna twist and shout his way out. Then he hit a really low spot and he was up to his knees in mud and water. That's when one of his triple tied shoes got sucked right off when he tried to lift it out of the quagmire. As it came off, there was this audible sucking sound and he shot forward into the mud and fell on his face. Nothing like the whole universe telling you how much you suck. I'm just glad it wasn't me, but I already know how much I suck. Klinefelter and Huber and some dude from A-C pulled him out, but they left him there to fish for his spiffy-ass superlite racing flat, which, apparently, was still at the bottom of mud lake. He finally finished in something like 24:25, behind Klinefelter and Huber. He'll be embellishing that story for his grandkids. Or maybe not. Maybe it'll be me.

I didn't fall down this time, but that was just a freak of nature. I usually wait until the sun's not out and we're at a big-ass invitational with thirty teams and 240 guys at the start. That's when I do my best falling down, so everybody can see it. Like the time at Quarryville Invitational when my rear foot slipped off the starting line and I fell flat on my face in the mud while everybody else took off, sprinting across the field into the woods. I'm sorry. I can't go on. Let's change the subject. Let's just say that for a sport with no spectators, there were a hell of a lot of people laughing their asses off when I was trying to get back on my feet. Now, that's entertainment. I would have laughed too if I were them. Come to think of it, I think I'm somehow still trying to get back on my feet. Like I said, I wait for the rainy day.

Oh, yeah, and then there was Ferris. It was unbelievable. I was the only one who got to see it, other than Ferris, and he was too stunned to know what happened. Annville – Cleona was one hell of a meet, if you're talking about major entertainment. Ferris had this spectacular fall/slide combo that he could never replicate if he tried. It happened just before the mile mark. I was right behind him, maybe five or six yards back. We both had on pin spikes, but they weren't doing much. Some of the mud had to be six inches deep, with water on top. We didn't yet know about the gigantic mud lake coming up later. We rounded a sharp bend to the left as we exited some woods, then the trail dropped off a significant slope. Ferris started to fly over the way-too-damn-steep-muddy-ass-can't-see-where-the hell-I'm-going-slope and when his lead leg hit the mud on the slope, he flew hard right onto his back. He stayed on his back for a good sixty feet, sliding rapidly down the slope, until he hit a small juniper tree on the side of the trail. Actually, I think the slide was faster than he would have traversed the same ground on foot. He was yelling something incoherent. He probably thought for a second that he was going to die: "Here I am, in the middle of freakin' nowhere, in twenty-third place in a stupid interscholastic cross-country meet, and I die of mud asphyxiation. Some obituary. What a way to go. The upside is: no more Winter! No more thinking for myself! No more Aristotle and all that crap. No more no girlfriend. Not to mention the fact that I'm in front of Tommie! Hey, where's the downside?"

Slam. His death reverie was preempted by his left foot slamming into the juniper, and his consciousness realizing that he's still right there in the mud, very much alive. When he hit the tree, it stopped his legs, but his head and torso went sideways and he ended up rolling over onto his stomach, facing downhill. It was awesome. When I passed him, I gave him a low five. He didn't respond. He was too busy flailing around in the mud, trying to get up. There was no way I could stop on the slope, so I had to be the bad Samaritan and just run on by. He'd do the same for me, I'm sure. Hey, it's all in fun until somebody breaks a femur.

And believe me, I was really moving, 'cause there's no way you can brake on a twenty percent grade downhill mud slope. Maybe it was then that the monkeys flew out of my butt, 'cause I slipped the whole way down and never bit the dust. Now that's weird. Something I'll always remember because I didn't fall. Maybe Ferris was the lucky one. When I hit the level, I looked back. He was up and moving. The thought of a grizzly crossed my mind, what with the mud from head to toe, or bigfoot. The price of glory.

Overall, I think he ran faster after that episode. His adrenaline must've been pumping like a steam engine. Even mine was pounding in my temples as I glimpsed his inauspicious descent. I was trying not to laugh, which was impossible. But when you're mired in anaerobic metabolism, depriving yourself of even more oxygen is just not a good idea. Not like that would stop us. In fact, there seems to be precisely nothing about this whole ordeal that sounds like a good idea. I mean, the whole idea of running over hill and dale in a monsoon seems kind of ridiculous, but we were out there, and for no particularly good reason.

Like I was saying before, the worse the conditions, the better for me. Let me get back to that for a moment. I'm referring, of course, specifically to cross-country, but maybe it's also true in life. Or, at least in a lot of other generally invisible human activities. The less talent, the more adverse conditions can tip the balance. That's why I'm the king of the shitty day. Let's put it this way: your shitty day is my golden opportunity.

Take Annville – Cleona, for example. I

finished fourteenth. It rained like it was time to build an ark. If it hadn't rained, I'd probably have been eighteenth, or twenty-fourth or something. If there'd been a 6.0 earthquake, I'd probably have come in twelfth. Earthquake and torrential rain together? Eighth. Earthquake, torrential rains over three inches and straight line winds? Fourth. Earthquake, torrential rains over six inches, mudslides and straight line winds? First place.

Ferris and Harlan had a pretty good day. So did Skip, Winterfield—come to think of it, it was a pretty good day all around. A bunch of talentless sloggers. Even talentless sloggers can get their day in the…not sun.

The Winterizer is back. How long have I been spacing it? Today, it's a pale green vest, black cuffed pants, black shirt, black jacket, black leather boots. No wonder he's called the Clint Eastwood of Philosophy. But he's still got Bette Davis eyes. And he entered with six shooters blazing.

"What is terrorism, ladies and gentlemen?" Holy crap, why couldn't we just take a break today and do something easy? But then, in this class, nothing is ever easy. We could talk about baseball and somehow things would get hard. It's never unlike the philosopher to ask the obvious, and then obfuscate to the point that the whole notion of obviousness is completely obliterated.

The last thing we'd want to assert is that anything on this godforsaken globe is obvious. That would just make livin' way too easy. John Raush broke the silence. One could only hope that the six guns were laid to rest.

"Terrorism is when you hurt innocent people who don't deserve to be hurt, just because you hate them. It's evil, plain evil." Raush looked pissed off.

"Are these people you know?" Winter inquires, raising his bushy eyebrows.

"Probably not, no."

"Why would you hate them so much if you didn't even know them?"

Raush spoke in a loud voice, with conviction. "Love is an action. It is a way to treat people. Hatred is also an action. It is a way to treat people. Love is when you try to make life better for others. Hatred is when you try to make life worse for others, or to take their lives away."

Raush made some sense. It still didn't answer the actual question: Why would you take hateful actions against people you don't know? Winter was walking around the back of the class, making us nervous. Why couldn't he just go up there and sit on the desk or something? Maybe he hates us.

Winter continues to dialogue with Raush. "As a terrorist, how do you express this hatred?"

"You could suicide bomb. Or mortar attack, RPG, small arms fire, any kind of home-made device, you know, Molotov cocktail, fertilizer bomb, knives, machete, fire, you name it. Anything you can do to hurt others. Hey, I play a lot of video games, so I'm up on this stuff. Most people in here would tell you the same thing." Raush looks around the room, but nobody says a word.

Winter is still not satisfied. "Class, how is this different from any other form of violence? Is all violence terrorism?" He was trying to get us to make a crucial distinction, or so it seemed. It always seemed to get harder and harder. How do you even know when a distinction has to be made? It's hard not to be insecure in conversations like this. It seems like a set up for failure. I feel like I keep shrinking down in my seat, at least on the inside.

Skip Garnet weighed in. "Not all violence is terrorism. If it were, then capital punishment could be considered state sponsored terrorism. That doesn't seem right." He was on it. His electrolyte balance must be back. Or maybe mine's low. Undoubtedly.

"Or state sponsored war? Assassinations? Genocides? Trade embargos leading to the deaths of men, women and children? Disappearings? Detention without charge or trial? Torture?

Drone attacks? Suppression of freedom of speech and of the press and of peaceable assembly on pain of severe and unspecified repercussions? According to the U.S. State Department, nations can be sponsors of terrorism, so there is a recognized category for state sponsored terrorists. Take Gaddafi in Libya, for example. He may be on the way out, but if you look at the Lockerbie plane bombing, we have very good evidence that it was ordered by Gaddafi.

"The list of historically known governmental actors ordering covert operatives to terrorize, harm, and kill is so long, we'd have to have a year-long course on this topic just to scratch the surface. This list would include governmental operatives in states considered by us to be democratic, and states considered nondemocratic—communist regimes, military dictatorships, or fascist regimes, you name it. If we just look at the actions themselves, it may not be possible to discern the difference between terrorism and nonterrorism. We need to look at the *goal* of the actors, the *intentions* of the actors. The goal will shed some light on the meaning of the violence in question.

"If we go back to Aristotle, we remember that all actions and all choices aim at some good, but that the good is in the eye of the beholder, and that the beholder can be egregiously mistaken.

Saying that all action aims at an imagined future is saying that all human behavior is teleological, which simply means goal directed. The terrorist, then, aims at something, something which he or she deems good. Remember also that the ultimate or final end of action, for Aristotle, is *eudaimonia*, which, you may remember, is living well, faring well, or happiness, broadly construed. The good life, you might say. We can now ask: What is the goal of terrorist activity?"

Winter keeps walking, up and down the rows of cement chair/desk combos, talking about terrorism. His gray hair is unusually disheveled. I really like his pale green vest. I'm not sure how it would go with my T-shirt and jeans, but it's cool on him. He repeats himself a lot, but I still can't remember half the stuff he says—and that's being optimistic.

"Well, the goal of terrorist activity would be the same as it is for the meth cooker: happiness." A familiar voice from the back of the room. It continued: "We all want happiness. We all want to live the good life. We all want to live well. So, if the terrorist chooses terrorism, the terrorist seeks happiness through the choice of terrorism. At least according to Aristotle." No need to crane. It was Monica spouting off again. Nice. Really nice.

"So, the terrorist ultimately has the same

goal as the meth cooker, the same goal that you have, or as I have, or as everyone else we know has?" Winter keeps breaking it down. Sometimes, it's not pleasant to see what you are actually thinking. I'll be more specific. Sometimes it's not pleasant to see what I am actually thinking. When I do, it often makes me wonder why I ever wanted to know. I do like to hear what Monica is thinking. Maybe it's just because we usually agree. I'm not sure if that's a good thing or not. Did he say that the terrorist has the same goal as you have or I have? I can't stop thinking about what he's saying long enough to actually follow what he's saying. I mean, I think I need a recording or a transcript or something.

"Exactly, yes, I think so."

"Thank you Ms. LeBlanc! Beautiful! Just beautiful. Let's say that happiness in this broad sense is the goal of the terrorist. So this is an internal, personal goal. What is the external goal?" Silence.

"External goal? Could you explain, Dr. Winter? Isn't it what John already said: to hurt or kill others?" It was Harlan brown nosing again. If he doesn't have any answers, he can always ask questions. Winter starts perambulating once again and Ferris kicks Harlan in the back of the calf. Harlan always deserves a good kick in the leg. He knows it too. It's like an act of justice.

"Is violence an end in itself, or is it a means to some other end, as yet unspecified? The meth cooking isn't an end in itself, so what about the violence?" I have the sensation of my brain being wrapped up like a pretzel, tighter and tighter. Finally, it gets so tight that my brain breaks into a thousand little pretzel pieces, with big crystals of salt falling from them into the black abyss.

"Violence is not an end in itself. It is a means to an end," says Ferris, speaking like the oracle of Delphi. His brain does not appear to be wrapped tightly, like a pretzel. At least not yet. I feel like, for some reason, I'd like to kick Ferris in the back of the leg, just on principle. I try to quell the desire. It is not easy. Winter is not finished.

"What, pray tell, is this heretofore elusive end, Mr. Ferris?" Why am I now feeling an ass cramp? Maybe I'm being punished for sins in a past life. I don't even want to think about this life. "The external end of terrorism is population control through terror, get it? It's about population control, pure and simple. That's about it. It seems pretty straightforward when you get right down to it." Ferris paused and cleared his throat. He seemed embarrassed to show too much intelligence. I suppose he decided the hell with that because he paused and then went right on. "It's about control: geo-political, economic, cultural, informational, but the root is: mind control, right? All of these forms of external control can be produced through terror. Terror is now a product marketed to those who seek to utilize it to achieve their goals, whatever they may be. Terror is required when other means are deemed insufficient to bring about the desired level of control. This is a key point when understanding the allure of terrorism as a technique, a tool, a product. The terrorist construes control through terror as a necessary component of the good life for him." Ferris trailed off and lowered his gaze toward his desk.

"Ferris. On your feet! Salute your own unlimited potential! Now!"

Winter looked radiant. I thought of the Madonna, with a ring of light around her head. Winter is four or five times as old, male—as far as I know—has this mangy-ass beard, is arguably ugly as hell, and is missing the ring of light. In all other discernable respects, he *is* the Madonna. I am awestruck. This isn't the same Ferris that slid sixty feet through the mudslide of el Diablo. Maybe I like that Ferris better. More comprehensible. In any case, this time I can't give him a low five. Logistics. My desire to kick him in the back of the leg has subsided to a degree, but not completely. He still placed seventeenth at Annville – Cleona. Loser. Mud Sasquatch.

Today, he is a superhero. Ferris recognized the demands of the situation, just like he had done on that rain-soaked bluff. He stood and saluted himself. The karaoke will have to wait for another day.

"Have a seat, Mr. Ferris!" Winter almost looks like he is going to cry. "Bear with an old man for a moment. Mr. Ferris, I would only like to say that I am proud that young men like you are inheriting the earth. Old men like me have screwed it up. Our collective behavior has been reprehensible, and for that I am truly sorry. I can't say how sorry I am…but I am proud to look out at this class and see the light of the future. I have hope when I look out. I know it is hard to have hope for the future, but I desire nothing more than for each one of you to have this hope as well. Don't give it up—for anything. If your hopes and dreams are stolen, you are an empty shell, a ghost masquerading as a person. Don't let that happen." Winter catches himself before he goes overboard with the show of emotion. "Okay, okay, you can relax, I'm finished with the motivational speaking for today. They used to call me the less motivational Chris Farley." I laughed at that. Only about three or four other people laughed. One was Monica LeBlanc. Who the hell in high school knows about Chris Farley anymore? I guess we're timeless, but at the same time teenagers.

"Farley was the greatest!" Kenny Zeferino yells out.

Winterfield comes alive: "Especially his ass crack. Real nice." Too much Peter Frampton, I guess. Only in this class could you get away with that. Or even get a commendation. Man that guy is retro. It's his Uncle Ray. That's guy's a trip and a half.

The direction of the conversation hangs in the balance. Winter goes with it. "Speaking of ass crack, I'm gonna terrorize you by turning the discussion back to…terrorism." The eyes are back, clear blue as ever. Damn. Once he finds his groove, he keeps at it. He doesn't let up.

It doesn't have the same feel as my other classes. Half the time I'm in here, I'm in a cold sweat, but at the same time I somehow feel ripped off that I wasn't able to take this class before. When you're really missing out on something, you don't even know it. I started thinking that thinking for myself was something I was missing out on, only I didn't seem to know it. I mean, I thought some things on my own, but there was a lot of stuff I could and should have been thinking about that just never entered my mind. It's kinda like sleepwalking. You think you're awake. I think I thought that myself. Did I? I must be drooling by now. No need to worry. Sitting near

Ferris and Harlan, it's hard to look bad. Anyway, I'm realizing now how preprogrammed my thought was. Even now, I don't seem to come up with the stuff I think about, let alone the thoughts I think about that stuff. That's hard to admit, but I think it means I am beginning to think for myself, so that's gotta be a good thing, I think, or I think I think.

Winter continued: "If the ultimate external end is control through terror, the means could be just about anything imaginable. The terrorist's use of violence is only a contingent condition. The *sine qua non*—the indispensable condition...people, pay attention now (he's frozen in place, actually at the front of the room)—is *production of terror*, not violence, if by violence we mean physical intervention. That is, the terrorist uses violence or physical intervention when it seems to be the best method—or the only method—available to bring about the desired end of control through terror. If other means are available and would bring about the same objective—control through terror—the terrorist *may* use them, if they seem better suited, more covert, or he may use them for any number of other reasons.

"For in the first place, it hasn't been established either that the terrorist necessarily uses violence to achieve his ends of control through terror, or secondly, that the terrorist wants to be known or recognized in any way. The terrorist, for whatever reason, may want to remain unknown, unrecognized. Thirdly, it may be the case that the terrorist doesn't want those terrorized to know that anyone is terrorizing them at all. What do I mean? I mean that the terrorist may even wish to create a situation of terror in which those terrorized do not recognize that they are living in a situation of terror. In this situation, those living in terror do not even know that they are being terrorized. This is a situation of subliminal terror.

"This latter situation may in fact be the ideal for the terrorist, for in this way he may more effectively exert control through terror. I will even go so far as to say that subliminal terrorism is the most powerful, most pervasive form of terrorism possible: it is disempowerment without equal. Subliminal terrorism is the most effective means by which to control a population: since there's no problem, there's no defense against it. Some say high blood pressure is the silent killer. I say that subliminal terrorism is the silent killer. For it can be the cause of many things, including high blood pressure, heart attack, stroke, cancer, obesity, auto-immune disorders, depression, anxiety, suicide and so many more deadly or debilitating conditions.

"The terrorist may wish to produce in the mind of those terrorized a belief that the current situation is not the product of terrorism at all, but rather the product of market forces, geo-political events, human nature, historical exigencies, natural disasters, shortages of food or water, shortages of natural resources—including of course, petroleum-based products, etc. This list could go on. The claim would be that there is no group or individual orchestrating said disaster or disasters in question. At least, that would be the *claim* of those doing the terrorizing, for they wish to remain covert. It could be the case that the visible terrorist organizations are not the ones doing most of the terrorizing. Is this making sense to everyone? Yes? Any questions so far?"

I hear a muffled yawn coming from somewhere behind me, near the back corner of the room. It sounds like Lake or Zeferino. It gets really quiet, but nobody says anything.

Meanwhile, Winter is making his serpentine rounds. I'm wondering what's for lunch. Then I think to myself: pearls before swine? I mean, I thought I cared, and I'm asking what's for lunch? Whatever it is, it's pretty much gonna be swill anyway, so I'm thinking that I just don't really want to think about what Winter is saying. Maybe it's that simple. I like to think that I like to think for myself, but maybe that's just my own cover story so that I can save face in front of…myself. Out of the corner of my eye, I see Haley Cooper raise her hand. Maybe it's just me. I'm the swine.

"Dr. Winter? I've…I've got a question," she says meekly, with hesitation.

"Go right ahead Ms. Cooper. Spit it out." Haley looked like she totally forgot her question. After about fifteen seconds of twisting her hair, she spoke.

"I think I get what you're saying. That violence, violence is not required for something to count as terrorism. Okay, yeah, I get that part." Then she starts to giggle. That lasts for about five seconds. Then she sits up in her cement chair, clearing her throat. She tries to look serious. "But isn't the threat of violence required for something to be terrorism? If you don't have the threat of violence, how could something be terrorism? Where would the terror be if there's no threat of violence?" Damn. That's a good question. I wish I had come up with it.

"Ms. Cooper, that's a very perceptive question. Thank you." Haley slumped back in her chair and started twisting her hair again. Then she switched to biting her nails. Maybe she wasn't up to the question, so she slumped down. Still, she had the guts to ask. More than I've got. Well, and I didn't even come up with the question, or any question.

"Class, is violence or the threat of violence a *necessary prerequisite* for something to be considered terrorist activity? Think about this carefully. It's tough."

"Haley seems right. If there's no threat, where's the terror?"

"Thank you, Ms. Stoltzfus. Is the threat of violence required to induce terror? Isn't that the real question here?"

"Ah, well, I don't know. Maybe. It all depends on...what you mean by violence, I guess." Stoltzfus was on it. This was starting to feel like a cross-country race, where I see a crowd of people slowly receding before my eyes. The last thing I see is a bunch of asses fading into the horizon. Yeah, we need to establish some kind of working definition for violence, otherwise we can't answer our question. That makes sense. I get that. But by that time, I probably won't even remember the question. Leave that to Rebecca "Intelligentsia" Stoltzfus. Or the Winterizer. Maybe I just don't follow because I'm spacing on half of what's going on in here and now I'm spacing on the fact that I'm spacing. Who's the patron saint of lost causes? St. Jude?

"We could go back to the Latin root: *violentia*, but that's not going to answer our question. To translate violence back into Latin is simply to reask the same question without adding anything to our extant body of knowledge. So why then did I do it? I hear the laughing! Exactly. Maybe to exhibit for you the fact that you're not going to find the answer in a book, or on an internet site, and no expert is going to give you the answer. If we want an answer that we can accept, we are going to have to think it through for ourselves and come up with one. There is no short cut."

Skip Garnet surmounts his electrolyte depletion to utter two sentences. "I'm not sure what the question is. Could you please ask the question again, Dr. Winter?" The laughter of not-so-subtle mockery. I feel his pain. That's why it wasn't me who asked the question.

"Absolutely, Mr. Garnet. What is violence? I'll ask another question: does violence have to involve a direct physical assault? For example, if a person comes home to find their home burglarized, they may say that they feel 'violated' by the unwanted intrusion into their personal space, as well as by the theft of personal items. Could such a crime be considered violence against the property owner, even though there was no direct physical assault? Let's say that the burglar was not found, and that another break-in occurred, and then a third, all at the same residence. Could this be construed as a form of violence?"

"That's stretching it. Yeah, it's criminal, but it doesn't seem violent." I'm ready to kick Garnet in the back of the leg, but my leg would need to be about twenty feet longer to do it. Luckily, the moment Winter peripatets away from the scene, Winterfield gives Garnet a good foot to the calf. In a nonviolent way, of course. Garnet turns around with a grimace and slugs Winterfield on the shoulder. Winter is busy reflecting on violence, so he takes no notice. This is more than evident by the blank stare in those Bette Davis eyes. Winterfield looks like he is going to lose his breakfast, if he had one. All covert ops were successful. The clandestine operation remained so after silence was maintained. The tree did not fall in the forest because no one who mattered was there to hear it.

"Uhh, I would call that violent because you never know what could happen. The person is violating you by being in your space and stealing your stuff. Like, if they do stuff like that, what's to say they wouldn't do something to you if you were home the next time they broke in? Maybe the only reason you didn't get whacked was because you weren't there…" Rebecca breaks off, but then she decides to keep going. "You might have nightmares after that, even though you can't imagine the face of the perpetrator. It's violent because you are terrorized by what you imagine might happen if you keep living there. So, after six months of waking up in a sweat, you move out and put the house up for sale. Your behavior changed—because of your level of terror."

I hear an unfamiliar voice somewhere behind me. "Hey, I know about terror, don't I Rebecca? I had this guy stalking me for months last year, and I still feel scared, and I can't get over it. He never physically assaulted me. He never even threatened to physically assault me. But the situation was really scary, and can you really control your imagination? I haven't slept through the night for over a year, and like I said, the guy never touched me." I don't believe I've ever heard Courtney Weaver speak, other than to say "Here." No wonder. She didn't say much before she got stalked, and apparently now she says even less.

"You can't get away from the terror, even when you are asleep? So, your subconscious is still processing the terror, is still in terror, even though no physical assault or direct threat of physical assault occurred?"

"That's exactly how it feels. Bad. I feel like I want to physically assault the stalker. I even have fantasies of getting rid of him altogether, or having him get hit by a car or something. But I know those thoughts are sinful and that I have to forgive, so I keep praying about it."

"But your natural inclination is to want to fight fire with fire? Violence with violence, if in fact we've established that violence could include something other than a direct physical assault?"

"That's how I feel. If I could sleep, it might be different. But I don't know if I'll ever feel safe again. I've been robbed of something I may never get back. I know Jesus wants me to forgive him, but I wouldn't know where to begin. It would just feel so—artificial."

Courtney burst into tears, jumped out of her seat and ran out of the room. Rebecca Stoltzfus got up and walked rapidly to the door, catching it before it closed. Nobody said a word. Even Winter stopped the aerobics. I heard birds singing outside the window. The timing was auspicious. Just then, the bell rang. Nobody moved.

"Philosophers, it's now time to philosophize on the job. See you tomorrow," said Winter. I could have sworn I saw him wink as he said it.

I caught a final glimpse of the green vest as I filed out. I averted my gaze from the Bette Davis eyes. Blame it on the bossa nova.

24

LOVE IS FOR LOSERS

Yeah, we all want happiness. Right. But who the hell is happy? Crazy people? What's the difference if you're Aristotle or a meth cooker? I've got my thesis for my critical paper: *Why Aristotle Would Be a Meth Cooker* by Monica Annabelle LeBlanc. The whole goddamn discussion seems absurd if the carrot is always out of reach. The question isn't whether bad people can actually be happy. Winter's wrong on that one, and so is Aristotle. No, the question is "Can good people be happy?" or, more to the point, "Can any human being on this planet be happy?" It's a wretched planet of tragic lives, lost and squandered opportunities, hopes erased and dreams defaced. The answer is: Happiness is for suckers. Hope is for suckers. How about: Love is for suckers. And suckers are losers. 'Cause every time you think you're happy for about two seconds, it gets ripped right out of your hands and you're there with nothing but pain and emptiness and all you can do is curse yourself for being stupid enough to hope for anything except tragedy and that's not something you need to hope for 'cause it happens every day and you're right there in the midst of it no matter how hard you try not to be and how much you try to stay on the sidelines and how much you don't want to get close and if you don't it's even worse and if you do it's worse again and love is for losers 'cause you're gonna lose it as soon as you've got it, along with your hope and happiness. So fuck it.

Violence and terror? Isn't that what it's all about? Living is violent all by itself. You get violated just thinking about living, let alone actually trying to freakin' do any living. Nonviolence? Peace? WTF? The violence is built right into the goddamn system, it's fucking systemic violence, and if that's not enough for you, it's existential violence. You're violated...because you exist. You don't need all those goddamn man-made weapons. Not that we're not ingenious when it comes to weaponry. In fact, if you want to look at the real genius of man, look at his capacity for destruction.

Yeah, that's it: The quintessential genius of man is his talent for killing other men, if you can pardon my gender-exclusive language. Or, more to the point: his quintessential genius is his capacity to kill other men and somehow call it a good thing. My thesis: *The quintessential efflorescence of man is rationalized killing.* And every flower wants to bloom. He's always making the world safe for democracy, or fighting the war to end all wars, or killing to get rid of the communists, or the fascists, or the terrorists, or whatever. It's killing to end all killing, as if doing the wrong thing was somehow going to usher in the never-before-seen golden age of peace. As if doing the wrong thing was going to magically produce the right outcome. Yeah, we've seen that happen so many times before. Like none times before. Exactly none. Yeah, right, it'll happen *next* time. And I'm Mother Teresa. Or Pasty Candida. It's your choice of delusion.

The brilliance of man, the self-reflector, who has to lie to himself so that he can get blood on his hands. That makes lying the only vestige of and sign of his nobility, since he somehow believes that self-deception is still *necessary*. Pathetic beyond pathetic. Welcome to the party. It's been going on since Cain and Abel. And don't think I'm leaving women out. I'm just streamlining my argument. They suck just as much, only they've got penis envy too. Equal Opportunity Suck. Yeah, if you want to see the real genius of man, look at his destructive capacity. People say shit like, "Man imagines what is not, and brings it into being through his infinite creativity." I say, "Man sees what is and it pisses him off, so he, in his infinite creative genius, devises ways to turn what is into what is not, to turn being into nonbeing, to turn being into nothingness." Because being is imperfect. And this, of course, pisses him off. The Scholastics were wrong. You know, I mean—how could you forget: the Scholastics were all those intellectually celibate Medieval dudes who did covert theology and called it philosophy. All they were really thinking about was how to smuggle God in and kick man out, out of the Garden, that is. Man was out way before those dudes started their convoluted machinations. Anselm was all screwed up. There is no perfect being, not even God. Existence is imperfect *qua* existence. Just because something exists, it is *eo ipso* imperfect. Antoine Roquentin gets it right in Sartre's *Nausea*. Only that bastard Roquentin still harbored hope because he was a son of a bitch coward. No, existence is an imperfection and the only way we can clean up the scene is to fucking blast existence right into nothingness. It's not easy, if matter can neither be created nor destroyed. The project of humanity is to surmount this principle, to fucking destroy the indestructible, to create nonbeing.

And since only God surmounts this principle by being a creator, what does this make us? Exactly. We're in inverse competition with God. Since we can't create *ex nihilo*, we've decided to figure out how to destroy. I mean *really* destroy, so the shit simply isn't there anymore, to create nonexistence. Does that sound fucked up or what? What really pisses us off, what really burns us up beyond measure, what really chaps the shit out of our asses is not being able to destroy the fuck out of something, to take it out. No, not taking it out as in killing it, but taking it out as in blowing that fucker in question into *real* oblivion. Yeah, that's the Freudian libido and death instinct all in one. Hey, I didn't make this shit up. It's just what it is, dude.

Nothingness. Ideally, we'd fucking blast *the memory* of the shit into oblivion too, but since that's not so easy to do, that pisses us off too. To blast or not to blast. Either way, we're pissed off. Descartes was confused as hell. *"Cogito, ergo sum*: I think, therefore, I am." How goddamn fucking trite. Nobody got any goddamn awards for sitting around thinking. What he meant to say was *"I destroy, therefore, I am*. And the *more* I destroy, the *more* I am. The more I destroy, the more space I take up relative to everything that is left. Without destruction, I don't exist. I destroy, therefore, I am." Yee-hah.

But for Descartes, thinking *was* destruction. He razed it all. Action was not possible, so he took the wrecking ball to the whole goddamn conceptual world. Now we've got post-modernism, darker than a moonless night, a stream without water, a cold north wind bearing naught but ill tidings. Our timeless *inverse-God-project* is to create nonexistence. The only possibility of perfection is nonexistence, since existence is imperfect. And we'll do whatever the fuck we have to do to chase the dragon of nonexistence. We'll destroy the imperfect real to get to the goddamn illusory ideal. The real sucks and the ideal doesn't exist. Well, we'll bring the ideal into being, *as long as it can never be real.* We're not trying to be Gods, hell no. That was passé by the time Adam and Eve got kicked out of the Garden. No, we're trying to become the Devil. The only real power left is the power to destroy. Since God has already staked all the other claims. Listen to this shit. No wonder all I can do is daydream. I think I need some more of that goddamn Southern sweet tea, black as hell.

You could suicide bomb. Or mortar attack, RPG, small arms fire, Molotov cocktail, fertilizer bomb, knives, machete, fire... Come on Raush. Let's get goddamn serious. If you really want to terrorize, shit, you can do a lot better than that. If you really want to terrorize the living motherfucking hell out of somebody, you can do a lot better than your infantile stone age shit. What about unmanned predator drones, cluster bombs, chemical weapons, biological weapons, nuclear warheads, nuclear bombs, neutron bombs, hydrogen bombs and all the secret nameless shit that's in some underground site about three-hundred feet down somewhere in Nevada that we don't know a goddamn thing about? What about making health care so unaffordable that even if you worked your whole entire god forsaken life, you're still gonna end up broke and homeless just to keep yourself and your family alive? Oh yeah, and it's illegal to actually bump yourself off, since the insurance companies tell you how you're gonna live and how you're gonna die. How's that freedom workin' out for ya? Yee haw! Go ring your Liberty Bell.

Shit, let's get fuckin' serious, okay? The fuckers in charge since the Cold War have created a situation of constant pervasive terror for any motherfucker who happens to be alive and conscious. Why do you think every goddamn bastard who can avoid consciousness checks out at the first available opportunity? American Idol? All that reality show shit? Are you kidding? That shit's so unreal that now unreality is what passes for reality. Like, for example, the unreal claim that one can live without anxiety, without terror. Yeah, maybe, if you have absolutely no idea what the fuck is going on. And the billion scripts for designer psychotropic drugs? Oh yeah, that's all we're doing here in America, facing reality. Right.

As soon as you start thawing out, as soon as you start waking up, as soon as you put down your goddamn cell phone and quit texting, as soon as you quit surfing the goddamn Internet, as soon as you quit playing that inane video game, as soon as you turn off the goddamn television set, as soon as you quit streaming bootleg movies over your fucking laptop, as soon as you quit eating your fucking self to death, as soon as you put away the happy pills, as soon as you put down the bottle, as soon as you quit buying all that shit made in China that you sure as hell don't need, as soon as you quit your goddamn feeble multitasking, as soon as you freakin' take *one second* to quit all of that shit, you will find out just how fast the weight is upon you. Just how fast you will be crushed by the infinite darkness of a species who has become masters of destruction, masters of incipient destruction, masters of genocide, masters of the double silver tongued nondialogue, masters of war, masters of delusion, masters of false religion, masters of seeming but not being, masters of terror, the terror that is in the air we breathe, the water that we drink, the food we prepare, the ground upon which we walk and toil, the sky toward which we cast our nearly always downcast eyes, the terror that is in the sun through whom all things are possible.

Terror has replaced God as our closest friend, has supplanted the Holy Spirit in its power to indwell, has expropriated the Christ for all who call upon it as their God. The travails of the Masters of The Universe, Big Daddy suckin' at the trough! How difficult it must be for you to pretend that you are doing this all for us! You are stockpiling thousands of weapons that could blow the earth right out of its orbit, but you are doing it all for us! Oh, the benevolent mercies of the Masters of The Universe! Thank you, Big Daddy, for your loving kindness. Stockpiling weapons— just to keep us safe! Thousands upon thousands upon thousands of rusting, leaking weapons that *you* will recondition with our billions—just to serve and protect! And not only this. Your secret black site detention facilities are there for us, to keep us safe, to protect us! Oh, the benevolent mercies of the Masters of The Universe! Thank you, Big Daddy, for your loving kindness. Your police state of warrantless surveillance, phone surveillance, Internet surveillance, global positioning systems, infrared detection systems, all designed and employed to protect the populace of our globe!

Oh, the benevolent mercies of the Masters of The Universe! Thank you, Big Daddy, for your loving kindness. Your devices of torture, your electroshocks, your waterboards, your manacles, all to ensure the freedom of your people! Oh, the benevolent mercies of the Masters of The Universe! Thank you, Big Daddy, for your loving kindness. Your thousands of military bases and millions of soldiers in arms, all to protect the innocent and weak! Oh, the benevolent mercies of the Masters of The Universe! Your countless mercenaries travelling from continent to continent, at your beck and call to protect the voiceless! Oh, the benevolent mercies of the Masters of The Universe! Your secret and top secret and top top secret meetings and telegrams and diplomatic memos and documents, all issued neatly to us in digestible communiqués! Oh, the benevolent mercies of the Masters of The Universe! Your flexible notions of freedom of speech and of the press and of assembly, knowing when all must be suspended for the good of the people! Big Daddy, you anoint us with the overflowing oil of your loving kindness.

Oh, the benevolent mercies of the Masters of The Universe! Your boundless love for humanity! Your daily efforts to provide food and drink to more than a billion souls who are starving at this very moment, those who, without the aid of your long arm of altruism, would perish without memory! Oh, the benevolent mercies of the Masters of The Universe! Your tireless efforts to produce justice worldwide through the World Bank and the International Monetary Fund! Oh, the benevolent mercies of the Masters of The Universe! You who bring peace through trillions of dollars of stockpiled weapons, we salute your patriotism and love of man! Oh, the travails of the Masters of the Universe, that you must bear all these and other untold burdens upon your broad and beneficent shoulders, you few courageous souls who sacrifice yourselves for the good of all! Your universal love we can only hope to comprehend!

Out of love for humanity you imprison those who would harm us, you torture those who seek to do us ill, you disappear those who threaten us, you kill those who must for the good of the people cease to exist! Oh, you benevolent Masters of the Universe! Would that we see the world through your eyes, if only for a beatific moment, in order to understand your enlightened and bounteous mercies, mercies of which we can only hope to continue to be unworthy recipients! We pray for your strength and continued sagacity to lead us as you have done without question or thanks since time immemorial! You, the born Masters of The Universe! It is to you we bow in homage. We owe our lives to you. You have made *all this* possible.

25

I CAN'T TELL ANY OF THOSE FAT WHITE GUYS APART

I knew the bastard wasn't finished. Nothing like being back in the Winterzone. He's got something on the board about "terror" as a technique, a product, a technology, a tool, a weapon. What I'd like is a technique to transport myself straight from homeroom to lunch, so I could skip all these damn classes in between. And then from lunch to the end of last period. And they say that I'm one of the *good* students. Yeah, right. That's a joke. You know, if it's really true that I'm one of the good students, this country is in seriously bad shape. I mean horrendously bad. Does anyone take learning and thinking seriously anymore? Isn't it all just angling to persuade, without any regard for the truth?

Take Ben Bimberger, world famous AM radio talk show host. That guy used to be just a joke on a few radio stations. He had a great comedic wit. Now he's this guru on the Fux channel and a million radio stations and people take him seriously? Are you kidding me? He can't even take himself seriously long enough to make it through one of his own shows. He still has a great comedic wit, but does the guy know anything about anything? Would he even know the difference? But the fact is, in the climate after September 11, 2001, people started taking him seriously. He started earning street cred, you might say. Without having to spend a second out on the street. It's all rhetoric, posturing, timing, inflection, persuasion. Truth? Irrelevant. It's funny alright, but not in a good way. Even a kid like me could feel the change. Maybe that's because I'm one of the *good* students. It's been a cold wind blowing, and it's getting colder and colder.

For example? The hate speech propaganda? Where do I start? How about global warming. Left wing hoax. They hate big business, freedom, and making money, and they love the earth and actually being alive so much that they invented this preposterous idea that burning fossil fuels was making the earth's atmospheric temperature go up. Sissy Communist assholes. What's more, they added on the threat that even a two or three degree Celsius rise in temperature would cause catastrophic damage to the global ecosystem and displace and kill millions of people. Only people who hate freedom and democracy could be so nefarious as to invent this pseudo-scientific nonsense! Worldwide ocean level rise, catastrophic flooding, drought, famine, epidemics all over the place, breakdown of infrastructure leading to loss of power, potable water, food, fuel, you name it. Those damn tree-huggers would stoop so low as to invent all this just to scare the people into big government regulation and before long everybody's guns will be taken away because of some evil U.N. treaty and Americans won't have any freedom left at all. And I'm an American and I'm free to do whatever I want to do so if I want to drive a goddamn 6,500 pound SUV that gets 11 miles per gallon and piss all over the planet it's my goddamn right 'cause I'm an American and that means freedom and freedom means being able to do whatever the hell you want to do whenever the hell you want to do no matter what the fuck it does to anybody else and those hapless bastards in sub-saharan Africa are just victims of their own corrupt governments and those people were going to die anyway (besides, what did they ever do for us?) and this myth of scarcity is just that 'cause with human ingenuity resources are absolutely limitless but those goddamn tree-hugging liberal sissy assholes just don't believe in freedom and they probably just need to get laid and now they've got the whole world believing in this global warming shit and at least we here in what's left of the free world, we here in *America*, a lot of us haven't fallen for that bullshit hoax and we're still free and we love freedom so we've got to fight before it's all gone and we're in some do-gooder's FEMA camp in the Ozark Mountains getting served some thin, cold horsemeat soup right before they decide to take us out 'cause the world can't handle no seven billion people so somebody has to go and it must be your time 'cause you're the one in detention and the death panel decision is final and what happened to our freedom 'cause we're Americans and America is all about freedom and human rights like the right to bear arms and drive a goddamn tank of an SUV if that's your preference but if you can't do it anymore it's just a slippery slope and soon you'll be driving a Prius and next thing you know even that'll be illegal and you'll be on the solar electric death bus to hell, that concentration camp for patriots like me right in what used to be the heartland of our great country where freedom actually meant something but it doesn't mean much anymore and if we buy into the hoax of global warming you can just kiss your ass and your freedom goodbye 'cause you're gonna be next and don't take my word for it just look at the facts, facts like it was even warmer here on planet earth about six million years ago and besides that God can make it cool or warm whenever He decides to do it and that could be now or next week so all these freedom haters are just contradicting God and I'd say that's blasphemy no doubt about it, it's got to be blasphemy, what else would it be so it sounds like they oughta be the ones in the camp out there in the Ozarks not us Americans that love freedom and God the way we do but all those stupid people that make shit up like animal rights, climate science, economic justice—hell, we all know that's just their code for Communism—and education, like knowing more is going to change anybody's opinion when they already know that freedom is the way to go and there's no way you can stop it, in the end real Americans are gonna win out since let's just tell it like it is—God is on our side. Thank you, Ben Bimberger! How else could I navigate the straits of modern science without your guiding hand, without your voice to lead the way? So, my question is: who benefits from having a fat guy who doesn't know anything about anything spout off and be taken seriously by millions of Americans? Oh, you thought I meant Penford Owen Bleck? That other radio shock jock for the masses? Another asshole workin' for Big Daddy. Sure, funny assholes, yes, but assholes workin' for Big Daddy. They seem to be growing around here like weeds. Their humor is so dark that they make a black hole look like the noonday sun.

So, *who* really benefits? 'Cause from where I'm sitting, it sure as hell *ain't* the little guy. It isn't the guy who's one paycheck away from being broke and homeless. And that would be the vast majority of people living in this great land of freedom. So, *who* benefits? How about that bazillionaire that owns the Fux Network and all the elites who share the ten thousand bazillion dollars they make from peddling that fearmongering poppycock? If somebody walked up to you on the street and offered you two million bucks a year to go on radio and TV and say pretty much anything that came into your head, what would you do? Say "Hell no, I'd rather keep my nine-dollar-an-hour job with no benefits and no vacation. I'm saving up to buy a gun so that I can shoot myself, but for right now I'll have to keep working at the Broken Family Dollar where just about nothing's a dollar. I figure in about three years I'll have saved enough to buy that .38 special and about ten bullets, in case the first shots don't bump me off. I couldn't afford the gun safety course, but hey, you do what you can."

Is that what you'd say? Or: "No thanks, my life as an alcoholic suits me just fine. Ever since they busted our union—they said unions were for communists and somebody believed 'em—I've been working at the auto detail, and then I stop at the Minute Market about 6:00 p.m. and get me a six pack of beer, okay, sometimes two, and go home and drink those puppies down while I eat my frozen Mexican dinner and watch a bunch'a reality shows. My favorite's *Naked Nympho Babe Triathlon Island*. I'm usually drunk as a skunk by then, so it's all good."

Or maybe: "No thanks, I don't want to be made rich and famous, 'cause then all them gawkers would start showing up at my 1967 single wide trailer that I love so much and I wouldn't have a lick of privacy. Yep, I inherited the thing from my dad after he died in an accident at the plant, and I ain't givin' it up for nothing. With all them gawkers, after I was rich and famous and all, I couldn't even hide in my steel building out back, 'cause they'd find me. If I tried to go squirrel hunting, them squirrels would more'n likely all get scared off by all them people following me back in the woods for an autograph, and besides, somebody might git themselves hurt. If that ain't reason enough, the dirt road would have mud ruts two feet deep and everybody would be gettin' stuck and it would just be one helluva mess. No sirree, Bob, I'll be keepin' my day job at the charcoal plant and my privacy with it. I don't need no pepperrotzi followin' me all over the dang place."

Yeah, you'd say something like that, 'cause your life's so freakin' good you wouldn't need the two million bucks. Let's just say you lost your job at Broken Family Dollar or the car wash, or your uninsurable 1967 single wide burned up in a brush fire. What about then? Interested now, Jose? Thought so. Then that dude who walked up to you would say: "Excellent. But first we'll hafta run a few tests. Got it?" Then they'll take you to an undisclosed location and give you all these special tests. Don't worry, you don't have to jump rope or use a hula hoop or anything like that. It's strictly psychological. You're not gonna need to have any coordination for this gig. They'd wanna make sure that you weren't too smart, and they'd wanna make sure that you were very open to the power of suggestion and that you'd follow the rules that were never mentioned. What rules? Just asking that question makes you a candidate right there, as long as you believe there aren't any. And of course you've got to be funny, in a dark, black-holey kind of way. That's a given.

That is, if you're going to take the two million bucks. Then, you'll get ghostwriters for the inevitable book deals and you'll get another two million just off the books and merchandising crap that they intend to sell out the wazoo. You'll have your makeup and fashion crew to make sure you look your part, like you came from nothing but know everything. Then, if you meet the low-enough intelligence high-enough suggestibility tests, you'd be up for the most important test of all. Credibility. You've got to seem credible to the people who are gonna watch and listen: the people who actually have to show up for work and work for a living. Oh, and I forgot the sense of humor, the black-holey dark humor you've got to have as you mock and pull one over on those people who can't get enough of you, since you're their guiding light.

Picking a person like this is the hardest thing ever for those bazillionaires, since they don't actually *know* any people like that. They've got to hire people who will find people who will find people who heard about some people like that, you know, people who actually work for a living, and then they can go out and hunt for them. You see, it's a complicated process searching for what will appear to be uncomplicated, true, pristine, credible. They don't want the dude to look like a marionette. If the puppet *looked* like a puppet and somebody got a glimpse of the puppeteer, the whole thing would backfire and who knows what the hell might happen. God forbid that people should get to thinking that they are being manipulated. That would really screw it up. Remember what happened in the *Wizard of Oz*? Oh no! Anything but that.

No, this talk show dude must be the working dude's working dude, maybe even a guy with a Ford F-150 with oversized tires and a big-ass trailer ball. If he doesn't have the F-150 with the oversized tires and a big-ass trailer ball, it'll be part of his signing bonus. He's gonna need it. It's part of his getup. Could you imagine him driving around in a Prius? Hell no! He'd look gay! They'll get rid of that Prius fast. It's show business, remember. Only the show's never over, and all the world's a stage. Yeah, all the world's a stage all right. I keep trying to get backstage, but no can do. I'm just a guppy in a one gallon fishbowl.

Okay, back to show business, you know, the nasty-ass propaganda machine. Here's the really really important part. You've got to get your listeners all screwed up on what their interests are. That's the main thing. That's the main thing, and that's the most important thing. You've got to get your listeners to trust you, and then get them all screwed up on what their real interests are. You've got to silently—but in the most vocal fashion—replace your listener's real interests with the interests of your employer. And since you're now in *their* club, your employer's interests are now *your* interests. In order to pull this off, you've gotta seem trustworthy, credible, one of the guys.

And you're doing it all for the people, right? Oh yeah. It's an ingenious sleight of hand. Masterful. Truly creative. You've been converted. You have a reason to fight, a reason to live, someone to hate. Back to our friend, the master of irony, Ben Bimberger. He's doing it all for you. He loves you. He just wants to sound the alarm. He may be martyred for the cause, but he's doing it all for you. And he's doing it all for you because he loves you. The least you can do is love him back. Yeah, you've got to learn to love him back. Is that so much to ask?

God, where was I going with all this? I'm probably just trying to avoid thinking about the cross-country meet at Northern Lebanon. That thing was a freakin' disaster. Fifty-two degrees, light breeze, sunny. The worst weather imaginable, if you're a slogger like I am. It was hell. I was looking for the biblical flood, but noooo, we had to have sunny, awesomely beautiful weather that sucks like it always does when you've got a cross-country meet. But I know I won't quit. I'm probably just a nip too dumb for that. When it comes to next year, I won't be on the chess team or the debate team. No way. I'll be right back out there, torturing myself for forgotten sins committed in some past life. At least Ferris, Harlan, Winterfield, the Fabrons, Zeferino, Lake, Oberholtzer and a bunch of other dudes will be back.

Once it's in your blood, you're screwed if you quit and screwed if you don't quit. What the...? Man, this is a helluva flashback. But since it's in the present and the future, it just goes on and on and on. Where the heck is Winter? Still in the hall haranguing the innocent? Figures. The gun goes off and I see people sprinting their asses off straight across the field and into the woods. It's like I'm in slow motion. My legs feel like they weigh about two tons apiece. All that speedwork did me *so* much good. Face it, when you've got zero fast twitch muscle fibers, all the speedwork in the world is just going to make you...tired. I'm still running at the speed of a wounded water buffalo. Actually, I am creatively visualizing being passed rather handily by said wounded water buffalo. I'm gonna have to cut down on that creative visualization stuff. It never turns out well.

Anyway, there I am, careening forward off of the starting line so that I can stumble the shameful two-hundred meters across the open field. After which time I can hide in the woods and keep up the slog. Even Harlan and Ferris seem to have turbochargers up their asses. Usually, they've got something else up their asses, but here at Norlebco, it's turbochargers. Just don't tell 'em I said that. I was only joking.

My lungs are burning before I hit the woods. About that, I'm not joking. Two-hundred meters down. 4800 meters to go. No use going on with the blow by blow description of the other ninety-six percent of the race. Just another example of starting off slow and tapering off. Enough said. Maybe another time. No need to hear about my time. I wish I were in the Winterzone. I wish I were in the Winterzone. I wish I were in the Winterzone. I click my heels together and…Now, I'm here in the Winterzone and I'm thinking about running out in the woods. Do I ever dream of being where I actually am? Boy, even that question sounds screwed up. Well, look who's doing the asking.

"Okay, philosophers! Thanks for your patience!" Winter is standing in the front of the classroom with a big smile on his face. "I had to deal with a little situation out in the hall. Let's just say, young lust passing for young love. Some things never change. I can remember it myself." Winter's eyebrows went up and he looked around the room. "Hard to believe? I know, I know, but I remember a few things." A few people laughed. It was hard to imagine Winter at age sixteen doing the lip lock in the hall between classes. It was hard to imagine a lot of people doing the lip lock out in the hall between classes, but there they were, out in the hall, every day, doing the lip lock between classes. Existence can be downright sickening. Really.

"You've got plenty of time for that stuff when you're outside of school, correct?" Absolute silence. "That's what I thought. The philosophy class. A bunch of celibates. You probably don't even know what I'm talking about. Good. Very good. Plenty of time to screw up later. Plenty of time for regrets, heartache and pain. Plenty of time for venereal diseases. Today, we can go back to the fun we were having last time." I was working hard to try to remember the fun.

"What fun, Doc?" said Zeferino, ready to rumble. He said what twenty-six other people were thinking.

"Very funny, Mr. Zeferino. Let's get back to our previous discussion. You can help us out."

"Really? Sure." Zeferino looks like his brain activity and his blood sugar are both bottoming out.

"If you'll remember, ladies and gentlemen, we had asked whether the threat of violence is required to induce terror. Then we realized that we'd have to address the question of violence itself: what is violence? We then asked: does violence require a direct physical assault, or could it be something else altogether? Courtney Weaver was kind enough to share her traumatic experience with us. She argued that what happened to her was violent *because* she was terrorized. What I'd like to do is start here and move forward. If someone terrorizes you, then what he or she is doing to you is violent because you are being terrorized. If you are being terrorized, then the perpetrator has in the past or is currently committing an act or acts of violence against you. The terror itself demonstrates that the situation is one of violence. The *evidence* for the violence is itself the induced terror."

Winter was being emphatic, panning and staring with the Blue Dog Clint Eastwood Bette Davis eyes, as per usual, but with some serious intensity. I noticed that today he has on a beige vest. Same black jacket and pants. Same black boots. His beard looks recently trimmed. I wondered how anyone could trim something so well. It looked pretty damn ornate. I think I just spaced it. Holy crap, that's about all I do. "We know that not all violence is terrorism. But all terrorism is violence. Physical pain has its finite limits. Nonphysical pain and torment is limitless, it is infinite. This is the realm of terror. This is the realm of the terrorist. This is the all-pervasive, ubiquitous, infinite terror that is the violence of terrorism. The omnipotence of ubiquitousness. The omnipotence of omnipresence. Absolutely no escape. A feeling of powerlessness. The feeling of being seen, but not being able to see. The all-pervasive nature of terror. The battlefield is in the mind." I'll say. I'm trying to keep my mind conscious but I don't know if I can do it.

"So, you're saying that being terrorized is to be violated, and that this can be either a physical or nonphysical violation. Both types are violent, but only one type is physically violent in the sense of being a direct physical assault. But both types are designed to induce terror, and to the degree that they induce terror, both are violent?

Violence, then, is not always physical. Just as terror doesn't require a direct physical assault. Is that it?"

"Absolutely, Mr. Harlan. You've got it! Absolutely!" I can't believe it's Harlan. Winter looked proud. I thought of the Madonna once again. Still no halo. "Terror is the essential mark of terrorism, not violence. Terror is the necessary and sufficient condition for terrorism. Violence, defined in a temporal-spatial way, is neither a necessary nor a sufficient condition for terrorism. Control of memory, thought, imagination—that's where the real war takes place. Memory, thought, imagination—these are the terrorist's battleground. The real battleground is not in space. It is in conceptual space, psychic space."

"How do you fight a battle in memory or thought or imagination?"

"That's *the* question, Mr. Harlan. Philosophers, did you all hear Mr. Harlan's question?" A few murmurs in the affirmative. A few grunts and murmurs in the negative. "Would you repeat your question, Mr. Harlan?"

"Sure, Dr. Winter. How do you fight a battle in memory, thought, and imagination?"

"Thank you. Philosophers, this is your homework, to think about this question, in addition to the assigned reading of selections from Aquinas' *Summa Theologica*. You can do it, so don't bother with the theatrical suffering. You're still going to have to read it." In spite of Winter's injunction, there were copious moans. Ferris sounded like he was asphyxiating on chicken manure. "How do you fight a battle in memory, thought, imagination? Think about it until our next class. Have a safe and enjoyable weekend. I look forward to seeing you next week, ready to continue the smack down." Winter has a sly grin. It'll be a smack down all right. I can already feel it. But next week, at this point, still feels like the next century.

I look over and see Waylon Waites texting. He is probably sexting, what with his incessant between-class hall lip locking sessions with that new chick from upstate. She must be desperate. Or maybe he's just terrorizing her into it.

26

RATIONALITY DICTATES SUICIDE

Why do I feel the urge to stare at the sun every time I see it peak over the horizon? Kind of dumb, right? Death wish? Or do I just want to go blind so that I can get on permanent disability and be set for life? Who the heck knows? I don't even know if *I* know. I caught myself thinking about it this morning even before the sun was visible, so maybe I can do a preemptive strike against my irrationality. Probably not, though. My track record's not the greatest on that account. Come to think of it, from what I've seen, neither is the rest of humanity's. I don't want to get myself started down that road. I'll try not to think about it. It's an intellectual cliff and today I would never have the strength to climb back out. If I survived the fall. I got out here by 5:40 this morning. That's probably irrationality in itself, wouldn't you say? I've got a lot on my mind. It's a cloudless, calm pre-dawn. Lots of stars. I hear a couple of hound dogs off in the distance. It's a familiar sound. My mom was already getting ready to leave for work when I slipped out the back door.

Monica called last night. She said that her mother wasn't responding to the second round of treatments. At least, not responding favorably. Her mother is getting worse, that's basically what she said. That's what I'm figuring. I stopped over there last week after Monica and I had talked on the phone. We were going to take another walk down by the Conestoga River. Well, I rang the ornate bronze doorbell and Monica's mom answered the door. She stood there in the vestibule in her pajamas and bathrobe. She looked very weak. I don't think she gets dressed much anymore. She had dark circles under her eyes. Her entire face looked kind of dark. Maybe it was just dark in the room, but I don't think that was it. Her wrists looked like the wrists of a child. It kind of smelled like a nursing home, like the smell I remember when we visited Grandma in Hamilton Arms. She looked really thin, skeletal-like. It looked like there wasn't much there under her robe. Even her face looked sunken in. She did say "Hi" and something about it's good to see me and she's glad Monica and I are friends. She was kind of whispering, though, and she went right to the sofa after her greeting. She seemed out of breath. There was a little wooden table beside the sofa. On it were at least a half dozen medicine bottles, a ceramic mug and saucer, a beige box of tissues and a cordless phone.

When you get this nursing home feel and Monica's mom is only something like forty-eight years old, it can't be a good sign. She looked a lot older than forty-eight. And a lot older than the last time I saw her, which wasn't too long ago. A few weeks, or something like that. I stood there for a few seconds trying to comprehend the whole situation, and of course I didn't want to say anything stupid or insensitive. It was then that I got hit with a pang of sadness. It really felt bad. Almost like I was going to burst out in tears. I didn't do it, though. I just stood there with my hands in my coat pockets and tried to say as little as possible until I could get out of there.

Then Monica's dad came downstairs and said "Hello" to me and shook my hand. I could tell he was trying to be upbeat, but he looked tired as hell. I wanted to offer my condolences, but I stopped myself after I thought the better of it. To offer my condolences would have been to acknowledge what no one had yet acknowledged, and I didn't feel right about being the one to bring it up. So I just said something like "It's good to see you, Dr. LeBlanc," and then said something about it being a really nice evening for a walk along the river. He agreed, but said he hadn't been down there in a long time, but that maybe he'd go again sometime now that I mentioned it.

Finally Monica came down. I was probably waiting something like three minutes, but it seemed like hours. The tragic nature of the scene seemed frozen in time, frozen in my memory and frozen in my imagination, no matter how much I wanted to shake it. Monica is usually waiting when I get there. But that night it was different. Monica walked into the living room and said "Hi, Tommie", but she wasn't her usual smart-ass self. I could tell she was very upset, but she kept it mostly to herself. I think she does that whenever possible. The café crying scene was kind of an anomaly. But she had to get it out. Her mother is leaving in increments, but she's not even saying goodbye. Monica is trying to hang on, but her mother's life is slipping through her fingers, and all she's got left is an empty fist and a world of pain.

Whoa! I mean, whoa! Damn, that was a close one. I've got to think about cars every moment I'm out here, even if I haven't seen one in miles. I'd better cut back on the daydreaming. Or nightdreaming. Whatever it is. Some dude in a Pontiac Sunbird sleep driving to early shift. Forgot to turn on his headlights. All he's got on are parking lights. And it's this dark out here? How is that possible? What is he thinking? Maybe he's just not thinking—at all. That's kind of a scary thought. At least I've got my head lamp. That dude's eyes must be closed. I'll bet it wouldn't be the first time. I pivot around and watch the car fade into the distance. It's got taillights. Both freakin' headlights must be burned out, or he just figured he turned 'em on, but it was only the parking lights. But if that's the case, why can I see the taillights? Crap, I'm overthinking this. Well, yeah, that can happen when you have a near miss. But I'll still probably never know. "Yep, I've got to get to work in the dark, but I ain't got the money for two new headlights. Guess I'll just cross my fingers." Man, I hope not. Another dude who can't afford *to* have a car and can't afford *not to* have a car, since there's no public transportation here or just about anyplace else from sea to formerly shining sea—if that place doesn't have at least a couple million people—and even then it's spotty. Plus, he could have been sleep driving or sleep texting or both. Or just old fashioned talking on the cell phone of death. No need to get drunk anymore to drive like you're drunk. Just have a conversation on your cell phone. You could run over friends and neighbors, cherished pets, maybe your boss or a few family members and feel no guilt whatsoever. Why? Because you wouldn't even know it. You'd look back in the dark, after you heard the "thump...thump" and think "Shit! Musta been a big tree limb or something. Now what were you saying, Bob? You bowled a 733 triple! Holy Cow!" By then, the hapless schmuck would be half bled out and you'd be none the wiser.

That dude in the Sunbird sure as heck wasn't thinking about some crazy guy running out here on this crowned road before sunrise. I might as well be a Tibetan Buddhist monk on a 8,000 mile ascetic journey somewhere in the East. Make that an invisible Tibetan Buddhist monk. It wouldn't have made any difference, 'cause if your mind ain't here, your optic nerve ain't gonna be doin' you a damn bit 'o good! That's how foreign my world probably seems to that guy sleep driving with no headlights. Oh, make that my invisible world. Can it really be foreign if it's invisible? Then again, *I* could be *him* in a few years.

Put another way: to that sleep driver with no headlights, I am even more invisible to him than he is to me. In fact, if he were as invisible to me as I am to him, I would probably have been dead about eighty-five seconds ago. Owl Bridge Road road kill. And the sleep driver may or may not still be proceeding to work. I'd bet on the affirmative: still proceeding. Then the UPS dude would drive by and thump...thump...he'd grind me into the asphalt just a wee bit more. By noontime, people would think there was some ground up buck on the road—for lack of any other ideas—sans fur, looking really gnarly, with stuff leaking and oozing all over. The turkey vultures would be thanking the almighty for this fortuitous oh-so-tasty snack. By nightfall, the wetness would be all that was left. The bones would be in an adjacent cornfield, picked clean.

I could go on and on, extolling the benefits of the early morning run. If I don't get bumped off in the process. It's a little cold this morning. I'm guessing forty-four degrees right now. It feels good. As long as I keep moving after I break a sweat, everything's cool. The air has some weight. Everything is so much more pleasant than it was when we were at Northern Lebanon. Man, why did I have to think of that? Come to think of it, racing is often a great way to ruin a good day. Maybe if you don't suck, it's different. I'll probably never know about that. But running is something else altogether.

It's no wonder I'm out here running and daydreaming and almost getting killed by dudes in Pontiac Sunbirds. There's so much shit to daydream about that I never know where to start. I never know where to start because as soon as I think about it, I get a sad, helpless feeling, which I'd like to forget, but how do you stop yourself from daydreaming? If I don't have something to daydream about, I don't think I'll make it. Well, let me rephrase that. If I don't have something to dream about, I don't think I'll make it. I dream about a lot of things, but mostly about helping the people I care about. Call me weird or whatever. Maybe I'm just deluding myself. But it's all I know, so I'll probably keep it up even if I realize I'm deluding myself. For example, I want to help Monica, but I have no idea how to do it. Just another one of those crappy helpless feelings. I know the family has medical debt piling up. Sure, it's better with insurance. But if you've got a chronic, serious condition, the difference between having insurance and not having insurance is kind of like the difference between being thrown into a one-hundred foot hole and being thrown into a 1000 foot hole. Either way, you aren't going to be getting out anytime soon. To be more specific: if your family makes $80,000 a year and you have a medical debt of one million bucks, that sounds horrendous, not to mention the fact that somebody's got some major illness going on. Can't forget that part.

All that pain and suffering, and then a gigantic bill that you can't pay? It seems like some kind of a sick, twisted, cruel joke. Economic trauma on top of the illness. The economic trauma alone would be enough to make most people ill, wouldn't you say? And an income of $80,000 is only a dream for most families.

Okay, let's say that with insurance, your family is left with a medical debt of $100,000 from all the co-pays, percentages of services paid by you, procedures not covered, and all that. Under normal conditions your $80,000 a year income is pretty much all spent on living expenses for the four people in your family and the money left over *after* mortgage, food, transportation, clothes, insurances, taxes, and all that is on the order of $5000 a year. So, if you didn't incur any additional debt and there was no interest on your debt, and you used *every penny* of your $5000 per year to pay down your medical debt, it would take you twenty years to get out of your $100,000 debt. That's the one-hundred foot hole you'd be shoveling out of if you had insurance. That's twenty years if you didn't incur any more medical debt, which is unlikely, and if no other family members incurred medical debt, which is also unlikely, I'd say. And these calculations only hold true in the unlikely event that your income remained stable. Twenty years? Monica's parents would both be well over sixty-five before the debt was paid off. Then what? Keep working? That's if you're well enough to work. Or you haven't lost your job. It sounds like a crappy situation all around, and that's if, like I say, everything goes exactly as planned.

But let's face it: the actual situation is a lot worse. Monica's mom is too sick to work now. She's on unpaid leave. Now, the family's income is something like $40,000 and their living expenses are something like $75,000. So much for getting out of the one hundred foot hole. It might as well be a 1000 foot hole. They're incurring additional debt of over, let's see—$2900 per month, and that doesn't even include medical debt. Something is definitely screwed up with this situation. Even I feel helpless, and it isn't even my family. After all the number crunching, it seems hopeless, unless you are prepared to (1) Rob a couple of banks or (2) Work for Oldmensch Suchs in the shadow derivatives market or (3) Print your own money. Or, let's throw in (4) Win a million bucks in the lottery, which may or may not cover it. After the IRS has had its way with you, probably not.

It almost seems like the rational solution to major illness is suicide, given the economic exigencies of the American Medical-Industrial complex. I don't even want to call it health care, since it so rarely has anything to do with health. I'm not saying Dr. LeBlanc should commit suicide. I don't think she should. I also don't think she should be in a situation where the most rational thing seems to be that she should commit suicide. It's a damned if you do/damned if you don't situation. Some may accuse me of being an overdramatic whiner. Maybe so. But the accusers probably aren't in a similar situation. The economic situation doesn't seem to be an act of God. It is clearly a situation created by human beings. It is a matter of how we treat each other. The dilemma is not written in stone. The illness is harrowing enough in itself. Why consign four people to a life of economic hell just because one of them was unfortunate enough to develop a serious illness? So much for loving your neighbor as yourself. I guess here in America we no longer have any neighbors. Go figure.

Well, I realize I'm spouting off to the only person who would end up listening to the whole diatribe. That would be me. I must be addicted to daydreaming, to thinking about the way things should be instead of the way they are. The perils of youth, I guess. I'll go with it. I'm loping back up N. Duke Street as I see the tip of the sun peak over the horizon. I struggle against myself not to look at it. It looks like it's going to be an excellent day. Too bad I've got to waste it on school. Hanging out with everybody is cool. Winter's class is pretty cool. As long as I don't have to sing any more karaoke.

Cross-country practice is usually cool too, just painful. When we take a long run, that's my favorite. Then I might get somebody else besides me to listen to one of my long-winded diatribes. And you can bet, I always get an earful. Well, that's another aspect of the magic of long distance running: it's hard to launch into a long-winded diatribe when you're already using most of your oxygen for other things—like standing on your own two feet and trying to move forward at a reasonable rate of speed. Not always an easy thing to do, even without the diatribe. Yeah, but the thing is, we mostly go so slowly that it's not a problem at all. Except maybe for Ferris the wuss. Standing on your own two feet and moving forward at a reasonable rate of speed? That sounds a whole lot like just plain living.

27

HOSPICE HOUSE

I got the call before school. It was Monica.

"What's up, Vera?" At 6:47 a.m., I didn't think it was going to be something good. I mean, it's not like she calls me very often, and she definitely doesn't call at 6:47 a.m.

"Hi Tommie," she said, almost meekly. "I would have said something at school, but you know I'm not like that. I hope you don't mind."

"Mind what?"

"Calling you so early."

"Hey, it's no big deal. I just got out of the shower. I was already stumbling around in the dark on Owl Bridge Road before that. So what's up? Do you want me to do your Calculus homework or something?" Silence. "Hey, that was a joke. How 'bout if I cheat off of you, like I usually do?" Nothing. "Monica, are you okay?"

"Yeah. Good job on the run. I don't know how you do it. There's no way you could get me out there. I just wanted to ask you a favor. Do you have time to...to come over tonight after practice?"

"Ah, yeah, sure—after practice, sure. As long as I can cheat off of you, I don't need to do my homework. I can be over there by six for sure. Is that cool?"

"Yeah, that's totally cool. Thanks. It means a lot to me."

"That I cheat off of you? That means a lot

to me too, since you're about the smartest person in the whole school, if you don't count Ferris or Harlan." She did laugh at that. Nothing great, but I know she's got a lot on her mind right now. She really has got to be the smartest person at school, and she's gotta know it. "Oh, and Mike Kriddle."

"By the time you finish, there'll be about 1735 people on your list, making me just about the dumbest person in the school. You can just skip to the end, and I'll admit to it now."

"Don't forget the administration. Nobody can be that dumb. If you count them, nobody can be dead last."

"No argument here. Sometimes it's hard to imagine how they even manage to dress themselves."

"You mean: if they manage. And if that counts as dressing. Pretty scary either way. Makes you know exactly what you don't want to be when you grow up. See you at school, Vera?"

"Oh, yeah, Tommie. I'll be there. If I can manage to dress myself. See you in Winter's class."

"Yeah, looking forward to it. That's the only class I actually look forward to, even with the karaoke."

"I hear you, Tommie. My favorite class was you singing karaoke. See you at school."

We didn't say much to each other at

school, as usual. I guess we don't feel that comfortable talking at school. It can be pretty inhibiting. If you're talking about kicking Ferris in the back of the leg, it's fine, but for any kind of actual conversation, it's not so hot, if you want to know the truth.

Practice was pretty good, especially if you're a masochist. We did some warm ups and stretching, and then ran an easy six miles, followed by six quarter mile hills. We decided not to race each other, which was a plus. We usually have at least one day a week where we race each other, like it or not. That would be the meets. No need to kill yourself every day. Skip started talking about the rapture somewhere out on Walnut Hill Road. It was getting to be a regular event, Skip talking about the rapture. It sure made the miles go by fast. It went something like this: "And then the believers will just disappear and be taken up to heaven. The nonbelievers will stay on earth. Whatever you are doing, if you're a believer, you will vanish and be taken up to heaven." Skip is just floating along like he's jogging the warm up. He's going slow enough so that there are about fifteen guys bunched up in a pack. Some of them are struggling just to be up in the lead pack, getting to listen to the sermon. I'm pretty much in that group, but it could have been worse. Actually, today was pretty slack. Almost anybody could have kept up, maybe even some of the girls. Okay, maybe I'm exaggerating, but it was pretty slow for Skip Garnet. Since Skip's the fastest runner on the team, everybody basically defers to him when it comes to discussion topics while running. If you want to avoid his edifying discourse, you've got to drop back, but dropping back would imply that you couldn't keep up, and nobody who can keep up wants that, so we've got fifteen guys listening. It also means that if a car comes, it's gonna have to stop until the herd shuffles by, since we were taking up just about the entire road. And then there are two or three packs behind the first, strung out all along the hills and valleys of Walnut Hill Road. "That's what the rapture will be like," Skip says, looking around like he's on a leisurely stroll.

Nobody says anything. Just some heavy breathing. Then Bobby Fabron blurts out "Rapture? I think I got that last Friday on the date with Karen Lambert, back down on Creek Drive." A hot cheerleader and Bobby Fabron down on Creek Drive? No way.

"Shut up, Bobby, you dumbass. Karen Lambert. Right." It was his twin brother Billy. "You were probably down there doing it with a possum. There's no way you were down there with Karen Lambert," he said scornfully.

"Rapture?" says Lake. "I thought you said

rupture. Oberholtzer ruptured himself not too long ago and he's still here on earth, sucking at cross-country."

"Hey Lake, you're the one that sucks. Only you suck at life. Shut up, loser." It's Oberholtzer, about four yards behind Lake, at the back of the lead pack. Maybe Lake didn't know he was there. Or maybe he did.

"The rapture? Skip dude, what if we're running the Lancaster-Lebanon League Championship Meet when it happens? That would mean that only a nonbeliever could win the race, right? That means I might have a chance." It was Kenny "Sweet" Zeferino, Mr. Deep Theology. He was certainly chapping Garnet's ass, but Skip exhibited the patience of Job. Actually, everybody was chapping his ass, but Skip just let it ride.

"Kenny Boy, if you're taken up, you won't care who wins the race. 'Cause you'll be in heaven! No more pain, no more suffering." Skip looked over at Kenny through his dark gold-framed shades, totally copacetic.

Harlan jumped in: "I don't want to go there, since if there's no more pain and no more suffering, there's definitely no more cross-country. But I can tell you this, Sweet Boy will never win the league championship, even if everybody else in the race gets raptured and he's the only one left." Harlan, I'm sure, would give up cross-country if he could just get a little nookie. For the foreseeable future, he'll be running. Running with us, the poor bastard. "If everybody except Sweet Boy gets raptured during the league meet, or if everybody gets ruptured during the league meet, Sweet Boy will still lose. He'd probably get lost out on the course and end up in Mount Nebo with shin splits, calling for his mommy. Wah! Wah!"

Lake didn't miss a stride. "Maybe everybody will get ruptured before they get raptured. God could heal them all once they got to the pearly gates, no problem. All except Zeferino, I mean. He'd still be down on earth, all by himself, not winning the League cross-country meet. He'd probably trip over a root and break his ankle. After he gets ruptured."

"What's that supposed to mean, Lake, you loser?" I said. I had to chime in somewhere.

"God wouldn't allow it. He's got some standards, you know, even for cross-country, and even after the rapture." Not unlike Harlan, Lake is always pushing his luck.

"In heaven there's no more cross-country as we know it...Well, I don't know if there's cross-country or not, but there's no more pain and suffering." Skip expatiates on the unexpatiatable. Meanwhile, we still had over three miles to go.

Harlan kept it up: "If I run cross-country, I suffer. If I give it up and do not run cross-country, I suffer. Therefore, there is no heaven." If Harlan runs with us, we suffer. What a dipstick.

"Harlan, that's an invalid inference. You're only proving that you won't go to heaven, not that heaven does not exist." Ferris kicks some theological ass. "But who needs it, as long as we've got Walnut Hill Road?"

"What is *that* supposed to mean? It sounds like Harlan just proved that he's gonna suffer, no matter what," says Sweet Boy Zeferino.

"Exactly, dude. And if only nonsufferers go to heaven and Harlan is a sufferer, then Harlan won't go to heaven. But we all already know that," Ferris says in a raspy, self-satisfied voice. Harlan doesn't look too happy. But that's kind of par for the course when it comes to Harlan. Or maybe it's only because every time I see him, he's around us.

"What the? What are you talking about, Ferris?" says Lake.

"Heck if I know. But there better be a heaven," says Ferris. "There's gotta be something better than this. Too many good people getting the shaft. Too many bad people doing the shafting."

The dark, gold-framed shades glanced back at Ferris. "Vengeance is mine, saith the

Lord. God will mete out his divine justice, at the right time."

"Holy crap, Skip, what's he waiting for? Maybe he ought to do a little meting right about now, wouldn't you say?" Ferris was on to something.

Winterfield so far hadn't said anything, which wasn't unusual, but once he spoke, you knew he was holding back for good reason. "What if you're flying a commercial airliner and you get raptured and two hundred people go down with the plane? That seems screwed up. Maybe they ought to screen those pilots and hire only non-Christians. It's the only safe way to go." There was laughter amidst the foot pounding and heavy breathing.

"There's no need to worry about stuff like that, Winterfield. God will handle it. He has a plan, but he's not telling it to us because we wouldn't understand it even if he did." Skip just keeps on going with the explanations, very patiently. It crossed my mind that maybe the rapture had already happened and somehow we just didn't know about it. I kept that thought to myself. Anyway, the rapture/rupture conversation went on for something like four miles, until we were basically back at the school. The miles went by like nothing. It almost never seems like that when I'm by myself.

I rang the LeBlanc doorbell at five minutes to six. I had eaten a protein bar on the way over. Washed it down with a little iced tea. I was feeling pretty good. A good kind of tired. Monica came right to the door, walked out, and closed the door behind her. She had her coat on and was carrying her purse in one hand and her car keys in the other. I didn't get a good look at her eyes. I just saw the glare of the fat plastic glasses. She seemed kind of nervous and she kept looking at the ground. Well, one good thing was that I wouldn't have to go through another awkward scene with the parental units. That was a relief. That last time was awkward...and painful. There's just no way I'm gonna start crying right there in the LeBlanc living room. Not if I can help it.

"Tommie, we're gonna take a little trip, okay? Do you mind?" She was speaking very softly. She was making eye contact with my knees. "I'll tell you about it on the way."

"Okay, Vera. Sure. Did you eat supper?"

"I'm not really hungry right now. Did you?"

"I had a snack. I'm cool." We started walking to her car. I love that thing. I thought I detected some new body damage as we got closer, but I think it was just my imagination. It probably always looked that bad. I figured Monica was being quiet for a reason, so I decided to wait until she said something, even if it felt weird. I didn't want to start joking like I usually do, just to relieve tension. I noticed that my right calf and achilles tendon were really starting to tighten up. What else is new? The car smelled like fast food. I was massaging my right calf as Monica got the Subaru going—with a lot more finesse than last time. A lot more. Maybe we'll live.

*   *   *   *   *

This is crazy. Why did I call Tommie? He doesn't even have a clue where we're going. For all he knows, I got knocked up by some 98 pound pimply-faced freshman from Cedar Crest who doesn't even shave yet and we're going to Planned Parenthood to dump the fetus. Nobody could tell that I wasn't pregnant, so who knows what he thinks? What was I thinking? What are we going to do over there anyway? Shit. Holy crap, where's third gear?

"Crap, Tommie, I can't find third gear!" I'm grinding the hell out of the transmission, but I know there's no way I accidentally put it in reverse. That's down and third is up. That's when Tommie puts his hand on top of mine, pulls the shifter into neutral and tells me to push in the clutch. Then he pushes the shifter forward, right into third. I slowly release the pedal. The clutch engages almost soundlessly.

"How did you manage to do that, Dale Earnhardt?"

"You're the one driving. I'm just the co-pilot."

"Maybe so, but without you, we'd never get out of second gear."

"Maybe that's a good thing. Maybe you're not supposed to get out of second gear."

"Sometimes I feel that way. Like I can't ever get out of second gear, and if I try, I just grind everything to a halt." We're moving forward, still in third, about twenty-two miles per hour. If only I could do this well in life.

"Vera, are we just driving around tonight, or did you have someplace specific in mind?"

"No, no, we're going somewhere, don't worry."

"It's alright if we're not going anywhere. It doesn't matter to me. I can see you just wanted an opportunity to show off your new driving prowess."

"Yeah, that's it." Yeah, that's definitely not it. God life is hard. Does it get any easier? Am I really having the time of my life, like all those old people keep saying?

"I've got something for you, Tommie. Look in the back seat under that pile of papers.

Happy belated birthday. I know I'm over a month late on your birthday."

"That's cool. I didn't expect anything. But if you've got something for me, that's great. I'll take it!" Tommie turns back and rustles beneath the papers and pulls out a small box, about six inches square, wrapped in blue tissue paper. I know he's going to like it.

"Is this it? He holds it up while turning it over a few times. He looks at it like it's a two pound solid gold medallion.

"That's it, Tommie. Open it up now while you still can. I might need to shift soon."

"Hey, that was funny." Tommie starts ripping open the tissue paper. He spies the CD.

"Hey, thanks! Awesome! Maynard… Ferguson's…*Con…quis…ta…dor*. You gotta love anybody named Maynard, especially if they actually use their real name. It's gotta be his real name. May…nard. There's a nerd in there somewhere. Plus, I'm sick of always downloading stuff. You never get to see the cover, never get to read the notes like you can with an actual CD. Thanks, Monica. Thanks a lot. I get to read about May-NERD."

"Very funny. Anyway, it's May-NARD, not May-NERD. That's one of my favorite CDs out of the archive. It's like thirty-five years old or something. Maynard was a trumpet player from

Canada. The theme from *Rocky* is on there, the first *Rocky*. You know, the movie."

"*Rocky Horror?*"

"No, not *Rocky Horror Picture Show*. It'd probably go good with that too. The Sylvester Stallone movie about boxing."

"Oh yeah, my dad likes that. I can't remember seeing it. It's like a billion years old or something." The car is stuttering down George Street, about eighteen miles per hour, just fast enough to keep it in third without the rig stalling to a stop. It's pretty embarrassing. And I haven't even brought up the hospice house yet.

"Yeah, a billion or something, give or take a few million." Am I ever going to get to the point? I'm losing my nerve. I don't know if I can do it. I feel so comfortable around Tommie, and yet, I just can't tell him what's going on. I think my breath stinks. I didn't brush my teeth. I didn't comb my hair since this morning either. I suck. Why couldn't I just fade away, fade away into oblivion. It would be so much easier than...this.

"Thanks a lot for the CD, Vera. I know I'm gonna like it. Real music for a change. Not all that crap I keep hearing on the radio and on TV and everywhere I go and try not to hear. Some real music would be a nice switch. With actual musicians. What a concept. I guess we can't listen to it now. No CD player."

I've got to tell him. "We can't, you're right. But...but...listen Tommie, we are going somewhere and I've got to tell you where, but I'm having a hard time." I sound pathetic even before I tell him anything. That is so pathetic. Maybe I should just drive back home and forget the whole thing.

"Vera, I've got an idea. Pull in to the parking lot right up there, okay?" There's a Chicken Mountain Minit Market just past the ninety-degree curve, on the road that heads straight into Lancaster, on the right. I won't have to stop on the road or cross traffic.

"Yeah, okay. Do you want some snacks?" "No. You'll see." I pulled in and parked and left the engine running. Tommie looked straight at me. I felt a knot in my stomach.

"Now you can tell me where are we going, Vera. Alright?"

I've just got to get it out before I choke up.

"Tommie...Tommie do you know...what Hospice is?"

Tommie looked like he had been caught off guard.

"Not exactly, no. I've heard of it. A health care alternative?"

"Sort of, yeah. Uh, people who are terminally ill can go to Hospice instead of the hospital. They take care of you while you are there, but they don't try to keep you alive. They just make you as comfortable as they can for your remaining time. Something like…that."

My throat was feeling really tight and I was starting to feel hot and claustrophobic. I could feel my heart beat in my ears. My stomach was feeling tighter and tighter, like it was constricting into a ball, churning and hurting. Tommie looked serious.

"Okay, Vera. I understand. I'm listening."

Now I'm feeling lightheaded. This is not going well at all.

"Look, I'm gonna get out and come over to your door. You slide over to my seat and I'll drive. I've got my permit. You can supervise. You can tell me where to go."

He is being so kind. God, I hardly ever use that word, unless I'm mocking the shit out of somebody. Permit? I didn't know he had a permit. But how the hell am *I* going to supervise? I can't even deal with my own shit. I thought all the kindness had been sucked out of the universe a long time ago, before we were ever born. But there's kindness still, in this universe, right here in my Subaru. God I feel empty. I feel a knife edge of pain slice right through me. Not that that's new. It's just another reason for the blade. I can't feel the kindness. All I feel is the blade.

"Okay. Yeah." My voice sounds so weak.

It's embarrassing. I want to pull my coat over my head. I start to slide over to Tommie's now empty seat, but my left leg gets stuck on the shifter. Dumb fatass. I manage to get loose before Tommie gets to the driver's side. Tommie gets in the driver's seat and pulls the shifter into reverse. He slowly releases the clutch while backing up in a semicircle, then finds first and again engages the clutch. He's been holding out on me. He can drive a stick. A lot better than I can. I feel like I might throw up. I'm so glad I didn't eat dinner. Tommie's probing eyes are turned again toward me.

"Are we headed out Millersville Pike toward Lancaster?"

"Yes."

"Is your mother in hospice? Is that what you are saying, Vera?"

"Yes, Tommie. She went to the Hospice House this morning after I left for school. My dad called the school to let me know. I'm supposed to meet them in there. It's on the west side of Lancaster, I think. I've got the address." My throat feels like it's burning up. There is so much pressure behind my eyes. It feels like my eyes are going to pop right out of their sockets. Tommie is driving smoothly and slowly past St. Phillip's Catholic Church right on the edge of town. I always feel like I'm on some kind of edge. I knew

I had to tell him more before we got in there.

"When you're in Hospice, you can stay at home, or, if you need more care, you can go into the Hospice House. Mom collapsed about 6:30 this morning and Dad had to call 911. The ambulance took her to the Hospice House. I thought they were going to take her to the hospital, but they took her to the Hospice House. When I called you, I thought we were going to go to the hospital. God, I can't believe this is happening. Why? It makes no sense. It's not fair."

My body is tensing up and I feel like screaming and punching somebody, but I just sit back and put my head against the headrest. I feel a wave of exhaustion engulf me. I just feel so tired. So tired. Like I'm swimming upstream. Like I've always been swimming upstream. Like I will always be swimming upstream. I try to breathe deeply, but I feel like I can't get enough oxygen and I'm drowning slowly no matter what I do.

"I agree, Vera, it's not fair. We'll get you there so that you can see her. We'll be there in a few minutes. You'll feel better after you see her." I was hoping that was true, but how much better can you feel when you see your forty-eight year old mother in the Hospice House? I gave him the address and we were there, almost before I was ready. I'm hoping I can get out of the car and make it into the building without collapsing. The building was a nondescript three-story old brick structure missing a lot of mortar. That I remember. I don't know why. It sat back quite far from the side street on which it fronted. It really didn't look that different from any of the houses around it, but then I realized that people had lived and died in them all.

"Would you like me to wait outside, Monica? I don't mind at all. I can hang out on the porch." I actually really looked at Tommie for literally the first time today and he looked so earnest. In my head, I feel so thankful that he's here. But I just can't feel it. All I feel is a knot of amorphous pain.

"Yeah, that would be nice. Thanks."

I got out at the curb and tried not to fall. I was feeling shaky in so many ways. I suddenly got the thought that I feel like I'm in hell.

"Take your time. Don't worry about me. I'll find a parking space and hang out on the porch. Take all the time you want. I won't steal your car." I don't know what I'm going to have to do here, but I just don't know if I can do it. God, I wish it would all go away.

"Thanks, Tommie." My throat was dry and constricted. I steadied myself on the door jamb, turned toward the building and closed the door. I headed for the Hotel California—East. I thought about stabbing it with my steely knives, but I knew I could not kill the beast. Nobody checks out of this joint, that's what I hear. And apparently, whatever knives I had, they weren't particularly sharp. I was walking almost in slow motion, and then I stood in the vestibule for what seemed like an eternity. Furtively, before I entered the lobby, I looked back and saw Tommie on a rocking chair on the front porch. He was looking out toward the street, his baseball cap blocking the slowly setting sun.

28

SHUT UP LOSER OR I'M GONNA FART IN YOUR FACE

When I got back, I came in the back door as usual. The time at the Hospice House took away my appetite so I skipped my customary snack. I went straight upstairs. I could hear Sammie in the bathroom brushing his teeth. I don't see him much. Man, is that an understatement. It's almost like we're invisible to each other. We live in the same house, it's true, but we don't seem to live life together. I notice it, but most of the time I don't notice it. Does that make any sense? I wonder if Sammie notices it. He may only be a little over a year older than I am, but he's got his own friends and he hangs out with a different crowd. Someday we might regret it. Then again, maybe not. It's hard to say. When he finishes brushing his teeth, I follow him to his bedroom and stand there in the doorway.

"Hey Tommie, dude" he whispers, motioning for me to come in. "Close the door and come in here for a second." I'm glad he said that. I wanted to talk with him too, but sometimes it's rough trying to figure out how to do it. It's not like you can just walk up to your big brother and say "Hey, would you like to talk?" At least not my big brother or any big brother I know. If I tried that, he'd probably look at me like I'm from Mars and then start laughing and then punch me in the chest a couple of times. That would all be before he'd make a joke about me being gay.

"Yeah, Sammie. Sure." I close the door. He pulls out the wooden chair from his desk, turns it around with its back toward me, and sits down on it facing me.

"Hey, sit down." Sammie points to the bed. I sit down on the crumpled sheets and blanket. I don't think he's made his bed since sometime in Junior High, and that was only about once anyway. Probably the day he started liking Suzette Ryder. Unluckily, she didn't like him back, so he quit making his bed the next day. If you were a twelve year old boy and you were going to like a girl, Suzette Ryder would be the girl to like. I guess Sammie got shut down pretty early, like on day one. Ouch. It's a hard way to learn about competition and the laws of supply and demand. They didn't really seem like laws to me. Somebody's always out there priming the pump. Even in seventh grade. Probably why I don't have Sammie's natural optimism.

Anyway, he told me about his crush on Suzette after I had already found out about it. Me and the other million people at school. I think it was on account of the fight at lunch with Derik Feilmeier, the fight that left a bloody mess out there on the playground, on the east end of the basketball court. There are probably still some dark stains out there on the asphalt behind the Junior High. Legendary stains. Stains that could make mothers cry, even after all these years. I'm sure it was worth whatever in-school suspension he got. It didn't solve anything. We all still had to go back to school and act like nothing happened and sit in class for the next five and a half years. God, that seems like a lifetime ago. Luckily, now Mom just stays out of our rooms, so it doesn't really matter if we make our beds or not. We're the ones that've got to sleep there, so if we want to sleep in a crumpled mess, that's our problem. It's probably the stench that keeps her out anyway, not some closely held principle about adolescent privacy. I'll take it either way, and so will Sammie.

"What's up?" I say. He's looking serious, so I'm wondering what he's going to say. He's actually looking at *me*, which is kind of weird in itself.

"Did you...hear about Dad?" he says, whispering. He looks at the floor and then glances back up at me.

"No. What? What? Did something happen to Dad? Isn't he sleeping?" I'm trying to whisper, but I'm feeling a little edgy.

"Yeah, at least I *think* he's sleeping. We'd better keep it down." We were already whispering, but Sammie was acting kind of paranoid. Not his usual self, that's for sure. I notice that the sole of his right slipper is coming unglued. I'd probably trip and break a femur if it were my slipper.

"Mom didn't talk to you?" he asks quizzically. He looked at me with what seemed like apprehension. I immediately felt the tension, but I tried to look calm.

"No, I haven't been home since I left for school this morning."

"Okay, well…Mom was crying when I got home from football practice…about 6:30," Tommie said. His face looked kind of stretched out and, I guess…old. "Dad was in his recliner staring at the TV. The TV was off. He was just sitting there, staring, drinking a beer. I figured they had an argument. There was no supper on the table, but that's not exactly unusual. Actually, one of the things that was unusual was that Mom was actually home when I got home. Yeah, that was a little unusual. Well, anyway, Dad said hello to me and then sat there for an hour or so, and then went right to their bedroom and closed the door. He didn't even watch the game. I knew that was weird right there. Then Mom tells me Dad got laid off, and this time it's for good. Supposedly, he got some kind of severance—nothing much— but that's how he knows it's for good. They're not going to give you eight weeks pay to not work, and *then* call you back. I tried to get her to tell me more about it, but she started crying again. The only thing she said was something about how in the past if they were going to get rid of people they usually didn't call it being laid off, and if you did a good job, they wouldn't do that to you to begin with."

"Dad got laid off for good? What the—? What does that mean? He's already been laid off at least two or three times. Is that all you know? Don't you know anything else?"

"No, that's all I know."

"So we really don't know what happened. Crap. Maybe he has another job. Okay, I'm dreamin' there. This isn't good at all. He must be *really* depressed. Man, I'd be depressed."

"Yeah. I'd be depressed. And pissed off. Don't you remember? Only a couple of months ago they told them that *nobody* was getting laid off, that it was all a false rumor. That's how they got them to agree to another pay cut. I don't know how many pay cuts they got at that place. More than one, I know that. A lot more than one. It's gotta be at least three or four. And now, he gets laid off. Let's tell it like it is. This time, he basically got fired. That's why Mom is so freakin' upset. They do everything to get you to be loyal to *them*, and then that's how they pay *you* back." Sammie's whisper was getting just a little bit less whisper-like. His face started to turn red.

"Hey, don't talk so loud. Maybe it's

temporary, Sammie. Maybe we're getting pissed off over nothing, and he'll be back there in a week or two like nothing happened." I had no idea what I was saying, but I felt like I had to say something that sounded positive because I didn't want to think about what was really going on. I didn't know if I could actually understand the implications of what this would mean to our family. As I finished, it sounded—even to me—more like what I was saying was just a bunch of B.S. Sammie was charitable.

"That would be nice. I don't really know what happened. But if you would have been here and seen Mom's puffy face, you'd probably have a different idea. I hope you're right. That would be a first." He grinned at me and punched me in the shoulder, but he still didn't look very happy.

"Shut up, you loser! Maybe he'll be back at work in a few days. Let's just hope he is."

"Yeah. Hey, I don't think Dad wants to talk about it, so it's probably a good idea not to bring it up. Let Dad bring it up, okay? That's what Mom said." Sammie was finally back to a low whisper.

"Yeah, I see what you mean. Yeah, okay." I can't imagine Dad bringing it up.

"Hey, how was practice? Where'd you go after practice?"

"Practice was cool. Skip Garnet was

giving us this sermon on the rapture, and Zeferino and Winterfield and Harlan and Ferris— oh yeah, and Lake— were really mocking the crap out of him, pretending that he meant "rupture" and stuff like that. He'll still kick their butts in the next race. We ran a long run and then six hills."

"Better you than me. That sounds like a hard workout. I'll take the forty-yard sprints any day. At least the pain is over in seconds. Oh yeah, and you're right about Skip: he *will* kick their butts. You're right. Unless he gets raptured."

"Very funny. That's a good one. Or unless he ruptures himself. He'd kick your butt too—even with a hernia—if you were in the *real* sport."

"Very funny yourself. Where'd you go after practice? House of Pizza?"

"No, actually, I went someplace I've never been before. I went to this place called a hospice house in Lancaster, with Monica Leblanc. To see her mom." That seemed like about the last thing Sammie was expecting to hear.

"Whoa. What the—? You did what with who? His face screwed up like he had just eaten a monster jalapeño. "Hospice house with Monica LeBlanc? Why doesn't this sound like fun?"

"Her mom has cancer and she's in this place called a hospice house."

"What? Yeah, so? What do you have to do with that? It's for cancer treatment or what?"

"I was just keeping her company. She asked me to go. I don't think it's for any kind of treatment. It's for terminal illness, as far as I know. I was just going there with Monica to help her out. Her mom just went in there today. I didn't actually go in. I sat on the porch."

"Man, that's depressing. I thought it was bad with Dad. I guess everything's relative."

"I guess so. The hospice thing seems a lot worse. But neither one is good. Man, if these are the choices, they suck."

"Yeah. Hey, I didn't know you hung out with Monica LeBlanc. I know who she is, but that's about it. Fat plastic glasses, not too photogenic? She's in your grade, right? She's the smart chick on the chess team?"

"Yeah, that's her. I saw her at the Café deVille one time when I was in there getting coffee for Mom. We started talking, you know, making fun of all the people in there and stuff like that."

"Boy, that's pretty easy to do. A lot of posers in that place. A bunch of nerds who think they're so cool."

"I'll say. I can't even figure out how to order a drink in there. Anyway, I saw her in the Café deVille and we've kind of hung out since.

On and off. It's no big deal. What about you? What have you been up to?" Tommie shifted in his chair, his arms folded, his pectorals resting on the top of the chair back. He really does look a lot older than I remember him. When did that happen? He looks like—a man.

"The usual. Football season's almost over, if I can make it to the end. It's kind of a lot of pressure and you have to go to all these parties and all that stuff."

"You mean you've gotta keep up your image. Not too easy. You'll make it, though. Don't worry. It's just like cross-country. We've got all these parties and a whole lot of naked girls show up every time, and it's a lot of pressure to fight them off. Just kidding. I was hallucinating there for a moment. Thought I was on the football team. I think I need more sleep. And I think *you* need more sleep."

"Very funny, you loser." Sammie looked like he was ready to slug me, but he held back. You guys could barely get the girls if you paid for them. You can't even get the cross-country chicks to come to your stupid parties." He was right about that, pretty much. And we barely ever had a party, and when we did it was more like a loser's parade.

"Hey, shut up. I'll have to beat the crap out of you, and then I'll post in on YouTube.

We'll see who can't get the chicks then, you big loser."

"Dreamin' again, Mr. America Anorexic! Anytime, any place." Sammie definitely did not whisper. I hope Dad and Mom are both asleep. Sure, he's got me beat by thirty or forty pounds, but I'm definitely not anorexic.

"How 'bout if we postpone the smackdown. I'm tired as hell," I say.

"Me too, Tommie. Yeah, let's postpone it. Besides, we don't want to wake up Mom and Dad." Yeah, if we didn't already. Or maybe they never fell asleep to begin with, but were lying there awake in their bed, silent, sweating, filled with dread.

"Good point. If they're getting any sleep anyway. Mom still has to be at work at 7:00."

"Yeah, I know. If *she* didn't get laid off."

"Don't even say it, Sammie! If that happens…forget it. Don't even think about it. It's almost midnight. No early run for me. We'll be lucky if we make it to school on time."

"If you're having trouble waking up, I can come over and sit on your head and fart."

"You suck, Sammie. If you do that one more time, I'm gonna have to start locking my door."

"I'll just steal your key and make a copy. Come to think of it, maybe I have a copy from the last time I stole your key," Sammie said with a sly Grinch-like smile.

"You really suck, ass wipe!" I think he does have a copy, and yes, he did wake me up more than once by sneaking in and farting right in my face. Actually, it was right *on* my face. I think I got contact burns. Bastard. "Go to bed before I have to hurt you, loser."

"Better call Ferris, Harlan, Winterfield, Garnet, the Fabron brothers and a bunch of your other wussy cross-country friends to help you do it. Zeferino too. Oh yeah, he'd be no help at all— just like all the other wimps on the team."

"I'll call 'em tomorrow. Truce." He caught me off guard and punched me in the left shoulder. "Owwww. Cut it out, you're gonna wake up Mom and Dad."

"Okay, I'll cut it out…for now. Better wear a gas mask over there."

"Sure, butthole. I'll wear a gas mask. You suck." I get up from the bed and walk toward the door.

"Hey, that's my job, little brother. Just lookin' out for ya!"

"Thanks, Sammie. You're too kind."

"I know. You don't have to thank me."

"Goodnight, Bungholio."

"Same to you, Bungholio Jr. Maybe someday you can rise to a full fledged bungholio."

I slowly pull Sammie's door closed and tiptoe across the hall to my bedroom.

I felt like I wanted to fall into bed with my clothes on, but I ended up brushing my teeth and putting on the cotton sweats I usually sleep in. As I drifted off, I was thinking about Monica's mom, and then Dad, and then Monica's mom, and then Dad...I don't think I got much sleep. Come to think of it, I don't think any of us got much sleep that night. When I got up at 6:30, Mom had already left for work. When Sammie and I left for school at around 7:15, neither of us had seen Dad. We were afraid to knock on his door. We walked to school together. Eyeing Sammie, it looked like a short long night for him as well. We didn't say much. We definitely didn't say a word about Dad. There was still a pink glow in the sky. We just kept walking, silently, toward whatever future we had left.

29

THE KING IS DEAD. LONG LIVE THE KING

It was just another day of the same old same old. School, long run with the guys, and the walk back home in the fading twilight. His mom wasn't home yet and his dad was in the recliner in front of the TV watching some old Western. Tommie finished off what was left of somebody's refrigerated macaroni and cheese and found himself at loose ends. He said "Hi" to his dad and went upstairs to his bedroom.

Tommie knew he had a reading assignment for tomorrow's philosophy class. He also knew that if he didn't read the assignment, the odds were that Winter would call on him, and things would go downhill from there. Winter's class was nerve wracking enough as it was—in a mostly good way—but still, he didn't want to push his luck. The Blue Dog Clint Eastwood Bette Davis eyes transfixed upon him? No thanks. Too harrowing to contemplate. He'd rather run twenty kilometers naked through quicksand. Besides, he actually liked the readings, even if he didn't always know if he had a clue about what the hell was going on in the text. Usually he did, but he wasn't sure enough of himself to know that he did. The readings were short by most standards—ten to fifteen pages—but Tommie realized early on that ten or fifteen pages of dense philosophical reading could easily take him as long as fifty or even one hundred pages of fiction, and his comprehension on the shorter reading could be, shall we say, less than ideal.

Being the cross-country runner that he was, this provided a challenge. It was a challenge that he, of course, could not pass up. Masochism is a hard habit to break. Especially for the masochist. It was early, and for once he wasn't tired. An opportune time for the philosophical reading, in more than one way. If it was like most philosophical readings, it was a better soporific than a handful of sleeping pills. He needed something to take his mind off of everything that was going on. His dad, his mom, Monica's mother, cross-country season—he was starting to feel the weight of the suffering around him. He was even thinking about Harlan's dad and the debt consolidation scam. He propped three pillows against the wall and jumped on his bed. He slid the computer off of his nightstand and logged on to the course. It was only 8:14. Winter often posted supplementary reading assignments on the course site. Tommie located the reading for the day. He began reading.

TERRORISM AS A TOOL OF THE INTERNATIONAL POWER ELITE, WITH SPECIAL ATTENTION TO THE USE OF INVISIBLE VIOLENCE

RUTHERFORD URIAS AUGUSTUS WINTER, Ph.D.

Terrorism is violence, but it does not require overt physical violence or terror as they are traditionally understood. It is a tool, a technique utilized by identified and unidentified individuals and collectives to manipulate and control a targeted group of people. Terror, as such, is the mechanism by which terrorists exert control. Terrorism is a teleological procedure designed to control a given subgroup. Its aims transcend terror, thus terror is not the goal of terrorism. Its aims transcend physical violence, thus physical violence is not the goal of terrorism. It may even be stated that physical violence against the targeted group may be neither a necessary nor a sufficient condition to effect the aims of the terrorist organization in question, and may, in fact, be contraindicated. As such, neither conscious terror nor physical violence are required to effect the teleology of terror.

The principles of parsimony and coversion necessitate a minimum of physical violence, stressing instead the advantages of subliminal psychological violence against the intended victims. This is often most successfully accomplished through the induction of a radical sense of insecurity within the targeted population. To this end, all historically necessary means of self-preservation practiced by the targeted group must be destabilized, including but not limited to food, housing, energy, medical care, education, work, culture, leisure, and political enfranchisement and liberties.

Let us speak briefly of the United States of America with regard to these issues. Within the sphere of work, there is neither job security, collective bargaining or any other significant enforceable rights, nor any type of meaningful compensation should one find oneself jobless. Outsourcing, subcontracting, downsizing, rightsizing, and the use of undocumented workers serve to keep the wages of those "lucky" enough to remain employed at a subsistence level and to keep workers on edge, lest they be the next to go. Worker solidarity is replaced with acrimony, animosity and, above all, suspicion.

As wages are driven down through

induced insecurity, workers are increasingly forced to utilize institutions such as credit card conglomerates, payday lenders and title loan companies to maintain equilibrium. These lenders, without exception, charge usurious rates, rates effectively set by the international power elite. Meanwhile, the CEOs, CFOs, Members of the Board of Directors and other elites at these same firms are rewarded with millions, even as they lay workers off, drive wages down, and run companies into the ground.

Within the sphere of housing, the lender utilizes the mortgage acceleration clause to radically destabilize the market, allowing for the legal seizure of collateral without significant legal recourse for the persons who actually live in the home. This clause, rarely noted at any time during the transaction, allows the lender to call in the entire loan, often if the borrower is only a few days behind on the payment. The reason the borrower is behind (job loss, reduction in work hours, cancer, heart attack, stroke, death in family, suicide, military deployment, car accident, flood, fire, war, nuclear reactor meltdown, hurricane, tsunami, earthquake, terrorist attack) is irrelevant; the loan can be called in and another nameless someone will become homeless.

This produces yet another sense of radical insecurity. At one stroke, the lender regains the collateral, keeps all monies paid, resells the property, and keeps rental prices high (the nameless someone must reside somewhere—one would think—but in such a radically destabilized market, even this is not guaranteed). A stroke of terroristic genius—if you're the one with the money. But it doesn't stop there. These same power elites can then transfer these monies to offshore accounts in the Caribbean or the Mediterranean or into secret Swiss bank accounts, accounts protected by these same elites from the Internal Revenue Service. Only those who do not have the connections to allow for such foreign accounts must actually pay federal income taxes. If you are working for these elites as a fund manager on these accounts and have specific inside information on those breaking the law and you blow the whistle, you will be arrested and tried. Or simply arrested and not tried, but plea-bargained into silence and obscurity. The accounts will remain secret. The elites are self-exempting.

Since they also control legislation, including tax law, the situation is relatively stable for the power elite, allowing them to defund any federal or state program deemed by them to run counter to their teleology of induced radical insecurity in the targeted population (including defunding any program deemed too "educational"). Within the sphere of education, we see the power elite rewriting "education" policy to coincide with their corporate agenda, an agenda that institutionalizes subliminal terror as natural law, producing, if possible, a fully predictable herd animal. Such rewriting includes the colleges and universities that would traditionally have been in a position to dismantle the fictitious narrative of the power elite as they seek complete dominion over what passes for truth and knowledge. Finally, the Supreme Court decision in Citizens United completes the disenfranchisement and ensures the thoroughgoing muting of the voice of the subjected group. Legal and human rights no longer exist for the terrorized group, the group that comprises a minimum of 99% of the societal population. Recognition and internalization of this reality augments and solidifies the terror within the targeted group.

Thus we see that (transitory and ephemeral) governments are merely an epiphenomenon of the goals and interests of the international power elite. These goals and interests are advanced through the institution of a fully monetized economy. To effect this end, local nonmonetized traditional barter and trade economies must be destabilized and subverted via the introduction of monetization through organizations such as the International Monetary Fund and the World Bank, institutions which radically destabilize traditional homeostatic economies, undermine participatory government, and destroy the rule of law.

Add to this the inscrutable privately held Federal Reserve and the invisible violence perpetrated against the 99% is complete. The Federal Reserve is not accountable to any arm of government and operates with nearly complete opacity. It can print money and buy worthless fictions that are referred to as complex investment vehicles—all invented by the power elite— paying billions of dollars for these empty vessels. Thus the Federal Reserve transfers billions directly to the power elite in exchange for whatever accoutrements of power and privilege deemed by these same elites as timely and appropriate. The unconscionable raping of the working people goes unnoticed--for their needs, desires, rights, hopes, dreams and victuals are invisible to the power elite—except to the degree that they interfere with the teleology of this elite.

Meanwhile, those that actually work for a living are increasingly required to utilize the commercial lending system in order to keep up with basic payments to secure lodging, transportation, clothing, food and health care. This group is additionally violated by being held hostage to the credit score, another invention of the power elite, something now utilized by them not only for lending to the targeted group, but for insurance and even employment as well. The credit score may be accurately described as an individual compliance rating, or a docility factor.

At the same time, it must appear to the targeted group that those ostensibly in charge are doing everything they can to guarantee stabilization and equity in all of the aforementioned areas. Propaganda is the surest means to effect this end. Propaganda can take many forms: economic forecasts, weather forecasts, education, religion, worker's rights (this is particularly notable in "right to work" states), science, politics, culture. The common denominator: to be effective, propaganda cannot be seen as such, but rather, it must pass for the truth. The lie as truth is the technical commodification of terror, the requisite product by which an international post-industrial power elite subvert any purported democratic process. This would include the purported democratic process as currently installed in the United States of America, a prima facie constitutional republic. The military defense of this pseudo-inclusive nation state is relegated to the terrorized targeted group (who "volunteer" for service, many of whom have few or no other viable options), while the power elite dictate the terms.

Multinational corporate conglomerates who sell lies as truth produce the necessary and sufficient conditions to ensure the ongoing subversion of human rights and the democratic process, provided that the potential truths revealed through societal educational systems have been sufficiently propagandized. Put differently, the lie will be portrayed as "truth" through these pseudo-educational programs. Thus, the question of truth does not arise. This dually constituted program of propaganda, with its arms of news and education, thereby effectively seals the targeted environment from the contamination of truth. Truth would mitigate and attenuate the intended program of control through terror and must therefore be minimized, maligned, eliminated.

Control of information and therefore thought, to the degree that such is possible, requires control of all substantive media sources, including the Internet. The power elite in both Egypt and Libya recognized this long before the uprisings of 2011, but overt suspension of access was required as the movement of insurgency gained momentum. So it is with the power elite on every continent, regardless of the officially stated form of government (a position which in itself represents a subset of the campaign of misinformation).[1]

---

[1] That is, the stated form or type of government is in itself a form of propaganda, given that the power elite have always had a universal disdain for the sharing of power, relegating it only to themselves. The popular notion of bringing others into the umbrella of shared governance (as is purportedly the case in a democracy or a republic) is itself a fiction designed and promulgated by the power elite.

Sufficient control of information—lie as truth––is required in order to induce and control the prescriptive amount of terror, based upon the aims of the power elite. Even the thought or memory of terror may be sufficient to terrorize a given population, in which case the power elite have little to do but reinforce the simmering hysteria.

Historically, the aims of the power elite in every case run counter to the demonstrable interests of the non-elites.[2] If they did not, the

---

[2] This is the case only in regard to the power elite qua power elite. In cases where the elites seek the collective good, their interests are no longer antithetical to those of the non-elites. An inductive analysis of history clearly shows that instances of this type are so rare as to be anomalous, so the present analysis will proceed without regard to them. In such cases, adjustments will have to be made, but let the reader be cautioned that situations in which the power elite seek the collective good are highly unstable and may fall back into normal hegemonic socio-economic conditions at any time— conditions in which the elites exploit all others as much through their power as through the idealistic delusions of the non-elites. These delusions, of course, are generated and fostered by the power elite. They include belief in the possibility of socio-economic equality and equality of opportunity.

entire project of terror and control would be superfluous. The power elite rule through an unholy alliance of government and business (a subset being the business of religion), an alliance that produces the bureaucratic medical-military-industrial-complex. The government and military are subsets of the international business interests of the elite, an elite which utilizes the concepts of patriotism, human rights, freedom and democracy as tools to advance its interests without regard for the things themselves. Or rather, with flagrant disregard for the things themselves to the degree that patriotism, human rights, freedom and democracy interfere with the interests of said group.

Such a medical-military-industrial complex requires constant war or the simulacra of war as a tool of terror. Additionally, the elites that generate this multifarious complex need to dismantle any constitutionally protected rights in the name of said war. Terror and control would be incompletely realized without the double effect of endless war and the attendant stripping of all guarantees of human rights in the name of said war. Real war, then, is not a necessity, just as reality, as such, is not a necessity.

To go further: reality itself is a luxury the terrorists cannot afford. Or, to be more precise, reality is useful only to the extent that it can be utilized to go beyond itself to produce a manageable unreality that can be imposed upon the targeted group. Reality, per se, is an impediment to the propagandization of reality and therefore must be concealed while at the same time being conceptually amplified. The concept of reality has endless functionality in the hands of the power elite. At the same time, the incipient encroachment of reality must be eliminated by any means necessary and in accordance with the principles of parsimony and coversion.

A current example of such an aversion to truth is the reaction of the government of the United States of America to Julian Assange and the Wikileaks website. Reality is in contradistinction to the aim of the terrorists, as their ultimate telos is the manufacture and control of reality (lie as truth) as such. To this end, all discourse must be regulated. No unsanctioned discourse is allowed. The objectives of said terrorists (the controllers of the medical-military-industrial complex) are at odds with principles of freedom, democracy, and human rights. This group currently seeks extradition of Assange, a move designed to benefit their own terrorist agenda, a Machiavellian agenda at odds with the principles of freedom, democracy, and human rights.[3] The narration requires only that reality exist as a background concept. This formula is replicated ad infinitum. The faces change; the game remains the same. No unsanctioned discourse is allowed.

---

[3] See Niccolò Machiavelli, *The Prince,* trans. N.H. Thomson. (Mineola, NY: Dover Publications, 1992).

The simulacrum of war is generally a sufficient condition for the elites to control the targeted group through terror. The power elite can, of course, benefit from real war in two ways: economic gain and propaganda-induced loyalty/patriotism. Terror as a tool to subvert the interests of the targeted population in favor of the interests of the international power elite is the most closely guarded secret of this class. The first order of business for the power elite is to produce in the terrorized the belief that the power elite does not exist. Having successfully induced disbelief in said class, the question of terror as a tool of a nonexistent class does not arise. If those controlled remain noncognizant of their own induced (rather than existential) terror, no explanation is required. If the controlled become aware of their terror and determine that it is induced, some explanation is required.

Thus the need for a war on terror. This war must exist as long as terror recognized as such exists. Terror must be endless, as a built-in requirement generated by the existence of the power elite. Terror recognized as such will remain only a contingent condition to be exploited as deemed necessary by the power elite. Once terror is recognized as such, the question of the origin of terror will never arise, since it is already deemed to be addressed in the object of the war on terror. Such an object, of course, is anything but the origin of the terror the controlled group seeks to extinguish (at the behest of the elite) through said war on terror.

To repeat, the goal is control and manipulation through the technique of terrorism. This is best achieved by means other than direct physical assault, yet all terrorism is a form of violence. It strips those targeted of the possibility of a life of self-determination. It denies fundamental human rights and is one of the highest forms of disrespect against human life. Finite terror can be produced through physical and systemic violence. Infinite terror can be induced through propaganda and the attendant destruction of educational systems within the targeted group. Psychic terrorism is homicide by other means. It generates ubiquitous terror, a situation in which even the notion of self-protection is defunct, since self-protection is no longer possible. The victims of such ubiquitous induced terror, having no visible means of recourse, end by embracing the very group that induces said terror.

Thus the targeted group embraces and precipitates its own terror, its own demise, in the name of self-preservation. It drinks the poison, looking upon it as the antidote to that very poison. Within such a fully propagandized pseudoreality, there is no clear Archimedean point from which to leverage oneself and one's peers beyond the propaganda. Consciousness of the process of terror as a tool of the power elite is a necessary but insufficient condition to create fertile ground for democracy, human rights, and real freedom for all peoples. The front of such a real war on terror is fought on the fringes of human consciousness. The question here becomes notably broader: how does one bring to awareness that of which one is not aware, especially given that from one's perspective of nonawareness, one will generally infer that there is nothing about which one must become aware? Still, if one recognizes the possibility of such nonawareness, this does not for that reason induce awareness. But it is a movement toward the light.

These concerns raise larger questions concerning the nature of human consciousness, including but not limited to the question of self-deception. Within the realm of self-deception, the phenomenon of the Stockholm syndrome has particular relevance to our present discussion. These issues are beyond the scope of our present narration, and must therefore await a later elucidation. An exposition and analysis of self-deception and its subset, the Stockholm syndrome, are necessary to the full understanding of terror as a tool of the international power elite. At this juncture, we shall turn to a specific example of terror as a tool of the international power elite, with particular reference to induced terror through the use of invisible systemic violence.

Many specific concrete examples could be offered to demonstrate that the power elite utilize terror as a tool to control and manipulate the non-elite. From "too big to fail" corporate monoliths to the absence of habeas corpus, to dragnet data mining without the need for warrant or justification, to arbitrary curbs on free speech and free assembly, to Supreme Court verdicts installing American Presidents, multiple and pervasive constructed scenarios serve to undermine the very possibility of peace and to induce terror.

Let us take the absence of universal health care as one example among others, for this reality is a quintessential example of control through terror utilizing the principles of parsimony and coversion, a situation that clearly serves the international interests of the power elite. To begin, we must make a clear distinction between health insurance and health care, since the former is certainly no guarantee of the latter. Health insurance, per se, is simply not a guarantee of health care, but may in fact in some instances serve as a deterrent to health care. This discussion will focus instead on health care.

Without a minimal level of guaranteed

access to health care, a population lives with radical insecurity, a sense of insecurity well described by Thomas Hobbes in his LEVIATHAN (1652) as the state of nature, a state prior to the time in which a human being lives in a civil society, a society which would provide certain guarantees against the expected exigencies of solitary living.[4] One primary focus of civil and social society should be to alleviate the existential terror of everyday living through the sharing of resources, knowledge, power, and defenses. But a society where anyone is potentially one serious illness away from destitution, poverty, homelessness, starvation and death is certainly not a civil society by any account.

Put differently: a society that would allow anyone to lose anything and everything necessary to sustain human life when such a situation is eminently preventable does not meet the necessary preconditions for civil

---

[4] Thomas Hobbes, *Leviathan or the Matter, Form, and Power of a Commonwealth, Ecclesiastical or Civil.* See especially Part I, Chapters 12-15 and Part II, Chapters 17, 18, and 21.

society. No one would agree to such a situation in John Rawls' hypothetical original position, wherein we choose the basic framework of justice as fairness without knowing where we will be in the socioeconomic hierarchy, since this situation is neither fair nor just by any account other than that of the specious narration of the power elite.[5] A society where anyone is potentially one serious illness away from destitution, poverty, homelessness, starvation and death is certainly not a civil society by any account, and yet such is the present situation in the United States of America.

Such an uncivil situation clearly violates multiple articles of The Universal Declaration of Human Rights, adopted by the United Nations General Assembly on December 10, 1948. At that time, the Assembly called upon all member nations to publish and disseminate the thirty articles

---

[5] John Rawls, *A Theory of Justice* (Boston: Harvard University Press, 1971).

found in the Declaration, and "to cause it to be disseminated, displayed, read, and expounded principally in schools and other educational institutions, without distinction based on the political status of countries or territories." I will note only portions of two articles of the Universal Declaration of Human Rights, the content of which the United States is in clear violation, given the aforementioned regarding health care:

Article 3: "Everyone has the right to life, liberty and security of person."

Article 25 (1): "Everyone has a right to a standard of living adequate for the health and well-being of himself and of his family, including food, clothing, housing and medical care and necessary social services, and the right to security in the event of unemployment, sickness, disability, widowhood, old age or other lack of livelihood in circumstances beyond his control."

It is eminently clear that Americans have no such rights. For this reason as well as those drawn from Hobbes and Rawls, we see that America is in fact not a civil society at all. Such a situation is one of induced terror. It is a situation of systemic invisible violence inducing terror, based upon the principles of parsimony and coversion.

With few exceptions, economics rather than need is the determining factor when it comes to the availability of health care in the United States. Thousands die, sustain preventable permanent injuries, are made homeless or lose all of their savings and/or incur monstrous debt every year due to medical reasons in these United States of America, a country that gave hundreds of billions of dollars in bailouts to the very Wall Street robber baron financiers that precipitated the financial crisis that "required" the bailouts. The overt agenda of the power elite was operative here (placing them in a potentially vulnerable position), yet the dual propaganda campaign of commercial media and educational institutions was so successful in this instance that many of those terrorized praised the bailouts—immediately after the largest transfer of wealth in world history—as the right thing to do.

Meanwhile, tens of millions who work every day, year in and year out, could lose everything in an instant if they were in an automobile accident and required sustained medical attention (even if they were not at fault). This is an artificially created state of nature, a state of war of every man against every man, a state of terror. Pervasive terror is thus induced from the ubiquitous and seemingly irremediable artificially created situation of constitutive instability, a situation that cannot be rectified even in theory as long as the unstated fundamental tenets that precipitated the situation are not addressed. The putative intractability of the current egregiously unjust situation is part of the mythology of the power elite.

To return to Thomas Hobbes in LEVIATHAN: "To this war of every man against every man this also is consequent, that nothing can be unjust. The notions of right and wrong, justice and injustice, have there no place. Where there is no common power, there is no law; where no law, no injustice."[6] Hobbes goes on to assert that the terror of such a state is far greater than the terror of a unitary dictatorship, and yet we are in such a state. The existing artificially created state of nature is nothing less than a state of induced terror.

---

[6] Thomas Hobbes, *Leviathan*, Chapter 13.

Nothing can be unjust: neither death, nor famine, nor poverty, nor homelessness, since the onus to provide these essentials rests squarely upon the person who sustained serious injury in the aforementioned automobile accident, through no fault of her own. No one owes her a thing, not even to be left to die peacefully—from preventable injuries—on a public sidewalk, since "living" in said location could very well violate local ordinances. Nothing can be unjust: the denial of a medical procedure necessary for continued existence on planet Earth—if the patient in question has not made acceptable financial arrangements. Meanwhile, multimillion dollar bonuses to executives at the bailed out criminal syndicates on Wall Street and around the world must be paid due to "contractual obligation". Nothing can be unjust. Nothing can be unjust in the state of nature, since conditions do not yet obtain for justice to exist.

These conditions exist by design, as they provide the constitutive instability necessary to induce terror unrecognized as such. The targeted group cowers under the weight of the onslaught of the contradictory nature of its reality, a reality where freedom is trumpeted from every rooftop by the relentless corporate media and the corporate institutions of indoctrination that pass for schools and colleges and universities, while feeling somehow that it cannot find terra firma, that nothing is sacred because nothing is protected, that nothing is sacred because everything is negotiable, that nothing is sacred because everything is for sale. When nothing is sacred, the people, as such, perish.

The notion of a common destiny, the notion of brotherhood, the notion of sisterhood, the notion of statehood, the notion of statecraft, the notion of community, they are gone, gone in a sea of calculated verbiage. Living together has been replaced with competition unto death. In the final analysis, when nothing is sacred, the individual ceases to exist. The very possibility of personhood is eradicated. The use of systemic invisible violence as a tool of terror by the power elite makes it all possible. Hail to the new Masters of the Universe. The King is dead. Long live the King.

N.B. To all students: If you do not understand a vocabulary word, look it up and learn it.

Tommie closed his computer and slipped it under the bed, then got up to take a leak. It was only 9:37 but he was exhausted. He had actually managed to finish the reading. He stumbled back to bed and turned out the nightstand lamp. Soon the waves of fitful sleep were crashing over the embers of his consciousness.

30

BEAR CLAW

Tommie woke up early. Really early. Maybe it wasn't such a good idea to read that kind of stuff before bed. He liked reading it, though. He even managed to stay awake for the entire assignment. That was worth something in itself, but probably not much. No one was going to give him a medal or anything, that's for sure. He probably wouldn't even get a gold paper star. Those days are gone, those glory days of elementary school. Alright, so maybe they weren't so glorious, but neither was adolescence. And Tommie was beginning to wonder about adulthood. Sometimes just getting out of bed felt sort of...heroic—even if you *didn't* finish your reading assignment the night before. He tried to imagine how heroic it might feel to get out of bed at thirty...at forty...at sixty....at eighty. It was impossible. He had trouble imagining it at twenty. But he had almost as much trouble imagining his own past as he did his future. It just didn't seem real.

Even the present had a kind of twilight zone feeling of unreality. All this made him feel like he'd like to read more stuff written by philosophers, but he didn't know where to start. Just so he didn't have to read any more of that French dude named Derrida or Derrido or Derridodo or Derridada or Derrierre. Talk about a twilight zone feeling of unreality, but not in a good way. Somehow the name, whatever it was and whatever it might mean or not mean, seemed to fit. Five pages of that guy were enough to make anybody want to commit suicide. It was a comedy routine masquerading as deep thought. As long as people take it seriously, he thought. As long as people take it seriously, then what?

He realized that the thought was incomplete. As long as people take it seriously, then students like him will have to suffer through reading the swill in school, even if the emperor is butt naked, physically and metaphysically, which is a whole lot of naked, that's for sure. You couldn't get any nakeder. It was nakedness to the maximum degree of infinity, kind of like God in Anselm's proof for God's existence, only the opposite. Anselm proved that the God he had defined into existence in fact existed, since he had defined Him into existence. A tautology or what? He would never underestimate learning about the concept of "tautology" from Dr. Winter. It was everywhere he looked. Maybe Derriere or whatever did the same thing, Tommie thought. Derriere said something like the text is all there is, if we don't count everything else that isn't text, like you and me and what we had for lunch. And people were taking that shit seriously? Never underestimate the boundless gullibility of the human animal. Even Tommie was starting to have a hard time distinguishing where his thought ended and Winter's began. The part of his thinking that was confused as hell was probably all him, he thought, but maybe he was confused about that too. For example, Derriere proved that nothing exists outside of the text, and that the text doesn't exist, or, if it does, it always unravels in a particularly unseemly way. What the? It wasn't just Tommie's thought that was unraveling, it was his life, and like Derrida's text, it was unraveling in a particularly unseemly way. Everywhere he looked, lives were unraveling, and he felt like he was part of the mass, slowly sinking, their muted cries reverberating but ineffectual, each together drowning, slowly, in a brackish sea of despair and hopelessness. What good was it to think about all this stuff, if you couldn't do a damn thing about, if you couldn't do a damn thing to stop the slowly moving train wreck that had become his life and the lives of those around him? Even though it was early, really early, Tommie was more than awake. Maybe he was too awake. But there was no going back. And somehow he knew it.

Anyway, Tommie liked Winter's reading, even though it was kind of depressing. Maybe that's what made it philosophical, he thought. The essence of the philosophical: that which makes one depressed. Maybe he liked it because he stayed awake during the entire time he was reading it. Or maybe he stayed awake during the entire time he was reading it because he liked it. That pesky problem of causality. It's hard to know which came first—if either. Which was the antecedent and which was the consequent—if either. As for the depression? He was probably depressed before he read it, though, so maybe it wasn't the reading. No, it was probably his life reflected on in light of the reading. Who the hell knows? He was starting to wonder how much he really knew about anything that was actually worth knowing, or that anybody really knew about anything that was actually worth knowing, for that matter. Even about himself. Or themselves. Is there really any reflective self-awareness, or is that some kind of fancy self-deception too? Is there any way of knowing? The lucidity of the labyrinthine logic was languorously lacking. Luckily, Winter's reading wasn't fifty pages or anything, in which case it surely would have been a different story. He would have been in REM sleep on page twenty-two, even if it was Winter and not Derridada. Winter had a way of distilling and focusing on what seemed more like the vague impressions and undefined feelings that Tommie felt even in spite of himself.

And he knew they weren't just his feelings. That gave him some impressionistic feeling of solidarity with others, which wasn't a bad thing. He had some weird residual feelings from dreaming a bunch of surreal dreams, the kind where you know they're surreal but at the same time something about them feels eerily real. Well, he felt like he had a bunch of them last night, or more accurately, earlier this morning, right after he got up to take a leak—at 3:12 a.m.—and couldn't get back to sleep. That was the extent of it though, since he couldn't remember anything specific other than one scene.

In the dream, he was out in some vast, undulating, seemingly endless desert, way out there because he couldn't see any signs of life, and he was alone. He had on this long brown robe, tied with a yellow belt at the waist, fancy molded purple sandals, and a lavender bandanna over the top of his head and tied in back. He also had on a pair of black wrap around sunglasses with pink lenses. It was windy but not hot. In fact, he felt cold. He was looking everywhere and yelling something unintelligible, at least to him. As he continued to yell, his voice seemed to get softer and softer. It seemed to him, in the dream anyway, that he was trying to warn somebody of something. He was almost in a panic, but he woke up without ever seeing anyone, without knowing what he was saying, and without knowing what he was doing. He felt boundless, insatiable desire, but its object, to him, was unknown.

After he woke up, the remembered level of specificity seemed downright useless and more of an annoyance. Pink-lensed wrap around black sunglasses? But he couldn't shake the weird feelings of loneliness and dread. At least Harlan wasn't in the dream. Then it would have been a nightmare for sure. Harlan would probably have wanted to do a fifty-mile desert run or something and then the GPS would run out of power and there'd be this gigantic wind storm and they'd be out of water and then they'd get separated and then a Komodo dragon would show up on the scene... Hey, maybe that's why I'm yelling in the dream? Tommie thought. There could be so many reasons.

He was awake now, that's for sure. Anyway, he was going to do what he usually did in situations like this: go out and run. As to whether it solved anything—that's a different question. He just knew it was time to get out there and run, whatever time it was. He fumbled for his glasses on the nightstand, since he never slept with his contacts in. He looked at the red numbers on the digital clock he got for eighth grade graduation. 4:37 a.m. By 5:06, he had gotten on his running gear, did a little post-surreal-dream-state-pre-waking-sleep-stretching routine on his bedroom floor, and was out on the street. There were a hundred billion stars, and that's just the ones he couldn't count. It was thirty-six degrees. The ground was wet with dew. He was wearing a windbreaker, tights, gloves and a billed hat. He had his miniature clip-on LED headlamp on the bill of his hat. It was good for a couple of watts on the ground, but overall, it was pretty underwhelming.

He was glad that it didn't look like an endless desert when he stepped outside. He was also glad that cross-country season was over. Next year, the team would be so much better, even if they lost a couple of their best guys—like Skip Garnet. That's going to be hard, he thought. He was really going to miss Skip. Nine and nine wasn't a bad season, but they could do so much more. They could go fifteen and four in league meets if they played their cards right. But that's a big if, and the key was minimizing injuries. Next year, he'd be so much better too. He'd like to drop his best 5K from 16:26 to 15:29, at least, and his home course best from 17:53 to 16:59. Yeah, the home course was a tough one, with Cardiac Mountain and all. More self-deception? Who knew?

It then occurred to him that it didn't really matter if he ran 15:29 and 16:59 next year or any year, just like it didn't really matter that he ran 16:26 and 17:53 this year. But that didn't stop him in his tracks. He kept moving forward, down the driveway and toward the street. He wasn't really running for speed, victory, awards, or anything extrinsic. It was more like a lifelong vision quest. He saw the customary outlines of houses on Cottage Avenue, and even a few lights on here and there. As he walked out the driveway, he thought about where he wanted to go. The night was absolutely calm, so he could start out in any direction and he wouldn't have to regret it later. At least not as far as the wind was concerned.

He felt a pain in his chest, a familiar ache. He knew it wasn't merely a result of the weird dreams he'd been having. He wondered if the ache had always been there. He decided that as far as he can remember, it had always been there. He wondered if he could trust his memory. He had no answer to that one. The familiar ache was still there, just as it had been throughout all of his answerless reflections, reflections that went back into his childhood as far as he could remember. He began the familiar night death stumble on the razor's edge of life. He headed west, past his old elementary school. He remembered running his first cross-country race there. Three quarters of a mile through woods and a cornfield. It felt like a hundred years ago, not seven. There was so much that he didn't know then that it barely seemed like him. And not knowing how much he didn't know

now made him wonder if even now he knew himself.

For sure, the childhood Tommie didn't seem like Tommie at all. In a way, it felt like it wasn't really him, but somebody else. Most of his memories seemed detached, as if they didn't really belong to him. He felt the sticky wetness of damp earth as he turned off into the woods, hoping the moon and the feeble headlamp were sufficient to light his way. If not, he'd find out the hard way. His reflections accompanied him along the barely illuminated trail, a trail he'd traversed since childhood.

*   *   *   *   *

I have absolutely no idea what to do to help Dad. He hasn't said much of anything for weeks, and I can't talk to him because he doesn't want to talk. If I say anything, it just seems to make him angry. Even if it's not my fault, it doesn't feel too hot, so I just shut up and go do something else. I know he's left the house in the mornings a few times, and from what Sammie tells me, he's applied for a couple of jobs. At least I think so, since Sammie told me that Mom told him that. I think he applied for a job or two online, too. I never seem to get it from the horse's mouth, so I could just be blowing smoke. What else is new? Yeah, I'm probably blowing smoke right up my own ass too. I'm right here and even I don't know what the hell is going on, so I'm probably just full of shit.

If that's the case, forgive me in advance. Yeah, I live here, but I don't get much straight from the source. In fact, real conversations seem to be at a premium around here, a real anomaly. Everybody's too tired, or distracted, or upset, or afraid to talk about what's really going on. It hasn't been serving us well. I saw Dad in his recliner the night before last, just like most nights, with a beer on the lamp stand beside the table. He didn't turn his head, so I didn't say anything to him, and he didn't say anything to me. A lot of times, it looks like he's pretending to read the paper, but you can tell that his mind's just wandering.

There's no way he's going to find a real job in the classifieds. And the online ads aren't much better. About ten million people lying about themselves, desperate to get something to pay the bills and hoping nobody checks out their applications. What if you tell the truth and starve to death because you told the truth? I mean, what if you could have gotten a job if you had just lied on your application and resume, but you were against lying on moral grounds and because you didn't lie, people who did lie were chosen for the job and you weren't and you ended up dead because of it? Or your family ended up homeless? Not possible? Why not? Now who's the one who still believes in fairy tales? Get real.

The air feels so good out here. The coolness flowing into my lungs feels like a cleansing, a new beginning, a transformation. It gives me hope that we can work everything out, even if I don't have the evidence. Or, at least everything that matters. Even if it's a delusion, I still feel better with the cool air flowing through every capillary in my body. The sweat and oxygen conspire to elevate my mood.

I haven't seen Mom much either, because she's always at work. Her eyes were puffy the last few times I saw her, so I know she's still upset, but there's no way I'm gonna bring it up. The last time I saw her, she had two bear claws on a paper plate, and a big-ass bottle of generic diet cola. She had just gotten home from work. She was sitting in the waning twilight in the kitchen, with no lights on, staring at the microwave. "That's one hell of a dinner," I thought. But I didn't say anything. I knew she had stopped at the convenience store on Manor Avenue. There's no way in hell I'm gonna try to get my puffy-eyed mom to eat right. I'm sure she tells herself that when the pressure's off, she'll go back to cooking. But when's that gonna be? After Dad goes back to work? After Sammie and I are out of the house? After Mom and Dad have stable jobs? After all the debt is paid off? After she retires at seventy?

There's always some reason to eat two bear claws and wash them down with a liter of diet cola. It sounded like a good idea at the time. Or not. How many bear claws does it take until the mauling is somehow...irreversible? I think she's trying to pick up some of the slack from Dad, but that's a long shot, unless she wants to work more than two full-time jobs. She was working more than one full-time job before all this, and she was barely home then. I raked in a whole $1550 last year on my lousy summer job, and it seemed like I was always at work. That would help out just about...none. It never occurred to me until now that we might have to move.

Why do I have this pain in my chest? I could run or not run, and I'd still have this pain in my chest. I could run uphill with a pulse of 180 and I'd still have this pain in my chest, or I could run downhill, with a pulse of 125, and I'd still have this pain in my chest. I could stop running and start walking, and I'd still have this ache in my chest. I could lie in bed and stare at the ceiling, and I'd still have this pain in my chest. I could eat breakfast or not eat breakfast, have eggs or toast or cereal or soy milk or skim milk or chocolate milk or orange juice and still have this ache in my chest, and still have this lump in my throat. I could speak or not speak and still have this lump in my throat. I could speak or not speak and still have this pain in my chest. I could go to school or not go to school, and in the end it would make absolutely no difference. I'd still have this ache in my chest.

I haven't tried narcotics or meth or any shit like that, and there's no way I will. Drugs are just a bullshit nonsolution. Life is rough enough without tackling it with a screwed-up mind. And I'd probably still have the pain in my chest as soon as I came back down to earth—if I ever did. About the only time I haven't got the ache is in the middle of a cross-country race, and that's not because I haven't got it, it's just that I can't feel it, what with a pulse of 190+ and the sensation of a cattle prod up my ass. The lactic acid and oxygen debt pretty much zero out any possible sensation of chest pain from any other discernable source other than the sheer folly of running through the woods as fast as I can go. Every muscle is on fire, and that's *before* it gets really bad. And after a certain absurd level of senseless pain, there's a breakthrough: just stopping provides an unparalleled sensation of euphoria. It coincides with Epicurus' definition of pleasure: the absence of pain. The absence of pain is pleasure. No argument here.

I guess what I mean by all this is that's what I'm working on: the absence of pain. The pain in my chest. The tightness in my throat. The vague and not-so-vague sense of dread related to anything and nothing all at the same time. Absence of pain sounds pretty cool to me. If I can ever get there. Right now, it's just something I think about, something purely hypothetical. Will it always be that way? Whoa! Holy crap. Wow, I just about tripped on that monster root sticking out. That was a real six point power stumble over some monster root, and still I didn't hit the dirt. Some fancy-ass nonreflective footwork, that's for sure. With all the leaves, there's basically no way of knowing what's really under there. By the time it's light, I'll be in the shower. Somehow, a metaphor for life.

I have absolutely no idea what to do to help Monica. I think her mom's been in the hospice house for over a month now, maybe even six weeks. Yeah, probably closer to six weeks. The last time we drove around in her Subaru, she didn't say much about it. That was last week. We listened to some Queen City Rocker and talked about school. I asked her about her parents, but she didn't say much. I went to the hospice house with her after that first time three more times, I think, and just hung out on the porch as usual. I'd feel weird going in, and she doesn't ask me to go in, so it works out. We went after I finished practice, all three times. I sit out on the porch of the hospice house, facing west, and try not to look into the setting sun. We haven't been saying much to each other at school, but Monica texts me once in a while, and I text back. I guess we talk on the phone a couple of times a week too.

*   *   *   *   *

Tommie rounded the final curve on the trail and hit pavement. It was still as dark as it gets on a moonlit night. The LED was casting a dim light on the ground, but it was insufficient to see where he was actually going. Probably about as light as Limbo in Dante's *Divine Comedy*, the place where Plato, Aristotle, Seneca, Epictetus— all the decent Greek and Roman philosophers— end up. Light enough to know there's something there, but not light enough to see what the heck it is. Dante didn't have the stomach to make the philosophical giants suffer—they were in a painless state of dim light for all eternity. Their suffering, as it were, lay wholly in eternal separation from God. Being pagans, they were not able to rest in the presence of the Almighty Christian God. Reason, that gift of God most closely resembling the nature of God himself, produces the dim light by which the philosophers in Dante's Limbo live and philosophize, a light bright enough to illuminate the forest path upon which they travel, but not bright enough to tell them where, in the end, that path will lead. But this forest quest is not a painless state of dim light. The ache is still there as Tommie warms down in front of the house.

When he gets back to his room, he notices that he has a message on his cell phone. It is a text from Monica. "Would u meet me @ my house @ 6? Please." "Sure Vera. Looking 4ward 2 it." Tommie texted back, not too nimbly. That day, Tommie did not see Monica in Winter's class. He didn't see her in the hallway. He didn't see her anywhere on campus. He checked the absentee roster in Lebowski's room. Monica was absent.

31

HOSPICE HOUSE DENOUEMENT

Ferris, Harlan, Lake, Zeferino, Winterfield and I ran the nine-mile Walnut Hill Road course after school. We met at the locker room, stretched a little, and left about 3:15. Everybody on the team was invited, but since it's the off-season, only the really crazy runners showed up. Or guys that have nothing better to do: some other sport, after school suspension, work, musical rehearsal, Driver's Ed, stuff like that. Even walking or driving a hottie home—but it's not like anybody on the cross-country team would be doing that. The likelihood of walking a chick home is up there with getting hit by a meteor. Almost *anything* could pass for something better to do, and it's not like you have to make excuses. If you're not there, everybody gets it. It's the off-season. Of course, to the real die-hards, there is *no* off-season—every day you're not out there pounding the pavement is a day you're getting behind. I think I get behind by pounding the pavement. Skip wasn't there, but I think he has some hip flexor injury or something. That's what I heard. He always heals fast, unlike me. He'll be back out there kicking our butts in no time. Anyway, the six of us ran the same nine-miler we seem to run most of the time. Long enough to weed people out but not long enough, generally speaking, to kill you. On the road for nine miles, I get a lot of updates on what's going on at school, or, more precisely, what a few cross-country runners think is going on, which is probably something altogether different. What the hell do we know? Even the best of us is sadly out of the loop. We're so out of the loop that we couldn't even find it in an open field, painted with hunter orange. Cross-country runners are kind of like computer nerds—minus all the computer skills. Yeah, exactly: that puts you somewhere between in the way and just plain invisible.

What I'm saying is not too many people are gonna care about the stuff we talked about, but so what? I did find out that Kaitlin Ramsey is back with Mike Kriddle, which makes sense, since they're both desperate. I give it another three weeks, tops, and then a theatrical public breakup with a bunch of shouting. That's my bet. We all bet ten bucks each, so I could collect fifty bucks, but Winterefield won't pay up until...the next life. Zeferino bet on two weeks. Harlan gives it four. Ferris only bet on next weekend. Winterfield is the only sucker for romance. He thinks it can last. And so can gingivitis and gonorrhea. Lake thought they weren't really back together; he thought they were just posing for...exactly: nobody. Who the hell would shout over Mike Kriddle anyway? That guy looks like such a wuss, and with the turquoise spandex tights, it's unbearable. Oh, but without them, believe me, it's even worse. Oh God, I don't even want to think about it.

We're all under the mistaken impression, I guess, that somebody gives a crap about our tiny lives. I don't even know if we can admit that they're so freakin' tiny and that this little town isn't the center of the universe. You almost have to believe you're the center of the universe, at least when you're a kid or you kind of lose momentum and wonder what the hell you're doing. You wonder why you're here and the next thing you know it's an existential crisis and some powerful over-the-top antidepressants. So, we like to think we live big lives somewhere pretty close to the center of the universe. I mean, if you stop for a second and think about the little thrills we get and our at best pedestrian achievements, you almost gotta laugh. Why all the effort for such mediocrity? What difference does what we do actually make? C'mon, in the scheme of things we probably don't make a dent, not in anything.

So we don't think about that. We joke about Kriddle and his chicken legs in spandex, just to keep it all at bay. Yeah, it's fun to joke about it. It serves its purpose, no doubt. The Kaitlin Ramsey – Mike Kriddle smackdown. Nothing like Theatre of the Absurd. Just what we're getting in English Lit. In fact, adolescent love is pretty much just that: Theatre of the Absurd. As soon as I thought that, I realized we were out here, the six of us, on foot, about four miles from the high school, breathing in the smell of fresh cow manure. This struck me as about as absurd as you could get. I mean, why? And then Harlan was trying to rap something off Barnacle Soufflé's new CD: *It's gonnanana be be be...It's gonnanana be a fatty fatty fatty fatty fatty revolution...fatty revolution uh uh uh uhuhhaha...fatty revolution...* The good news was we couldn't understand much of anything he was saying, but then again we all knew the lyrics to *Fatty Revolution*, especially since the whole song has like forty words. The bad news was it was Harlan...trying to rap something off Barnacle Soufflé's new CD. Freakin' pathetic. That guy takes uncoolness to a whole new level. If we had just been able to pick up the pace, he wouldn't have had enough oxygen to keep it up. On foot, four miles from school, Harlan imitating Foobar Freshass? Theatre of the Absurd? Would we know it if we saw it? And we're out here doing this?...why? Voluntarily, for fun? Really? Zeferino starts pointing to a stock pond just inside the cattle fence beside the road. "Hey, Harlan, ass wipe, go jump in that pond...Hey, hey dumb ass...jump in that pond, will you, dipshit?" Harlan, of course, didn't shut up. And he made no effort to jump in the pond. Oh no, in fact, Winterfield and Lake actually joined in with

Harlan for the next chorus of *Fatty Revolution*. The thought that went through my head was that no matter how much this scene might have sucked, some day we were gonna miss it. Maybe this was it. Maybe this was the best it was ever gonna get. And we're going to look back on it and try to get it back. Even try to claw our way back.

I got to Monica's house about fifteen minutes early. Her Subaru was in the driveway, looking forlorn as ever. I knocked once and she came to the door with her purse, her coat already on. She closed the door behind her, and then turned toward me. She didn't look good at all. She had black circles under her eyes. Her hair was greasy and sticking out all over, in clumps.

"Thanks for coming over, Tommie."

"Well, sure. It's no big deal, Vera. Are we gonna take a ride?"

"Yes. Let's take a ride." She pulled the key out of her purse. She had on brown jeans, red tennis shoes, a gray sweatshirt, and a half zipped lined blue University windbreaker.

"I can drive, Vera. How about if I drive and you relax."

"Okay. That's cool." She handed me the keys and I opened the passenger door and then walked around and got in. I'll never get over how much I love the automatic seat belt shoulder harnesses. They go up and down all by themselves, just in case you forget to strap yourself in. Not like life at all. There, you can forget all kinds of important stuff and then you've got to suffer the consequences. Or maybe you didn't know that important stuff to begin with. You still aren't off the hook. You can't claim ignorance. You still suffer the consequences. I figured we were taking another trip back to the hospice house in Lancaster, so I started her up and headed toward Millersville Pike. Monica didn't say much on the way in. In fact, she hardly said anything. Less than I can ever remember. After we made it all the way out of Millersville, I figured it was time to say something.

"I didn't see you in school today, Vera. Are you sick?"

There was a long pause.

"I wasn't there. I guess I'm not technically sick. But there are a lot of ways to be sick."

"That's true. I feel sick every time I look at Harlan."

"I'm starting to feel sick every time I wake up in the morning." Monica spoke slowly and deliberately, like her throat was tight and she was feeling a great deal of anxiety. I glanced over at her. The dark circles under her eyes were the worst I've seen, and her face seemed as pale as ever.

"That sounds like morning sickness,

Vera." I immediately regretted joking around.

"Mourning with a u."

"I hear you. Hey, I'm sorry for joking around." She didn't say anything. I didn't want to bring up her mother right then, but it was the big elephant in the...Subaru. We'd be at the hospice house soon enough, and she seemed like she was very shaky. "Did you eat supper yet? We could stop afterwards, if you feel like it."

"Ah, I don't know. Thanks, Tommie." That was a first, Monica not wanting to get something to eat with me. I know *I'm* always up for it. She's really having a bad day. I kept heading east on Millersville Pike. My skills were improving even without much practice. It wasn't long before I found a space right across from the hospice house, a space long enough to pull right in without having to parallel park. My skills on that still need some work. I got as close to the curb as I thought I could, straightened her out and turned off the engine.

"I can wait on the porch. I'll walk you up to the door."

Monica was sitting still, looking down at her hands in her lap.

"Okay. Thanks."

We waited on the curb together until the traffic cleared. She was hunched over, and looked so much smaller than I remembered. I put my arm around her back as we navigated the busy street. When we got to the door, she told me she'd be out in a while. I sat on the porch swing and faced the setting sun. The sun was already behind the city skyscape, no longer visible, yet it was still light. I sat there for maybe fifteen minutes or so, and then I pulled my cell phone out of my pocket. Maybe I was trying to distract myself from that familiar ache. If so, it didn't work. It never does.

No messages, as usual. Once in a while I'd get a message from Ferris or Harlan, but that was about it. Oh yeah, and Monica, of course. I kept fiddling with my phone for lack of anything better to do. Wouldn't want to just sit here and think too much. I could see what time it was in Beijing or Rio de Janeiro or Helsinki or Bangkok or Belfast or Mombasa or Asuncion or Lima or Tokyo, I thought. Boy, that's a useless function. Did I need a calculator? Right there in the free cell phone. Or, I could connect to the Internet and check out the five-day forecast. But it's gonna cost me. It's not included in my plan.

At the rate things are going, there will be a whole lot more that's not included in my plan. My whole plan may no longer be included in my plan. The plan, as such, may no longer exist. A plan is just something made to be broken. But it's gonna cost you. And roaming charges can really bite you in the ass, if you know what I mean. At some point, it's impossible to know if you are or are not sticking to the plan. And there's something you've *got* to do, so you deviate (or not), depending upon whether your well-laid plan is (or is not) in fact on the plan. How in the heck are you going to know?

I think I pushed just about every freakin' button on the stupid cell phone. Of course I don't know why. Probably not on my plan, so it's gonna cost me. I probably accidentally called a 900 number at fifty dollars per second and it's been charging me since a week ago Tuesday. I was pushing a lot of buttons then too, waiting for Monica or Godot or something I know not what. After I get the ten bazillion dollar bill ("those services were not on your plan") I suppose I could work it off at the burger joint for seventy seven years, after which time my indentured servitude will be, shall we say, over. Terminated in so many more ways than one.

I think I'm just worried about a lot of stuff, not the least of which is the situation right here at the hospice house. That's a little weird in itself. I mean, I don't really know what it's like in there, or what goes on. I just sit out here on the porch. I might freak out if I went in there. I actually feel relieved that I don't have to go in. Monica does alright, I guess. It's kind of hard to tell. Her dad never seems to come in to visit when she does.

How long have I been sitting out here? Longer than usual. I feel like I've been sitting on the porch for three of Lebowski's biology classes. That would be close to three eternities. The damn cell phone says it's only been about an hour and fifteen minutes or so. When Monica comes out, the sun is down, and the moon is rising.

"Hi Tommie. Thanks for waiting." Monica came over and sat on the swing before I could get up. I think my quads were shot from that hill work yesterday. They give me intimations on mortality.

"No problem. Are you ready?"

"Let's just sit here for a minute, if it's okay with you." She was almost whispering.

"Sure, Vera. This is a great swing. I'd like to have one if I ever buy a house. Porches are very cool."

"Yeah, I like porches." Monica was looking at the porch floor. Her hands were in the pockets of her windbreaker. She was barely audible. We sat there for a while in silence, not unlike our drive in. I checked out the moon sliver a few times. It seemed to be changing color constantly. Finally, I figured it was time to speak. "How's your mother?" It looked to me, out of the corner of my eye, like Monica winced. Maybe I'm mistaken, but that's what it looked like. Kind of a big shudder. I think I felt it myself.

She didn't respond for what seemed like an eternity, but I didn't want to push it and break the silence. We both kept staring straight ahead, both with our hands in our coat pockets.

"Do you believe in an afterlife, Tommie?"

"I guess so, yeah. I don't think it has streets of gold or a bunch of harps, but I guess I believe that we go somewhere after we finish our time here. Otherwise, it's even harder to make sense of it all."

"I don't know. I'd like to believe that, but wishing doesn't make it true."

I looked over at her. There was about a quarter moon, and with that, the porch light and the streetlights, I could see her face. She looked so old, like there were wrinkles everywhere, like she'd been through it all and lived to tell about it, but for those very reasons wasn't able to tell about it.

For what seemed like the first time today, she looked over at me. Her eyes were bloodshot. Every muscle in her face and neck seemed tense, contracted. Her skin looked blotchy. The pain and confusion were right there. I felt the familiar ache in my chest, more pronounced, more insistent. Her voice was shaking as she spoke her endless suffering.

"Tommie, my mom died this morning, before sunrise."

32

HIGH BROW UTILITARIAN RATIONAL HOMICIDE, OR WHY IMMANUAL KANT WOULDN'T BEAT HIS DOG

I drop Tommie off and go home. Dad is on the phone with my Aunt in Charlotte. He's made a hell of a lot of calls today. Better him than me. There's no way I could do that now. Call up your friends and relatives and tell them your wife died of breast cancer at forty-eight? Shit. I think I'd rather do almost anything else. What kind of goddamn planet is this? He's probably about ready to keel over. I don't think he's eaten anything all day. As a matter of fact, he hasn't eaten much since Mom has been in the hospice house. Even before that, as far as I know. He looks like skin and bones, with sad sad eyes. Way back sunken into his skull. Makes you think about the fragility of life. If something happens to him, I don't know what I'll do.

I walked in the back door. Dad looked over and we saw each other. We didn't say anything. What is there to say? I go up to my room. I walk around in circles. I sit on the bed. I get up and walk around the room some more. I look out the window. I lie on the bed and try to read a magazine. It's hopeless. I'm feeling restless. I get my purse and jacket and go back downstairs. Dad is still on the phone, with someone else, back in the kitchen. His voice sounds weird, like there are two voices instead of one. Really weird. Maybe it's the superaudible overtone series becoming audible. I go out the front. 8:45. I drive to the grocery store on the edge of Lancaster for a few items, the place over on the other side of Bausman. I don't want to go to the store in Millersville and bump into someone I know. I drive right past it.

I'm feeling a little paranoid. I think it's going to be a long night. I turn off my cell phone. I don't want to hear from anybody. I have thirty-five dollars in my wallet. I park about as far away from the store as you can get, way the hell out there, almost past the lighted area. I start walking up to the store. My legs feel stiff and rubbery all at the same time. My chest feels tight. I feel fat and ugly and I don't want to be seen. Believe me, if they delivered, there's no way in hell I'd be here. I feel a general sense of disgust, with no clear focus. It's ubiquitous, with no object.

Maybe I just hate myself. That's what happens when your IQ is too damn high. You hate yourself. It's inevitable, really. You can see through any shit you feed yourself or anybody else feeds you that might talk you out of the self-hatred, so what's the use? You've got to accept it. Whether my IQ is 167 or 174, either way it's in the range of inevitable self-hatred. Part of the family curse, I guess. Mom always quoted 174. That was the score from my second test. But does it really make any difference? And why the hell she cared is another matter. It's high enough to be condemned to a life of self-hatred. I know that much.

And high enough to know that the Big Daddies suckin' at the trough don't give a rat's ass about anyone but themselves. That the world is a zero sum game. Not because it has to be, but because the fuckers in charge want it that way. But you don't need me to tell you. Don't take my word for it. Just look at the evidence. I'm gonna hazard a guess. If you count preventable deaths due to starvation and eradicable diseases, add on World War I and World War II, then add on the Holocaust and Stalin's purges and the Gulag and Mao's Cultural Revolution and the killing fields in Cambodia and the Korean War, Vietnam, Gulf Wars I and II, the Afghan wars—first with the U.S.S.R and then the USA, and add on genocide in Bosnia/Kosovo, the Rwandan genocide, genocide in Darfur, and all the other hundreds of wars and genocides just in the 20th Century, I'm gonna say we killed well over two billion people since 1900. I'm using the term "we" loosely here, but you get my drift. Don't write me off. Just think about it for one minute. That's all I'm asking. Just think about it and add up the numbers. And remember, you could be next, so show your work when you do your math. Show your work.

Oh yeah, we killed two billion people, no

doubt. And when I say we, I mean the one percent or even a fraction of the one percent—probably more like *one hundredth of one percent*—aided by the propaganda-fueled serfs who have no idea what's good for them or their planet. Preventable death due to starvation and eradicable diseases would be over 1.5 billion, easy. It would be between 12.75 million and 15.00 million per year, *minimum*, at a rate of 35,000 to 41,000 preventable deaths per day. So, in a century, you've got somewhere close to 1.5 billion bumped off needlessly just because the powers that be somehow couldn't get their shit together. Or, rather, they *did* get their shit together, and this is *exactly* what they had planned. It's the rest of us that didn't get our shit together and put a stop to it. That's a lowball death estimate, to be sure. Well, hey now, I'm just being conservative, so that when I'm finished, there won't be a single person with any vestige of brain activity left who's going to be able to refute my argument. I'll say it again: these are preventable deaths, you sons of bitches. Mostly women and children. I guess we're gonna have to stick my mother in there. Just another statistic for your for-profit death machine. God, I feel sick. I feel so sick. Like I could vomit forever and it would never be enough. How am I ever going to get over it? There's no way. Oh, yeah, and the most helpless of helpless men.

Don't forget them as they soundlessly perish.

And I'll go on to bet that my number is low. Maybe a billion people low. Maybe two billion. But just like Stalin and the US military, you don't do body counts. Just ask General Tommy Franks. Just like Stalin, you count up the loss of livestock, because they have some value to you. But you don't add up the loss of human life, because clearly, it is of no value to you, except as raw material for your monolithic death machine.

God, it hurts so fucking bad and nobody can do a goddamn thing to make it any better. And how many people have to go through this? And it wouldn't have to be this way? I just don't get it. Some people just can't be human. I mean, how could you do this to another person? Just let them die when they could have lived, or act in such a way that you pull a bunch of strings that set in motion a series of events that actually bumps them off, so you can have something you want more than letting them live? Why are some people allowed to have that kind of power? Where's the civilization in that? I just can't see it. I'm too young, I guess. Not cynical enough yet. Maybe I'll realize that what passes for civilization is just war by other means. It just hurts so bad. And that's only one gone. Two billion gone is beyond belief. And "we've" done it to…ourselves? What a fucking toxic species.

Maybe God shouldn't have tipped Noah off and just flooded the whole planet before he knew what the hell happened. I mean, no other species likes us either, and we sure as hell don't like ourselves.

Don't argue with me, motherfuckers. The evidence is overwhelming. You had no defense. You have no defense. And you will have no defense. Women, children, old men, crippled, blind, lame, their lifeless decaying bodies piled high to the heavens, with the stench pungent in the nostrils of those who loved them. The Tower of Babel, constructed solely of human corpses, piled to the heavens, the foul odors of malevolence stinging one's nostrils. If we stacked 'em up, the two billion corpses, and let's say, they averaged nine inches thick each, we've got a tower over 284,000 miles high, straight out into outer space, our spectacular Tower of Babel, our little God-project right there in front of us, for all the gods to see. You'd think the gods would kill us right then, right after they see (and smell) the tower, just to stop the killing. It would be the only *just* thing to do, wouldn't you say? A tower of corpses 284,000 miles high, who could believe it? And it's getting so much higher...every...single...day. One must avert one's eyes, or risk instant insanity. One must avert one's eyes, or risk instant death. It is like gazing into the face of God—no one shall live—only it's not the face of God. It is the diabolical face of pure evil, instantiated in the world through the fruits of those who love darkness, those who worship their own masterful creation, the Golden Calf of Death.

Those blind, lame, poor, weak, stupid, confused, mentally ill, heart broken, crippled, hapless sons of bitches? Fuck 'em, right? Don't like my language? Too offensive for you, cock suckers of the universe? That's what I thought you'd say. 1.5 billion dead, two billion dead, no problem. Four letter words? Time for a burning at the stake. Well, it is your style. Killing. That is your real genius. High Brow Utilitarian Rational Homicide. It's what makes the world your playground. No need to explain it to us. We don't matter anyway. What can we do about it? Darwinian economics, Darwinian politics, Darwinian culture, right? Exactly. The state of nature? Oh, I meant the 20th and 21st centuries, here on planet earth.

In the end, they amount to exactly the same thing. So much for NATO, The United Nations and The United Nations Universal Declaration of Human Rights, Greenpeace, Amnesty International, International Law, the Geneva Convention, Democracy, Freedom, Liberty, Truth, and Justice. You've got them covered, Big Daddy. They are just little problems to be solved. Selling weapons and sowing discord, that's what you do. Those humans who aren't anything more than a fucking contagion won't be using them on you. They'll be using them on each other, after being carefully coached by you—subliminally and liminally—Oh Omnipotent Masters, Big Daddies sucking at the trough. My IQ might be 167 or 174 or whatever the fuck it is, but I'm not smart enough to figure out how to take you down, you sons of bitches. You mother fucking one percent of one percent that make the planet a living hell of terror for everybody else, we who live at your pleasure and only at your pleasure.

God, I hate myself. I get a cart and start down aisle one. I want to make it fast and get the fuck out of here. I try not to look at anybody. I end up with three plastic bags full of shit and get the hell out. I've still got $4.08 left. On the drive home, I start daydreaming and almost run into oncoming traffic. Pretty damn stupid. I can barely drive as it is. I just can't concentrate anymore. Then I sit at this light after it turns green. Some asshole in a goddamn monster truck starts honking like he's gonna be late for the birth of Queen Elizabeth. I wanted to go back and punch the guy in the face about a thousand times. I started to wonder what I'd do if I had a gun.

God, I feel tired. When is it going to be the fuck over? When is the nightmare over? Then I notice my gas gauge. It's almost right on E. Awesome. Fuckin' awesome. I pull into the minit market on Millersville Pike in Bausman. The last thing I want to do is look at yet another goddamn human being. The clerk looks at me funny when I ask for $4.00 on pump four, but he doesn't say anything. I felt like telling him to fuck off and go to hell, but I didn't say anything. He's the fucker working all night at his shitty job. Probably has to steal shit from the store just to make ends meet. Poor bastard.

I get 1.146 gallons of gas. I'm gonna have to get another job. This summer job shit and part time job shit during school just isn't gonna cut it. Maybe I could steal the night shift job from the fucker here at the minit market. It's just screwed up that I would have to work more than I do right now and still go to school full time and be expected to learn a goddamn thing. I mean, when the hell am I supposed to study? Any ideas? Maybe you can fuckin' feed it to me in my sleep. If I'm just training for the great big universal army of slave workers, then why the hell would they want me to know anything? Exactly.

Hence, it's set up so that it's impossible to learn anything because the *last* thing they want you to do is to get a notion in your head that you can better your condition. No fuckin' way. Way too subversive. Way too 20th century. They killed

1.5 billion people, but that was the century *before* all hope died. That shit's over. The whole fuckin' *civil* rights thing is over. The whole goddamn *human* rights thing is over. Now you've got to beg the masser to pick *you* as the slave. And if they don't pick you, go right ahead and starve the fuck to death down on what used to be some public sidewalk—since they took out all the benches to discourage your kind—somewhere in Detroit or Selma or Cincinnati or Houston or Pittsburgh or San Diego or Atlanta or Denver or Tampa or Chicago or Memphis or Dallas or Lancaster or Millersville or wherever the fuck it is that you're gonna starve to death. Just don't make a big scene, don't make a big racket, 'cause there are pretty people all around, shopping and dining at all the right places, and you wouldn't want to put them out. Wouldn't want to ruffle their chicken feathers. No, you've got to do your livin' and your dyin' in the right, prescribed way, even if the dyin' part is way before your time. You've got to do your livin' and your dyin' in a quiet-like kind of way. Don't make a scene. You'll just make it worse for all the rest of your people, the ones that ain't been snuffed…yet.

It could be Bangalore or Jakarta or Manila or San Juan or San Salvador or Guadalajara or Kandahar. It doesn't matter which fuckin' sidewalk it is, the sidewalk where you starve to death, or whether it's just a strip of dirt, as long as the Big Daddies suckin' at the trough don't have to step over you on their way to something important, like a meeting on new ways to fuck the world. What fuckin' difference does it make when we're all subhuman cogs in the fucking machine, the machine tuned to feed the endless blood lust and greed of the goddamn one percent? Race, sex, ethnicity, religion, who the fuck cares? We all burn the same, my brother. We all burn the same, my sister. We all burn the same, my child. So just shut the fuck up and get in line. Okay, I'm in line, but how the hell do I stay off the sidewalk? Maybe I can sell my soul on eBay. I'd probably still need to get another part time job. Surrogate motherhood, after I turn eighteen? It won't be long now. Who knows? Yeah, all we need are more motherfuckers on this planet, 'cause for some reason, seven billion ain't enough. We try to keep it down, that's for sure, what with all the calculated starvation and killings and all. Yeah, of course, those millions of kids and millions of adults that starve every year, and those one billion who get too little protein to have normal brain function? That's all calculated to benefit that one percent of one percent. It's old news, but here in the good old U.S. of A. nobody seems to get it. They're all sitting in front of their monster flat screen entertainment centers waiting to win the goddamn lottery. Their last hope is the myth of social mobility, since they can't hope in anything that's actually based on their experience. Oh, or having Jesus magically feed 'em a happy pill, right after they get downsized and their utilities get shut off. What I'm saying here is oh-so-not-radical. *It's so freakin' obvious.* When are people going to wake up? Talk about denial. But why deny something if you'd be *so* much better off not denying it? Other than fear? Oh yeah, fear can really create a sonic wasteland where everybody's talkin', but nobody's sayin' a thing. The whole goddamn global economy is calculated to benefit the infinitesimal sliver of what I'll charitably call humanity. And the sliver's about as happy about the situation as bad people are ever gonna get. They love the shit out of it. The only downside for them is they can't kill the plebes fast enough. I'm sure they've calculated the exact optimum ratio but it's not easy to keep on top of it, what with conditions constantly changing on the ground, especially since you've got to get the plebes to fell the axe. Maybe that's their number one logistical problem. Birth rate's too high, right Big Daddy, Big Daddy with the baby soft hands?

It's a combination of systemic, globalized, institutionalized active and passive euthanasia. That fraction of one percent, they need just the right amount of slave labor, so you don't want to kill off too many. You want to kill off just the right number, so you've got just the right number left. The right number requires a continuous surplus of labor so that you can force workers to compete with each other, attack each other, and think of each other as the enemy. This keeps their thoughts off of you, the sliver of one percent. This surplus of labor has the added benefit of driving wages down, down, down. Down so fucking low that after you've busted the last mother fucking union on the face of the earth, workers will fight to the death over a job that will not even allow them to remain alive. Ironic evil genius.

It's all for Big Daddy, that glorious fraction of one percent! They need the new bigger-than-an-island-yacht, to go along with their old big-as-an-island yacht. And don't forget the new jet, lest they wish to dine this evening in Brussels with some old friend who just received a Nobel Peace Prize and who made his money fucking over women and children. Yeah, you want the right number of slaves, but absolutely no more, because to tell the truth, you can't stand the sight of them. You'd replace them all with robots if you could. No chance of the truth dawning on a goddamn robot. No chance of a revolution.

You can't stand the sight of your slaves, without a doubt. But you do enjoy hurting them just because you can. In fact, it seems to me that you enjoy nothing more, not even your boats or planes or cars or houses or property, or jewels or gold or silver or complex investment vehicles or honors or vacations. No, there's always something you seem to enjoy *more* than all that shit, and that's fucking the helpless *just because you can*. The meek will inherit the earth, since you're the fuckers who are gonna be sure to put them six feet under. Robots will not allow you this privilege. Thus, humanity is spared.

In order to ensure an endless supply of people you can fuck, you do everything you can to enlarge the ranks of the fuckable. Without, of course, allowing for *too many* slaves. They all serve at the pleasure of the king, so you keep just the right amount in reserve and systematically enforce your global program of passive and active euthanasia. Why waste a bullet when you can just starve the fuckers to death? Why waste bombs, tanks, munitions of all types, chemical and biological weapons, when you can maintain the scientifically correct number of herd animals to do your bidding, whether as factory workers, Ivy League economists, academics, White House spokespersons, or journalists for major media outlets? The really smart part of your nefarious plan is getting the slaves to kill each other, while you watch the rollerball competition from the sidelines, for pleasure, of course, but also just to make sure it turns out as rigged. The Romans sure didn't have nothin' on you.

To do all this, you've got to be very careful in your calculations. All those fucking economists and political scientists and historians and philosophers and other pseudo-thinkers at the colleges and universities and goddamn think tanks all across the land of the free and the home of the brave? Just pay 'em off and they not only do all the calculations, they go the extra mile and provide you with the cover story so that no one will know! Same with your journalist lackeys! In fact, after all the seeds of terror and desperation have been sown by you, the Mother Fucking Masters of The Material World, you can get just about anything you want.

I know, poor babies, if there's something you *can't* get, you're gonna get more pissed off than God. And then your merciless wrath will descend. At least you'll kill, maim, starve, torture and burn your way as far as you can get. Meanwhile, I'm still trying to pay my goddamn bills. I'm just trying to make it to fucking adulthood without you killing me or the people I care about. You fuckers sure did a great job on the health care thing, with your new patsy in the White House. Thanks a lot, motherfuckers, for killing my mom and then sending my dad a bill for your evil homicide. If she would have gotten the tests and treatments she needed *when* she needed them, instead of jumping through months of goddamn hoops and red tape so that you could end up denying treatments, she'd be alive today. Today, she is dead. She was alive yesterday. God, do I feel empty. It's a painful soul-deadening empty. A searing, ubiquitous hunger.

Fuck it with having kids. Who would put their kids through this shit? If you get sick, the kid has to watch you die from a preventable condition. Yeah, that's post-civil civilization. Goddamn one percent. I know your stock went up, ever so slightly, because you were able to deny needed services for my mother. Yeah, your stock went up because you killed my mom. Yeah, your stock went up because you committed active euthanasia. Your stock went up because you killed my mother, you goddamn monsters. Fuck, I've got to get out of here. I'm just trying to survive, and you're making it, well, basically impossible.

I'll probably have to say ixnay on the surrogate motherhood. I'd probably starve as a prostitute, so that's out. Shit, with all these options, the sky's the limit. But first, I'll have to rack up $50,000 in college loans. And that's if I go to Fuckin' Homegrown U. right here in Bumfuck and sleep in the same bed I had since I was four—if nobody carts it away. The state's given up on the idea of actually supporting state schools, so I guess they're public in name only. Not a very good marketing ploy, if you're looking for prestige. Probably better to abolish them altogether. Rather, probably *necessary* to abolish them, to save what's left of the bought off state.

A planned inevitable consequence of public school privatization? No. It's can't be! So nefarious! Who would have thought of that? *Is everybody that's still human always ten steps behind?* Wake the fuck up. If I go somewhere else—God forbid a private school, then the debt's gonna be $200,000. I'll have no trouble digging out of that economic shithole by the time I'm— well, let's see—best case scenario—forty-five, no problem. Worst case scenario—after death. Welcome to Fucking America. Welcome to our goddamn planet 2011. Welcome to 21st Century Planet Earth, where we've reinvented slavery and called it freedom, so that a sliver of one percent of the world's population can live like fuckin' Big Daddy-O Masters of The Material World.

Those fuckers are livin' large, all right, larger than God. God's just a fucking concept they use to bludgeon the slaves into submission, if you get my drift. Better than a goddamn tazer. A hell of a lot longer lasting. Better to invent replicants, you know, like in *Blade Runner*, if you could even trust *them*. Technology is one hell of a thing. You invent it for yourself, and it ends up taking you captive. The point is, Big Daddy's got to have slaves, but as the world's greatest philanthropist, the world's biggest micro-lender, the world's cultural curator, he's got to call them something else, like employees or citizens. The only problem is, when you treat everything like shit, you turn into shit yourself.

Even Immanuel Kant knew that, and he was a real piss ant. He told you not to beat your dog *not* because the dog had a right not to be beaten, but because when you beat your dog, it makes *you* cruel, it twists *your* character. It makes *you* a piece of shit. It's still all about *you*. He didn't give a shit about the dog. The finest philosopher of ethics in the last five hundred years and it's still all about you and to hell with the victim. So say the fraction of one percent, as reflected in all credible academic opinions. Therefore, don't beat your dog. A fine piece of reasoning, if all you give a shit about is the powerful. But the powerful do beat their dogs. They just call them by a different name. Fuck it.

Back to *Bladerunner*. If you haven't seen it, get the director's cut. Before it's too late. In the end, the replicants were more human than the humans who used them. And the replicants were goddamn machines.

Speaking of machines: I walk back to my

car on my stiff and at the same time rubbery legs. I get back in the car and it doesn't start. I'm sitting at the goddamn Chicken Mountain Minit Market in Bausman at 9:35, the night is turning cold, and the car doesn't start. It's such a surprise, that an eighteen-year-old car with more miles than God doesn't start. It's not the first time. I wait in the car for about ten minutes, staring through the buzzy fluorescent light and the carbon monoxide. I wonder why we need to imagine a hell that's...somewhere else.

I think about calling Tommie, but I just saw the guy not two hours ago. He was out there waiting for me for a hell of a long time. I wouldn't even have blamed him if he took off. But he just sat out there on the porch. I wonder what he'd have thought if he knew Mom wasn't even in the hospice house. She'd been dead for twelve hours. She was already at the mortuary. I was just sitting in what used to be her room, staring. I needed to be there. Why, I have no idea. The only good thing was that nobody else was in there yet, so I could hang out.

I think about calling someone else, but I can't think of anyone I want to talk to. Now is not the time to be honest. I get brave and turn the key. The car starts. I gun the engine and jam it into first. I head back toward Millersville. This day is still not fucking over. It feels like a hundred years.

When I get back to the house, dad is still on the freakin' phone. I can see him through the kitchen window when I park in the driveway. I don't want to go through the kitchen. I go around to the front and carry the groceries up to my room. I change into my sweats and think about washing my face. Why bother? I decide not to. I remember to lock the bedroom door.

I dump all the shit out onto the bed and start lining it up. A box of individually wrapped cinnamon and sugar snack cakes. One box of apple with vanilla frosting toaster pastries. A bag of chocolate chip cookies. A bag of spicy tortilla chips. A dozen peanut butter cookies from the bakery. A bottle of mouthwash. A box of thick pretzels. A bag of red licorice. A six pack of 12 oz. diet cola. A six pack of 12 oz. diet root beer. A roll of paper towels. A pack of Klein's spearmint gum. A bottle of liquid ibuprofen capsules. I line the shit up on the far side of my bed, the side furthest away from the bathroom. I use the bathroom. I turn on the lamp on the night table and turn off the overhead light. I get ready to get into bed when suddenly there is a knock at the door. It wasn't totally unexpected, but it startled me just the same.

"Monica. Are you alright?"

"Yes, Dad. I'm fine. Thanks for asking."

"Can I come in?"

"Ah, well, I'm in my pajamas and I was just getting into bed—" There is a pause.

"It's okay. I'll see you tomorrow. If you need anything, let me know. Sorry I was on the phone for so long."

"That's okay dad. You had to tell everybody about Mom." Another rather long pause. He's still standing outside the door. I'm sure I remember locking the door, but I still feel nervous.

"Are you...sure you're...alright, Monica?"

"Yes, dad. Are *you* alright?" I hear the old floor creak outside the door.

"I'm...makin' it. It's been a long day. It's been a long year and a half." He sounded so exhausted, like he could sleep for a million years and still not be rested.

"That's true. I hope you can get some rest, Dad. There's nothing we can do now."

"I hope that you can get some rest too, Monica. Let me know if you need anything."

"I will, Dad. Don't worry about me. You've got enough to worry about. Good night."

"Good night, Monica."

I hear footsteps slowly recede into oblivion. I go over one more time to check the lock. I wash my hands again and then get into bed. I prop three pillows behind my back and open the package of chocolate chip cookies. I know I have to pace myself, or I'll get really sick. I get six or seven cookies down, fast. I don't do a lot of chewing. The cookies stick in my throat. I pop open a diet cola and wash the cookies down. I fumble for another and stuff it into my mouth. I feel a pang of something, but I don't know what it is. I finish off the package of cookies and pour the remainder of the can of diet cola down my throat. The fizz burns as it goes down.

Then I open the cinnamon snack cakes. It pisses me off that I'm getting crumbs on the bed, but I'll just have to clean it up later. I've already got at least six paper towels on the bedspread, but somehow, don't ask me how, the freakin' crumbs just jump somewhere else. I start thinking that Mom won't like it when she sees all the….freakin' snack cake crumbs. The damn things are individually wrapped, which I thought was a good thing. I open the second and cram it into my mouth. I try to chew, but it's sticking to the roof of my mouth. I pop open another diet cola and suck it down along with the snack cake.

All of a sudden, I decide I'd like an apple toaster pastry. I open the box, open the stupid inside wrapper, which is a pain in the ass, and take one out. No need to toast. I alternate large bites of apple toaster pastry with the rest of the second diet cola. I'm starting to feel full, but so what? I rearrange the three pillows and then open the spicy tortilla chips. I use the scissors I keep in my night table drawer to open the bag. If I opened them by hand, it could make a loud pop, and the last thing I need right now is Dad coming back and standing outside my door. I don't hear any noise over there, but I doubt if he's asleep. He hasn't been sleeping right for as long as I can remember. I don't like salsa or cheese dip. It's too messy, especially in bed. I eat a bunch of tortilla chips, two or three at a time. Maybe half the bag. I open the night table drawer and take out a clothes pin and pin it on the folded top of the bag. Then I open the peanut butter cookies. I feel like talking. I look at the clock on my cell phone. 12:14 a.m. Probably a little late. I can't think of anybody to call anyway. I put the cell phone back on the night table and pick up a peanut butter cookie. I don't think I'm tasting anything. That's okay. It's not that important. I eat three cookies and then seal the plastic wrap back up.

I feel like I'm getting a headache, so I pop the top off the liquid ibuprofen and take two 200 mg. gel capsules out of the bottle. I wash them down with the third diet cola. I wish I had some sweet iced tea, but it probably wouldn't make any difference. This diet shit sucks. Then I open the red licorice. I decide to read a magazine while I'm chewing on the licorice. I've got *Chess*

World, but I don't feel like reading that. I could read *Harper's*, but I'd have to get out of bed and walk over to the desk. What the hell, I get the damn magazine, along with copies of *The Nation* and *Rolling Stone* and throw them on the bed. Besides, I need to empty my bladder.

I feel pretty shaky when I get out of bed. I lean my hand against the wall as I make it to the bathroom. God, the toilet seat's cold. My stomach's making a lot of gurgling sounds. I stumble back into bed. I feel lonely. My phone says 1:37 a.m. I decide to open the bag of thick pretzels. I take the scissors out of the drawer on the night table and carefully cut the bag. The salt stings my mouth, but I like the feeling. I pop open another diet cola. I start thinking about college. Maybe I'll get a scholarship. There's got to be somebody or something out there who wants to give me money. 'Cause with the $7.25 an hour job, I'll need to save for about two decades just to pay the bill.

Yeah, I'll get a scholarship! Go to Pine State or somewhere else that's not this town. I take a few swigs of the diet cola and have a licorice stick. I start thinking about Pine State. I don't know a thing about it, so the thinking is purely imaginative. It's kind of exciting. The only thing I'd really miss is Tommie. Maybe he could go too? I wonder if he likes me, but I guess it's obvious. I'm not really likeable. Nobody's drooling over me. No man in the universe ever drooled over a chick because her IQ was 167. Or 174. I'd be better off good looking with an IQ of 74. That way I'd never be alone.

I have another thick pretzel. A bunch of big salt crystals fall on the bedspread and not on the paper towels. So what? Tommie is cool. He probably thinks I'm cool. Or maybe not. Maybe he thinks I'm a basket case, just a big charity case. That's gotta be it. It's always *him*, doing something for *me*. I'd like to do something for him, but I have no idea what it could be. I finish off another diet cola. I use one of the plastic bags for my trash bag. I'll separate the recyclables later. I'm feeling pretty sick to my stomach. I guess it's time.

I stumble back into the bathroom and turn on the sink faucets. I turn them on as far as they will go. I wash my hands, splashing a bunch of water all over. Does it really matter? I leave the water on full blast, just in case. I go over and lift the toilet seat with my left hand, and then stick the index finger of my right hand down the back of my throat as I kneel before the porcelain. I vomit the undigested remains of half-masticated saliva-soaked junk food. It spews forth from deep within.

I feel at one with my vomit. It is hot and

caustic. The stomach acid burns in my throat. I feel fire in my nostrils. At the same time, I break out in a cold sweat as my body wracks itself, seemingly without mercy. It feels like some kind of religious ritual, or the closest to religious ritual that I've experienced in many, many years. It seems like an eternity since I've gone to those church services, those Sunday school classes. I convulse just enough to push out the remains of the contents of my stomach. I wipe my mouth with a paper towel and hold on to the toilet as I raise myself up. Then I go to the sink and rinse my mouth three times, throwing the paper cup into the waste basket. Then I brush my teeth, very carefully. I've got a hell of a headache.

I stumble back to the bed. I can barely wait to get under the covers. I feel so weak and exhausted. When I wake up, it's 8:27 a.m. The bed is strewn with cinnamon and sugar snack cake wrappers, peanut butter cookies, a crumpled bag of thick pretzels, a partially full box of apple and vanilla toaster pastries, mouthwash, a bunch of crumbs everywhere, a warm six pack of diet root beer, one warm diet cola, a bag of trash, a half eaten bag of spicy tortilla chips, a bottle of ibuprofen, and a bunch of paper towels. My throat feels like a sewer pipe. I feel like shit. I know Dad's at the mortuary, and I don't have to go to school today. The house is quiet. I don't have to go back until at least next week. Four more days of this and I don't know if I'll make it.

33

SATANIC GPS

Ferris picks me up in his '95 Chrysler LeBaron convertible and we head over toward Harlan's place. The LeBaron is a piece of crap. The suspension is shot so bad that every little bump makes it rock like we're in a typhoon, going around the Cape of Good Hope. The red paint looks so not red that it isn't even funny. Let's just say that it exudes a faint recollection of red, but that's about it. The only thing good about the LeBaron is it's got a Mitsubishi engine, and that's marginal, seeing that it has 262,507 miles on the clock, and that's only if nobody set it back. It burns a shitload of oil and gets about twenty miles per gallon, if you're light on the pedal. Ferris isn't light on the pedal.

That's why I hate it when we've all got to chip in when he drives up to the freakin' pump. It could even make big boys cry. Harlan just does a lot of bitching and whimpering. It would probably be better for all concerned if he just started crying and kept his lips sealed. But that's never gonna happen. You'd just have to know Harlan. Fillin' up that thirsty sucker is all of $65.00. Bail out Chrysler? Hell, somebody should bail out everybody who *drives* a Chrysler, and even people whose *friends* drive a Chrysler. Damn. Even split two or three ways, it's painful. God, is it painful. That's all of four large pizzas at the House of Pizza, with extra cheese and three toppings each. It's ridiculous. Almost makes you want to walk. Since we've got those wars going in Afghanistan, Iraq, and now Libya, gas has tripled in price. Awesome. If it triples again, it'll cost just about two hundred bucks to fill up that thirsty beast. I think I'll get myself a moped. My dad didn't have a moped, but he did have this 1971 Hodaka Ace 100 B+ that got like a million miles per gallon. Okay, it was probably more like a hundred miles per gallon, but still. At least a hundred, for sure. It was this little single cylinder two-stroke deal that sounded almost like a chainsaw, only a hair friendlier, but not much. The only problem was that you had to mix the oil with the gas, and it burned some oil, let me tell you. I remember when he still had it running. That was a while ago. If it was still running, I'd probably be out there on it right now. I'd be the coolest dude…well, I'd like it. It had the smell of adventure. Or incipient disaster. Depending upon your perspective.

Because of all the pollution from burning all that oil, the new two strokes aren't legal on the road anymore unless you've got an old one that's still running. Fair enough. But you can get a small four-stroke motorcycle that's a heck of a lot quieter and gets awesome mileage too. Just don't go on the highway, unless you've got a death wish, and then it'd be more than a wish. Plus, riding around on the small ones is fun as hell. If you think riding around in a convertible Chrysler LeBaron is fun—which it is, believe me, as long as you've got some Dramamine—you should ride around on a small moped or scooter or single cylinder motorcycle. You almost laugh out loud. Unless, of course, you dump it, in which case you'll be doing a few other things out loud.

I'll tell you how I know. I was over at Ted Metzler's last summer and he let me ride his Suzuki 125 dirt bike. They called it a DR-Z. I sucked at first, but then I...sucked. That was even after I'd gone back a bunch of times. Metzler is a charitable fellow. Or maybe he was taking bets on when I was going to run into a tree. It happened like this. There's a bunch of woods and fields behind his house and Greg Schleffler showed up with his brother Dave. They had some nice rides too. Kawasaki KLR 250 and Yamaha TTR 225. Personally, I was glad to be on the DR-Z. Those other bikes looked a little too big for me, maybe more than a little. Any dirt bike more than double your weight is just a bad idea waiting to happen. I wouldn't have said anything, though, if they wanted me to ride their bikes. Saying something wouldn't have been cool. Always gotta step up to the plate when it's your turn at bat. No flinching. You know what happens if they smell blood. Or tears. Well, I won't go into it but you won't get invited back. It's all for your own good, of course.

They didn't invite me to ride those big ass bikes, and that's probably why I'm still alive to tell the tale. As for the 250 or the 225: I probably would have figured out how to get on it, just barely, and then I would have dumped it back in some mud hole in the woods. They'd have to call the sheriff, and finally the United States Forest Service. They'd use cadaver dogs. My body wouldn't have been found for three years, two months, and eleven days, but who's counting? My skeleton would be right underneath the KLR, with the rear brake lever stabbing through my chest, right between a couple of broken ribs. I'd be the talk of the town for all of...three minutes. So much for my fifteen minutes of fame. Luckily, those guys didn't ask me to ride their monster bikes, so my life—and my masculinity—were saved.

On the other hand, Metzler's DR-Z was just awesome. And I don't say that a lot, not even with reference to God. That weekend powwow was the testosterone event of the season. There were all these guys coming out of the woodwork, you might say. Bruce Heinreich showed up on his Honda CRF 80. Eighty freakin' cubic centimeters of raw power. Less than five cubic inches. I didn't feel so bad. That thing was little. But a guy on a little motorcycle is still cooler than a guy with no motorcycle at all. Hands down. Then Ron Shyver. He had some weird looking thing that I barely got to see because all I saw was his fat ass and a bunch of smoke. That's right: his fat ass blowing smoke. It looked like an antique, but then again, I didn't get a good look when it was flying by. I later heard Shyver call it an ass hole. When I asked him what he meant, he said "Let me spell it out for you—O-S-S-A, sphincter brain". It went something like this:

Ron, pointing to his parked bike, cigarette in hand: "My ass hole might be old and worn, but it's still mighty fine."

Me, a bit incredulous: "Your ass hole is mighty fine? Maybe you've come to the wrong place."

Ron, pissed off: "Let me spell it out for you—O-S-S-A, sphincter brain."

By this time, Heinreich, Metzler, and Schleffler and Schleffler were laughing their asses off, but I had this bad feeling that after our little break, I might be eating a lot of extra dust. But with my riding prowess, it's always difficult to discern whether I'm eating extra dust or just the usual amount. So it was an OSSA. Whatever the heck that means. After the break, I did see a lot of Shyver's fat ass blowing smoke. I can tell you that much.

Maybe it's short for OssaPieceofShit. Okay, I take that back. I saw his fat ass like ten thousand times, and I know the DR-Z ain't shit, so his ride's more than okay. Just tryin' to be fair. Of course, if I was riding it, it might be a different story. I don't know exactly why he was blaming me for not hearing, after we had all those bikes out there making a buttload of noise. Just turning off the engines made the silence seem...loud. Weird. Just remember, the senses can deceive you. And it's a good thing too. And getting back on that DR-Z seemed like a good idea. Duh.

Anyway, they had this little enduro course back there in the woods. Kind of like a cross-country course, only less painful. Or, hopefully less painful. No guarantees. Just one wayward ground hog and you're toast. We rode around the serpentine dirt trails, trying to avoid the plentiful hardwoods. Yeah, it was hard to find space with all those trees. Sounds like a set up for something funky waiting to happen. I'm not even sure where all those freakin' trails went. I just know that when I saw a trail crossing the trail that I was on, I got a mite nervous. Without a doubt I was the slowest bastard out there. I know it wasn't the bike. It was me. My reflexes were like... whaaaaaaa happpeeeennned? Yeah, that's what I mean. That would be after I missed the S curve and crashed into the blackberry thicket. It's not the best kind of thicket to crash into if you're going to have to crash into a thicket. Real nice, if you know what I mean. I could have been riding the world's fastest dirt bike, and I'd manage to get my butt kicked.

I can envision Greg Schleffler roaring by me on a CRF 50. That thing's got about ten inch wheels. And forty-nine cubic centimeters of throbbing power. That's about three, yeah, three cubic inches. It's made for guys that are just out of their diapers. Or maybe old guys that are just getting back into diapers. Anyway, I could be on like the liquid cooled six-speed Kawasaki KLR 250 and Schleffler'd blow by me on the midget CRF 50. His wake would shake me up so much that I'd steer straight into a thirty-six inch white oak. I slam into it at my full speed...seventeen miles per hour. See, the DR-Z doesn't have a speedometer. In fact, it doesn't have much of anything, other than a kick-starter and some handlebars with grips. Oh, and a kill switch in case you get yourself into a pinch. You can cut the engine just prior to careening over a fifty-foot embankment, for whatever good it'll do you. Me, I'd just let the engine run, for two reasons: First, I'd never be quick enough to shut the damn thing off. Second, if the engine keeps running, maybe somebody'll hear me down there in the bottom of the canyon and I'll get rescued before the thing goes up like a Roman candle. Of course, the wolves and mountain lions could also be alerted by the sound, in which case, somebody may inherit a pretzeled but otherwise awesome DR-Z 125, if you don't count all the dried blood.

Oh yeah, back to the no speedometer. With no speedometer, I'm flying through these labyrinthine hilly as hell trails, and I'm thinkin' that I'm really eating up the terra firma like nobody's business. I'm thinkin' I'm going…fast. Then we all take another break back in Metzler's back yard. Heinreich whips out his wrist GPS and velcros it to Metzler's handlebars, which for the moment are my handlebars. I go back out on the trail. I think I'm cranking the windy hilly serpentine suckers like I know what I'm doing, like I've got talent. Holy crap, I'm cranking it and the GPS says 19.2 mph, then 18.8 mph. Sharp corner. 9.0 mph. Dip and left 90 degrees: 12.6 mph.

It was demoralizing. I could imagine some dude from Kenya running right behind me. I get to a sharp 115-degree curve, and he passes me on the inside. Damn. I suck. Okay, I got it up to 26.7 mph on that one straightaway, but it was only for about one second, and then I instantly sunk right down below 20. The speed scared the hell out of me, but it was exhilarating all at the same time. It's not like a car. It's not like a car at all.

It's more like a magic carpet ride. I'm back to 14.2 mph as soon as I hit the underbrush. At one point, I was going up this rather steep embankment, at a weird angle, and I managed to downshift into first gear. As I crested the peak, I noted the satanic GPS: 3.4 mph. Then Heinreich and Shyver and Schleffler and Schleffler show back up on the course, piped with Mountain Dew. It was so sad. Even the CRF 80 blew by me with amazing speed. I sucked so bad. I sucked so bad it was astounding. Good thing there weren't any girls out there, or I'd have to quit forever and move away just to retain my sanity and my honor. Oh, I forgot: I'm a cross-country runner. This is nothin'.

34

EMPIRICAL YET DEFINITIVE PROOF FOR GOD'S EXISTENCE?

I'm jolted out of my egregious reverie. Ferris is driving up the two-inch bump that leads into the Chicken Mountain minit market parking lot. The LeBaron starts shaking like it's possessed. Ferris pulls up into a space and stops, but the car is still rockin'.

"Dude, let's get out before the thing explodes," I suggest.

"Hey shut up, Tommie. Where's your car? That's what I thought. It's invisible."

"That's true, but shut up. I'm working on a moped. Maybe I'll get a moped."

"I always knew that you wanted to commit suicide, but do you have to be so obvious about it?"

"Wanting to get a moped is my cry for help."

"I'll say. And you need it, too. Let's get some tea."

"Oh yeah." Ferris jumped out just as the car stopped rocking. I knew we couldn't ever go straight to Harlan's joint. How could we do a long run without proper hydration?

We pick up a gallon of the regular stuff and head over to Harlan's. Now, they've got something like 10,000 flavors, so if you want some regular ass tea, you've got to wade through a sea of weirdness just to get to the real thing. By next week, they'll probably add Strawberry Kiwi

Melon Cucumber Cherry Papaya Ohio Buckeye Cinnamon Mango Lemon Sugar Free Decaf Tea, because I didn't see that one today. What's up with that?

By the time we get over to Harlan's, we're so late that he's actually ready. I mean ready to run. Not ready for life. Or for anything else that actually matters. His dad lets us in. He says "Hello" but doesn't look too stellar. We mumble "Hello" back. We probably don't look too stellar either. We file up to Harlan's microroom. He's playing some good shit, as per usual. But it's not antediluvian fossilized shit, it's something that's actually from after the double millennium.

Money be honey, upside down flags

"Dudes, you suck. Thanks for the tea!" Harlan tries to grab the gallon jug out of Ferris's hand. No can do. You'd need a team of Harlans to get that job done.

Are red, black and blue

"What're you playin', player?"

"You mean you don't know, Mr. America? Give me some tea, Ferris dude, and I'll let you know." Harlan drives a hard bargain. He's still gonna end up begging for the tea. Ferris doesn't move. He doesn't say anything either.

And you got the electric hall

"You mean you don't know, Ferris? Where've you been? Oh, yeah, out trying to finish that 5K. It's Bobby Skulls, dude, with The Yowl." Harlan pontificates like everyone on the planet who has any sense ought to know.

"Bobby Skulls? That Neanderthal? Well, at least it's not from the last century like all your other shit. Are you buyin' after we get back? Two large pizzas with everything, on you. You get to pay just because you're you, sphincter."

"Where is my other running shoe?" Harlan asks, half under the bed. Ferris and I just stand there, staring at nothing in particular, shaking our heads. He fishes it out from a dark place, under the bed.

We got the cannon balls

"Whoever sucks the most today gets to pay," I suggest.

"So, you're saying that Ferris is paying. Yeah, I'm down with that," Harlan spouts. Ferris makes a face like he's gonna pound somebody, mostly likely Harlan.

"Hey, if you guys are ready", I say, "let's get the crap out of here." Ferris takes a few long swigs from the tea and passes it to me, while Harlan eyes it with envy and dread. "We'll save you a couple of drops, don't worry, Harlan." Not like he deserves it. Then I pass him the bottle before I drink.

It's hard-on wallets and hard-on greed

"Dude, Mother Teresa!" He chugs all he

can in fifteen seconds and the coldness nearly knocks him out. "Holy crap, that's cold. That hurts."

Harlan's neck is so skinny that I almost feel sorry for him, but I hold back.

"That's the way it is when something's good. It hurts," says Ferris, letting us know it's going to be one of those days.

It's what you need, what you need, God bless America

It doesn't take long for us to polish off the jug. Ferris does one of his signature plastic jug crumples, then slam dunks it onto Harlan's bed.

Suited Hitlers in the bank with the rank smell

Harlan retrieves the jug so that he can dump it into the recyclables on our way out.

Of corpses of lost city streets in the country cells

After we've all taken our final whizzes, we file back down and out. You can always create your own adventure. With or without a moped.

"Shoes double tied, rock stars?" I ask. Ferris and Harlan grunt. "Okay, cool."

We hit the street and start slithering into a run. Don't want to get Ferris into a tizzy. We head south. It's a great day, just a little windy. About forty degrees, sunny, bright blue sky with a few puffy clouds, but not many. It smells like hope and an endless future.

"Where are we going, anyway?" asks

Harlan in his usual nonspontaneous way. He's so anal, having to know where we're going. Our pace is sluggish. It's pretty obvious that it's the off-season. Of course, our pace sucked during the season too. But let's not get into that.

"In life?"

"Shut up, Tommie. You know what I mean."

"Stoney Lane Loop?" I suggest.

We're basically going that way now. Ferris and Harlan don't say no, and we're on the first mile of the thing anyway, so it looks like that's it by default. Another fantastic life lesson. Nine miles to go. Maybe more, if we add the extra Owl Bridge section. Our masochism meters must be low today, or we would have picked Silvermine Road. The last time I did Silvermine with Harlan and Ferris, I should have brought a buttload of diapers, 'cause those guys were just freakin' infants waitin' to get potty trained. All I heard was "bitchbitchbitchbitchbitch" for almost two hours. Do I really want to hear if Harlan has a "Ohhh hot spot…Ohh…hot spot?" He's like a 98 pound loud mouth baby wuss.

Yeah, yeah, for the uninitiated, a hot spot is what you call something before it turns into a blister. A pre-blister, if you will. Well, the pansy ass Harlan was bitching about "Ohh hot spot… Ohh hot spot" for mile after mile and I was hoping it'd just turn into a damn bloodly blister. Not that *that* would have shut him up, but he would have quit yelling "Ohh hot spot...Oohhh hot spot." Now, you don't want to hit the guy, him being such a wimp and all, and besides, we're in the middle of a fourteen-mile run. So, you just have to listen to it and imagine silence.

Well, that's pretty hard to do, what with Ferris slapping the hell out of the archaic asphalt. It would be bad enough if the slaps were somehow even, rhythmic. But hell no, they're so not even that you have to keep looking over at Ferris, just to see how he manages to keep upright. With slaps and scrapes like that, you'd think he was having some kind of a seizure. But no, that's Ferris on a long run. Keeps Asics in business. You'd think with the sound of the carnage, he'd need new shoes just about every other day, but he's still got on the same pair he had before the cross-country season. Go figure.

When I'm out running with these guys, I just imagine that I'm running with a couple of mentally handicapped dudes—not that it's much of a stretch—and then I break out in a smile. And finally a laugh. Yeah, I laugh out loud, right in the middle of the Silvermine Road course or whatever. Both Harlan and Ferris look over at me every time, both pissed. They know I'm laughing at them. But it can't be helped. I think anybody that sees us thinks that there are three mentally handicapped dudes trying to get in shape. Or some proselytes doing penance. Anyway, they give us a really wide berth. That's how I know. Not that giving us a wide berth is a bad thing. I, for one, would rather not get run down out here. Ferris is slapping the shit out of the asphalt and Harlan is yelling something about hot spots. Damn. It's a fine day for a run. Speaking of slapping, Ferris isn't doing it—yet—today. He pipes up about the reticence of Harlan's dad.

"What's up with your dad, dude? He hasn't even told us a joke in like, three weekends."

"Yeah, I know. It's the university. He didn't get a contract yet for next year. He could still get one, I guess. It's kind of early. But since they've started advertising nationally for his crappy one year position, it kind of means that he didn't get the job."

"Damn, Harlan. What are you saying? Didn't get the job? I thought he already had the job. Why didn't you tell us?"

"Tommie, there was nothing to tell. It's just like every other place everywhere else. It's nothing special. Typical university shit. He didn't get notified that he doesn't have a job, or anything like that. They don't let you know if you're *not* getting a contract. They only let you know if you *are* getting a contract. So you can always wait and hope that you're getting one, even if they have no intention of giving you one. Like I said, there's nothing to tell. They don't have to 'let you go' because technically, you were never there. Never there as a permanent hire, that is, no matter how long you're actually there. And it could be decades. So when you're 'let go', so to speak, all you "hear" is this really really long silence. You listen to it for the rest of your life, I guess, and hope it doesn't drive you insane. Yeah, I've got to listen to it all the time. All the time. I can't remember when I didn't have to listen to it. My dad's always stressing about it. The whole thing really pisses me off."

We're cresting the hill at Prince Street. Ferris is still right there, what with our geriatric slog.

"When do they usually let you know, I mean, if you're going to get a contract?"

"Tommie, dude, my dad's been at so many places I can't even remember anymore. But they always advertise nationally before the end of the fall semester, you know, for the jobs beginning the next fall. Every school pretty much does that. So if you don't have something by the winter semester break, you're screwed, basically."

"Harlan, Ferris and I will buy the pizza." I meant well, but after I spoke, I realized that my utterance could be taken in at least two ways, one of them a bit less than charitable. Before I was able to make a save, Harlan was on it. He sounded pissed.

"To celebrate our next move, our move out of town, you bastard?"

"No dude! Okay, you still get to pay, Harlan. Forget what I said. Forget it." I look over at Harlan looking at me and he looks hurt and angry, like he doesn't know what to believe. Now I'm feeling like a giant asswipe.

Right about then, Ferris stumbles over an ant or something and yells out. Maybe today he won't even make it out of Millersville. He could always crash at the House of Pizza. Given that we're just about passing it now, maybe he's faked his little stumble as a strategic way to preempt the remainder of our lovely adventure. But who in his right mind would do that?

"Oooowwwww! OOOOooowwww! Crraaapppp!" It's Ferris, catapulting to the asphalt, once again. It's part of his routine. My dad calls him the Jimmy Carter wanna be, just not to his face. We stop, quickly, in the middle of Prince Street. It's one way, south to north, so we only need to observe one direction to note by which untoward vehicle we are soon to be crushed. Luckily, the road is clear. Ferris is face down on the road. Already, there is blood. "Stupid street! Stupid potholes! Crraaapppp!"

Ferris is up, walking agitatedly in small circles in the middle of the street. Blood drips from his right knee where the tights are ripped, and both hands. Fortunately, there is still no traffic. It's an auspicious start.

"Are you alright, dude?

"Yeah, just get going. I'll get over it, Tommie. Just get going, will ya?" Ferris sounds mighty pissed off, for Ferris. He's generally on an even keel—with notable exceptions, like when he is catapulted into the street—something you can't always say about Harlan, the professional whiner. All of a sudden everything goes quiet.

Harlan is just standing there behind his shades, for once in his life mute. Ferris is already starting to jog slowly and unevenly down Prince Street, pulling the spandex wedgie out of his ass as he stumbles forward with the wounded water buffalo style, his classic. He gets blood on the back of his tights. Nice. Really nice. I'm wondering what people are going to think when they see two guys running, with a bloody guy running in between. We already looked like the special needs parade, and that was *before* all the blood. It doesn't sound like you could draw a very favorable conclusion. Of course, we keep running anyway. Maybe we should start carrying a little first aid kit, velcroed behind our windbreakers or something? Nah, probably fall and obliterate the very thing you needed to save you. That would be awesome. Somehow, the story of humanity in a nutshell.

By the time we get back, Ferris could have an infection. And that's only if he doesn't fall again, in the event of which he may be the next candidate for the transmigration of the soul. Harlan and I are extra careful. We know that pride goeth before a fall. And so does apathy, inattention, inflexibility, lethargy, muscular weakness, electrolyte imbalance, glycogen depletion, low blood oxygen, potholes and just plain stupidity. By the end of this run, most likely we'll be poster boys for everything on the list. We turn onto Frederick Street, and single file it onto the sidewalk, heading west out of town. Nobody says anything until after we make our next turn, a left onto South Duke. We try not to look at Ferris's oozing wounds. Suddenly, as we crest the small hill on South Duke, we spot some amazingly hot chicks, so it's hard to keep quiet.

"Dang, I hope I get a date before I'm thirty," says Ferris.

"Don't worry, Ferris, you're attracting them with…blood. See, they're already salivating. Maybe if you pose as a vampire, you'll get lucky, 'cause otherwise you can forget it. Then again, bloody spandex is pretty irresistible in itself."

Ferris's feet have started to slap just enough to get the attention of the girls. Almost immediately, they seem to lose interest. What am I doing out here with these losers?

"Shut up, Harlan," Ferris almost whispers. "They're looking over here. I know it'll be hard, but don't be an ass, dumbass. *You* sure ain't no babe magnet. Chicken breast."

"Hey, if you don't get a date by thirty, you can just turn gay."

"Harlan, you're getting on my last nerve. Shut up."

This is bad. Harlan is on Ferris's last nerve, and we've still got eight miles to go. It could be a WWF smack down. I'm trying not to look like an ass, which, somehow, I find remarkably hard to do. I have to admit, these are some really hotties. Smokin' hot.

"That's my proof for God's existence!" I say, trying to observe without gawking.

"What's proof for God's existence? Harlan's chicken breast? That's more evidence of the Devil."

"No, shut up, Ferris, you know what I'm talking about. Holy crap. *How* could *that* be an *accident*?"

By now, as we approach, we are all doing the impolite thing: staring. Luckily, the girls are on the sidewalk on the *other* side of the street. I imagine Ferris staring, missing the upcoming driveway dip in the sidewalk, and careening onto the cement. Or it could have been Harlan. Or me. The view really was unbelievable. If that's an accident, I'm gonna have an accident in my pants, just out of sheer disappointment. That '71 Hodaka Ace 100B+ looked mighty fine, but there's no way in any possible universe it could hold a candle to either of those hotties. It's almost like instant love. I think we were all getting almost dizzy. Maybe we were actually taking in too much oxygen, what with the unconscious hyperventilation. The chicks were just walking, right on the other side of the narrow street, one tall with black hair and one shorter with brown hair, both with their little backpacks on. It ain't easy getting too *much* oxygen when you are out running long distance. No, it ain't easy at all. But hotties like this, strategically planted along the course, could precipitate a dramatic drop in times, and who knows? A world record. Any of us would have passed out for sure if we actually had to speak to either of those babes. Twenty five seconds and it was over. Only tingling muscles and goggly eyes as reminders. And a whole lot of silence. But of course Harlan can never shut up for long.

"There ain't *no way* I'm gonna turn gay!"

"Too late, Harlan. Maybe you're just bi."

"You're just bi, Ferris. BE-ITCH!"

We've made it past Funk's fruit farm without a smackdown, the hot chicks burned into our subconscious. At the same time, I know we'll probably forget by mile three. Ferris's foot slapping has magically stopped.

"You make a grown man cry…You make a grown man cry…"

It was Harlan channeling Mick Jagger. At least *he* thought he didn't suck. That song was about hot chicks, without a doubt, but with Harlan's rendition, he couldn't even attract a chicken.

"Just because you cry doesn't make you a grown man, Harlan. You think you're so…metrosexual, when you're clearly ruralsexual, which means you like anything with four legs." Ferris is back, blood and all.

"Shutup, loser. *You're* ruralsexual. Make that just plain rural. That means you were born with an ATV up your ass."

"Ohhh. That hurts so bad….lardass wimp."

"What, the ATV? I would imagine so."

There was a lull. Actually, most of our conversation could be considered a lull, but in this case it really was a lull in what passed for a conversation.

We're finally warmed up. Only 7.5 miles

to go. At this pace, it'll be nightfall and then some, especially if the run continues to be punctuated by Ferris's gymnastic prowess. I was thinking about God, the hotties, the hotties, and God. Amazing. Without a doubt, God's revelation is ongoing. And if the creator is at least as great as the created, holy shit. Revelation? Speaking of revelation, right about now I'm looking for a revelation about what's for lunch.

"Ooohh…hot spot…hot spot….Ohhh."

Holy crap. Not again. El Diablo knocketh at my door, in the form of emaciated wussass Harlan.

"Shut up, Mr. America Anorexic. You signed up for it. *I'll* give you a hot spot."

"*You* shut up, Tommie. You'll miss me next year." I have to admit that that will be true. I hoped, however, that his dad would get the new contract. Since I deemed such an expression too corny and sentimental, I said, rather:

"Really? If you say so, Harlan." We slogged across the Conestoga River at Slackwater and up the Stehman Road Hill. There was another lull in the conversation, if we were having a conversation, rather than a WWF sonic smackdown.

"Someday, we're all going to miss this," says Ferris, out of the blue. As bizarre as that sounded right at that moment, we all knew it was true. Kind of like basic training, at least, if what my dad tells me is true. Only at the end, you don't know if you're ready for the real thing, or even what the real thing is or if you'd know it if you saw it. We saved the rest of our oxygen until we crested the hill at Long Lane. That's a three quarter mile hill. And we say we're out here for fun. Nice cover story. We braced ourselves and prepared for the attack of the miniature geriatrics, those two dogs that terrorized us before, more than once.

"Get a stick or a few rocks, sports fans."

"Oh, yeah. Tommie is right. It's those dogs," says Harlan warily.

We survail the roadsides until we each acquire an acceptable weapon of choice. I've got a pretty long stick and so does Harlan. Ferris has picked up a few rocks, in addition to the ones he's got in his head. As we approach the farm, we hear the barking. Those dogs are doing their job. What the hell are we doing? It's hard to say. We keep moving forward, rather slowly, with our weapons du jour. It never helps that this is another uphill stretch. I kind of drag my stick along the road and it makes a distinctive sound. Harlan imitates me, as he is wont to do—and not such a bad choice, I might add, and drags his stick on the asphalt.

With the sounds of two dragging sticks and Ferris the human catapult ready to spring into action, the dogs decide not to run out onto the narrow road that looks more like a path to nowhere. It would have been great for a horse and buggy. Too bad we haven't got them now. So much more fun, and less risk of rabies. The miniature geriatrics keep running back and forth along the road, making as much racket as doggedly possible. If there's one thing they show us, it's that a geriatric dog with six-inch legs can still run circles around us, guys who think they can run. We survive the ordeal. After three hundred yards or so, the dogs break off and go back to the shade of the porch. We go back to contemplating existence.

"Who's gonna buy the pizza?" The lower his blood sugar gets, the more Ferris gets fixated on the pizza. All of us together may not have enough cash to go over to the House of Pizza.

"How much money do you guys have? I've got like ten bucks."

"Eight bucks, Tommie. Ferris? How much have you got?"

"I don't know. Not much." That means nothing or something like $4.67.

"We might be able to scrape enough together, but then we won't be able to go out with those hotties back there."

"Yeah, like *that* was ever an option. Shut up, Tommie, " Harlan barked.

"If we can't scrape enough together, I know we've got peanut butter and jelly and potato chips at our place. And we can get some more tea."

That was the last thing that Ferris and Harlan wanted to hear, but we've done it a bunch of times before. Going to the House of Pizza turns out to be a bluff about eighty percent of the time. But we're always hoping for that twenty percent. I look over at Ferris. He looks crestfallen. Harlan has a palpable look of dejection as well. Given that we're barely on Stoney Lane, it's gonna be a long six mile slog back. Without hope, glycogen don't mean a thing.

"Okay, dudes. We'll find the dough. Maybe Sammie can loan us a few bucks."

"Or, you could just steal the change off of his dresser, dude. That's what you meant, right?"

"Yeah, I know *you'd* do that, Harlan. *You* can do it, sure." I know he won't. These dudes are painfully honest. That's one of the things I like about them, but I wouldn't want to actually tell them that. That would be way too awkward. One of those sickening metrosexual moments. It would go something like this:

Me: "Ferris, one of the things I really like about you is that you are so honest."

[Twenty seconds of silence]. Ferris slowly stares in my direction.

Ferris: [Uncomfortably] "Tommie, one of the things I really hate about you is that you are so honest."

[Sixty seconds of silence]. No eye contact. Both of us are looking straight ahead.

Me: "Want to go to Chicken Mountain and get some iced tea?"

[0.5 seconds of silence]

Ferris: [With boundless enthusiasm] "Oh yeah!"

We're passing those trailers on Stoney Lane, and then the cedar grove.

"Harlan, if your dad's contract isn't renewed, do you think there's a reason?" queries Ferris, very carefully.

"Well, yeah, I guess there's *always* a reason, but it seems like it hasn't got jack to do with my dad or even with education. It's all about the bucks, dude, from what I see."

"I mean, like performance evaluations or something. Don't take this the wrong way, but you guys have moved an awful lot of times," Ferris continued, slowly.

Tell me about it, dude. I wake up and slap myself, and then ask myself what state I'm in. Once in a while, it takes me some time to remember, I'm not kidding. It's a really disorienting feeling. My dad's only performance evaluations come from the students. That's right:

the students, and that's it. I'm sure it's another awesome cost cutting measure. This state used to provide well over half of the money necessary to run the state university. More like seventy percent, if I remember correctly, back in the day. That's what I heard. Today, that number is twenty percent, and the asshole governor wants to lower it to ten percent. C'mon.

"Everybody will become an adjunct at that point. That will be the end of what's left of faculty governance, tenure, and free speech in the university. And free speech in society at large. We're just about there now. Maybe we are there. Then, the colleges and universities that are left will only exist to the extent that they are able to pander to the corporations that *allow* their continued existence. That will be the end of education, which also means the end of democracy and the end of a free society. Yeah, right now, only the 'consumers' do evaluations of the professors, consumers who every day know less and less about anything that matters.

"Basically, the more you give the students what they want, the higher your performance evaluations. It's that simple. Not like that's a surprise or anything. I mean, even I can figure that out. Hey, we know it from our classes at Pine Manor. Nobody wants the hard teachers. Winter might be an exception, but you know what I mean.

And God forbid that you get a complaint at the university when you're on a temporary contract. Any issue whatsoever—even like holding a student responsible for flagrant cheating—could be enough to ensure your termination. Therefore, we may say conclusively that real education is no longer possible. It is a game set up to keep those in power happy, so that they can get what they want out of everyone else. Hence, my dad's contract may not be renewed." Harlan really sounded angry. He coughed, sniffed a couple of times, spit into the ditch, and then continued: "If he's *too good*—that is, if he actually makes people think and learn to read and write and have an opinion, well, that's ample grounds for termination right there. The colleges and universities are there to perpetuate themselves and to support the egregiously inequitable power structure. The elite want, first and foremost, to ensure their own self-preservation. And secondly and as a means to the first, to generate revenue. The universities and colleges have become one more venue to achieve these ends, not unlike wars or strategic famines. To achieve these ends, the needs of those in the universities and colleges— whether the professor or the student or the janitor or the food service worker or the guy who works for grounds and maintenance—their needs must be sacrificed. Their needs are irrelevant. That's right: even the needs of the student are irrelevant.

"You've got to give up the naive illusion that educational institutions today are here to educate. To miseducate? Absolutely. To self-perpetuate? Exactly. To generate revenue for a few? You've got it now. Even the medieval monks and scribes who kept truth and learning alive in their monasteries had an overarching belief in something greater than themselves. Today's educational bureaucrats? Absolutely no way. Educational institutions have an accidental relationship with education, at best, and educators must attempt to educate in spite of the covert agenda of the institutions in which they operate. There are no longer any transcendent ideals, let alone humanistic ideals. The university has become, to put it bluntly, one more arm of the global propaganda machine, a machine in the service of the power elite." Harlan paused as if he was going to keep going, but then he just looked down and kept running.

"Holy cow, Harlan! Dang! My brain was cramping up just listening to you," exclaimed Ferris. I looked over at Ferris, who was looking over at Harlan in astonishment. At least the blood on his hands, arms, and knee was dried, so Ferris wouldn't bleed to death. At least, not today. As Harlan was finishing his sermonette, we were slogging our way into Rock Hill. There were five or six cars at the tavern, even before noon. Maybe it's never too late to get an early start. I guess it all depends on your perspective. We muscled over the corrugated bridge and up the steep hill toward Walnut Hill Road. I started thinking about Monica's mom. As we topped the hill, Harlan and I were about twenty meters in front of Ferris.

"Harlan, dude. Let's slow down and let Ferris catch up. C'mon."

"Okay, yeah, why not? He's buyin'." We kind of ran in place in our usual clandestine way for about twenty seconds until Ferris caught up. No need to bruise his ego. No need to induce combativeness. We loped together down Walnut Hill Road. Three miles or so left in our adventure. Monica's mom was still on my mind.

"Dudes, you know Monica LeBlanc, right? Her mom just died on Wednesday. She had breast cancer."

"That's terrible, Tommie. I didn't notice Monica in Winter's class lately. In that class, it's obvious when she isn't there, I mean, she's the best in the class. She gets it."

"That's for sure. I didn't see her either, Harlan. That's really bad, Tommie. Sorry to hear it. Some people are saying Three Mile Island might have something to do with all the cancer around here. You know the government and the corporations kept quiet about Chernobyl. They didn't tell the truth. Now, the Japanese government and Tokyo electric aren't telling the truth about Sendai. Do you think our government was telling the truth about Three Mile Island? Most people don't seem to think so, but what can you do?" Ferris was voicing that helpless feeling so many seem to have on issues of public health and safety—issues of grave public concern. The helpless feeling is often expressed by…silence.

"The funeral is tomorrow afternoon." Death seemed so remote, an abstraction really. But it was also the ever-present backdrop of daily life.

"Are you going to go, Tommie?"

"I don't know yet, Ferris. I guess I'll call Monica today and see if she wants me to." The hospice house seemed surreal at this point, almost like some kind of a dream. Was I ever really there? When I get to the end, if I get a chance to look back, maybe I'll say that about my entire life. *If* I get a chance to look back, and *if* I remember anything. I'd like to remember this day, with Harlan and Ferris, when we were alive and feeling the effort of running the whole freakin' way out to Stoney Lane and Rock Hill, for no particular reason other than we liked to be together and bullshit and have a few minutes of real conversation and feel the wind and the sun and smell the cedar and fend off the miniature geriatric attack canines and feel the pain in our feet and the burn in our lungs and the sense that we are alive and that life is worth living and that we are living and that we are living if only for this moment and only for this moment this moment right now when we are living.

We managed to limp our carcasses into town, scoping for the evidence of God. We found some, but the case wasn't as strong this time. And we did figure out a way to eat at the House of Pizza. We supplemented our $22.14 by borrowing a little spare change off Sammie's dresser. I figured he'd agree with it in principle, so what the hey.

35

QUALITY TIME

It turns out that Monica did want me to go to the funeral. It was down on Blue Rock Road. The casket was closed. I wore the only suit I had, but I didn't look too good. At least Dad helped me put the Windsor knot in the tie. Mom had to work, so Dad and I went together. I guess he had some kind of a vague association with the LeBlanc family, but he didn't really know them. I hadn't seen Dad get dressed up in a long time, probably not since he got laid off this last time. He looked great. A lot better than he does sitting in the recliner in the dark, staring, beer in hand. I'm glad he went with me. I don't know if he feels the same way, because he didn't say anything to that effect. He doesn't usually say much. I think it was good for him to have a close shave, wash his hair, put on some black argyle socks from the back of the drawer, and wear his black suit. Somehow, it seemed like a cleansing thing for both of us.

On the short drive over there, we didn't say much. I was thinking how few times Dad and I have actually been in the car, just the two of us. I have no idea, really, but it seemed like I could count them on my fingers, especially if you just add up only the last five or six years. If you're talking me, Dad, and Sammie, the number isn't really much larger. Maybe add four or five times. That was a sad thought. I wondered what he was thinking on the drive over. I'd have to keep wondering, 'cause he's perfected the fine art of keeping it to himself. No use in asking.

When we walked in, some super well dressed guy in a black suit and green tie with a black vest was handing out these kind of cheesy five by seven funeral programs. Annette Louise LeBlanc. January 28, 1963 – November 17, 2011. 1963? She was almost three years younger than my Dad. Weird. Then it had a short bio, like you could sum up somebody's life in 127 words or something. After that, it said something about the family requesting that all donations be sent to the Cancer Research Foundation. A priest gave a short speech that was pretty vague and boring. Even though it was only about five or six minutes, my mind kept wandering all over the place. It seemed pretty generic. I wondered if he had even met Dr. LeBlanc.

We sat in the second row of folding chairs, behind Monica and her dad, but over about a half dozen seats, so we could kind of see their faces. Monica looked back as we filed into our row and sat down. When she saw me, she kind of smiled a mournful, awkward smile, and I nodded to her and tried to smile back. That was about it. At least she knew I was there, for whatever that was worth. I don't even know if she recognized Dad.

The service was depressing, sad, and awkward as hell. Not to be callous, but it also gave me a vague impression of theatre. Mostly a bunch of professors from the university going on about celebrating Dr. LeBlanc's life and not her death and that kind of stuff. They were saying stuff about her "groundbreaking work" on narratives of oppression and something about giving a voice to the voiceless and neocolonialism and other stuff along those lines. It seemed like we were now the voice of the voiceless, and that included Dr. LeBlanc. I really pitied her dad, having to sit there and listen to the summing up of his wife's life in something like forty-seven minutes. It's got to be literally unbearable. But he sat there in the front row and didn't pass out.

I wondered how many university administrators showed up for Dr. LeBlanc's funeral. You know, the ones that terminated her salary and put her on unpaid leave for the last who knows how many months. I'm sure that helped her recover. I'm sure that helped her recover real good. I was also wondering just how many health care executives and insurance adjusters showed up for Dr. LeBlanc's funeral. You know, the ones that denied her certain tests and preventative care all along that may have averted the whole disease and death thing. Yeah, those people. The ones that work for a corporation that has the audacity to call itself a member of the health care field. That's a real euphemism if ever there was one. It has that clever ironic twist of seemingly providing the exact opposite of what it euphemistically purports to provide.

Making a profit off of the sickness and death of others. What a great idea. Yeah, it's a great idea. Whoever came up with that should be patting herself on the back right now, it's just so goddamn awesome. I'd call it vulture capitalism. You just need people with the balls to ensure that you will actually make a profit, since that's your real goal. And the way you do that is by addressing your corollary goal: providing as little health care as possible, at the cheapest possible cost. You just need people with the balls to ensure that you can cut corners and deny care—and profit as much as possible off of those illnesses and deaths, many of them preventable. Apparently, if you need people like that you can always find them, provided you pay them a shitload of money, like twenty or thirty or forty or fifty or one thousand times what the average person makes.

People are always pretending that these executive positions require some kind of esoteric specialized knowledge, but I don't think that's it at all. You just need somebody with the balls to kick somebody else when they're down. And the balls to keep kicking and kicking and kicking. You might even have to keep kicking until they're, well... let's face it... dead. That's the truth of the matter. Pardon me, I misspoke. *You* don't actually do the kicking. You've got to order *others* to do that. You've got your army of people who will kick those people—the customers, or clients, or whatever they call them—who are down, and those people you order around will kick those people who need kicking. They'll kick them real good, for as long as it takes.

Well, I was thinking all that and trying not to cry, which was hard as hell. I looked at Monica about ten minutes into the service. I could see the side of her face. She had a stoic, hard profile, inscribed with anguish. The anguish of youth grown old, never to bloom again. It was then that I felt a hot tear running down my cheek. There were quite a few of them after that. I didn't even bother to wipe them away. It felt like a release of tension and pain and grief, but I felt ashamed anyway.

I think I was too afraid to call attention to myself by moving. Luckily, Dad didn't look over at me. I didn't look over at him either. I just didn't make any loud sobs or anything. Nobody did, really. I never did see Monica cry, or her dad.

There weren't too many people from school. I saw one or two from the chess club, but that was about it. There were a few other people in the front row on the other side of the aisle, but I didn't recognize any of them. I'm guessing a few were grandparents, but I really don't know.

The service itself was really hard to take, but the reception line was worse. I don't know who invented it, but it seems like a way to really twist the knife on the grieving family, to really get in the final unbearable torture. Monica, her dad, and five other people that I presumed were some sort of family lined up at the back, right near the doors, so you kind of had to go past them. I think there were a few side doors, but that would have been pretty obvious, so Dad and I lined up to shake hands with the family and give our condolences. The waiting was really painful, to tell you the truth. It seemed like there were even more people in line than there were in the service, but they were clearly just more proximate. My Dad said "Hi" to a few people he recognized, but all of the acknowledgements were more or less subdued, as appropriate.

We stood in line for what seemed like ten hours but was probably more like ten minutes, and then we got to Monica and her dad. Both of them looked hollowed out with grief. The anguish and loss before us was palpable, searing. When you want a solution and there is no solution, what do you do? When you need an answer and there isn't any answer, where do you go? When the truth is no longer palatable and lies are no longer possible, where do you turn? Dad went first. He shook

Monica's dad's hand, then Monica's, and said "I'm very sorry for your loss" and then took two more steps to the other waiting relatives.

I looked at Dad's shoes. I always liked them. He was wearing these black leather Rockports. Then I had to look up. God, it hurt. I can't even imagine how it was for them. I shook Monica's dad's hand with both of mine, but my throat closed up so I didn't say anything. Then I got to Monica. I gave her a hug, the first ever. She wasn't crying. She was shaking. We made eye contact for a split second. That was enough. Neither of us spoke. It was about then that I wished I could have beamed back to my starship, to travel to my planet far, far away. But instead, Dad and I shuffled through the rest of the receiving line and after another grueling five minutes or so, we were greeted with the bright November sun. I folded my program and put it in my left suit jacket pocket. Dad gave me his and I did the same thing with it as well. We walked slowly back to the car.

"Tommie, would you like to ride up to Central Manor Mart and get a sandwich?"

"Sure, Dad. Good idea."

The funeral home was already on the way, so it wasn't long until we pulled into the small gravel lot. The Mart was still open. Being on farmer time, it closed early: at 5:00. Opened early too: at 5:00. We both ordered the same thing: a shifter, fries and a cola.